CUT OUT COOKIE

CUT OUT COOKIE

AUNTIE CLEM'S BAKERY #17

P. D. WORKMAN

Copyright © 2022 by P.D. Workman

All rights reserved.

No part of this book may be reproduced in any form or by any electronic or mechanical means, including information storage and retrieval systems, without written permission from the author, except for the use of brief quotations in a book review.

ISBN: 9781774682265 (KDP Paperback)

ISBN: 9781774682289 (KDP Hardcover)

ISBN: 9781774682234 (KDP Large Print)

ISBN: 9781774682241 (Kindle)

ISBN: 9781774682258 (ePub)

ISBN: 9781774683439 (Lulu Paperback)

pdworkman

ALSO BY P.D. WORKMAN

FIND MORE BOOKS AT PDWORKMAN.COM

Auntie Clem's Bakery

Gluten-Free Murder

Dairy-Free Death

Allergen-Free Assignation

Witch-Free Halloween (Halloween Short)

Dog-Free Dinner (Christmas Short)

Stirring Up Murder

Brewing Death

Coup de Glace

Sour Cherry Turnover

Apple-achian Treasure

Vegan Baked Alaska

Muffins Masks Murder

Tai Chi and Chai Tea

Santa Shortbread

Cold as Ice Cream

Changing Fortune Cookies

Hot on the Trail Mix

Fateful Plateful

Cut Out Cookie (Coming Soon)

On the Slab Pie (Coming Soon)

Recipes from Auntie Clem's Bakery

Reg Rawlins, Psychic Detective

What the Cat Knew

A Psychic with Catitude

A Catastrophic Theft

Night of Nine Tails

Telepathy of Gardens

Delusions of the Past

Fairy Blade Unmade

Web of Nightmares

A Whisker's Breadth

Skunk Man Swamp

Magic Ain't A Game

Without Foresight

Careful of Thy Wishes

Time to Your Elf

Undiscovered Tomb

Missing Powers (Coming Soon)

Thrice Spared (Coming Soon)

Kenzie Kirsch Medical Thrillers

Unlawful Harvest

Doctored Death

Dosed to Death

Gentle Angel

AND MORE AT PDWORKMAN.COM

For those with warm hearts and warm cookies

CHAPTER 1

Erin heard Terry's truck engine as he pulled in front of the house and parked. She rubbed a hand across her forehead, trying to ease the muscle tension that was giving her a headache. Orange Blossom meowed a protest as she got up out of bed, removing his favorite warm body. She scratched his ears and continued past him to the front door. She reached it at the same time that Terry opened the door and put out his hand to enter the security code into the burglar alarm panel.

Her presence there made him startle, and she saw his hand jump to the holster on his hip before he was able to process who it was and that he was safe. He let out his breath and let K9 in before shutting the door behind him.

"Scared the crap out of me, Erin!" He punched the code into the alarm so that the siren wouldn't start blaring, then took her in his arms and gave her a firm hug and a kiss on the top of her dark hair. "What are you doing up?"

"I haven't been able to sleep. Too restless. I thought I'd get up and have a cup of tea with you and see if that would help me settle in."

Terry nodded and escorted her, one arm around her shoulders, into the kitchen. His brown eyes were smiley and he kissed her on top of the head. "Always happy to have a bit of company. But you need to make sure you get enough sleep."

Erin pushed a dark lock of hair back from her face. "I'm not sleeping right now, whether I'm in bed or out of it, so I might as well do something to help myself relax."

There was the patter of footsteps as Blossom realized they were in the kitchen and galloped in looking for food. He started to yowl noisily for a treat.

"Calm down," Erin told him. "You'd wake the dead."

"Or at least the neighbors," Terry agreed. He shifted his duty belt before sitting down. "We don't need any more nuisance calls because you're making too much noise."

Erin went into the pantry to get a treat for the noisy orange feline and skimmed a few across the floor for him to chase and gobble down. She grabbed one of the gluten-free dog biscuits they offered at Auntie Clem's Bakery and gave it to K9, who was standing patiently waiting for it. He took it politely in his lips, then stretched out on the floor beside Terry's chair to munch on it. Orange Blossom arched his back and hissed at K9, but the dog took no notice.

"How about you, Marshmallow? Do you want a carrot?" Erin called out. There was no movement from the living room, where the bunny was probably snoozing behind the couch. "You see? Marshmallow knows that it's time to sleep, not to eat," she told Blossom, who yowled for another treat. She gave in and got him one more.

After that, she closed the pantry door to signal that there would be no more treats. She washed her hands and put the kettle on, then got out their favorite mugs and put a basket of assorted teabags on the table.

"How was work?"

Terry ran his fingers through his short, dark hair. "Pretty quiet today. A couple of reports of a prowler, but nothing there when we checked it out. Kids, maybe. Or just shadows in the trees."

"Any of those reports from Adele?" Erin asked. Adele lived in the summer cottage in the woods behind Erin's house and acted as a groundskeeper, ensuring there were no trespassers or teens hanging out, causing trouble. It was an arrangement that gave Adele a place to live and the ability to practice her Wiccan observances in private so that she wouldn't be driven out of town by her Bible-thumping neighbors, as she had been from other towns.

"No, nothing from Adele. She can take care of most trespassers on her own."

A shotgun in hand was a remarkably effective deterrent. There were other places to hang out and be rowdy.

As Erin poured the boiling water into their mugs, she saw Terry's eyes jump to the window. Looking out from the brightness of the kitchen into the dark night, they couldn't make out very much, but Erin saw the ghostly glow of a white dress drift across the yard. Blond hair, a slim figure. Victoria Webster, Erin's employee and best friend, in her nightgown, taking Nilla out for a tinkle, she guessed.

"It's just Vic."

Erin put the kettle down on a hot pad and went to the back door. She opened it and turned the back door light on. "Vic?"

"Sheesh, you trying to scare the life out of me?" Vic's voice was sharp, a departure from her usual calm Southern drawl. She swore under her breath.

Erin's stomach tied itself in a knot. Everyone seemed to be jumpy. "I'm sorry, Vicky. I didn't mean to startle you. I was just up with Terry, and…"

"I wouldn't be up if I didn't have to take this critter out for a walk," Vic growled, reaching down to pet the fluffy white dog. "I'd be in bed, where you should be. I know it's not a regular day at Auntie Clem's, just the ladies' tea after church services, but you still need to sleep sometime."

"I couldn't sleep tonight. Figured I'd get up and have some tea with Terry."

"And wake up half the neighborhood with that cat."

Erin shook her head, surprised by Vic's response. She was

normally cheerful, even when she was short on sleep. A calm, grounding presence, which was just what Erin needed most of the time. Even though Vic was younger than Erin, she often seemed more mature. Maybe because of the life she had lived with her family, part of the notorious Jackson clan, or as a result of the discrimination and even hate that she'd had to deal with after coming out as transgender.

"Do you want to come in for some tea?" she offered. "Valerian or chamomile?"

"No. I'm going straight back to bed as soon as His Majesty is finished with his business out here."

Erin nodded. "Okay. Sorry about scaring you; I didn't mean to."

"I know. It's okay. You just startled me with the light suddenly going on."

Erin gave Vic a little wave and shut the door. She hesitated whether to turn the light off or leave it on, and decided to leave it on. She would be able to see that Vic was safely back in her loft over the garage before she and Terry went to bed.

Terry raised his brows as Erin returned to the kitchen table and sat down. "She seems a little on edge."

Erin nodded. "Nilla probably woke her up. You know what it's like being awakened from a sound sleep."

"Yes, I suppose. But she's usually more in control than that."

Erin sipped her sleepy tea, hoping that it would calm her overactive thoughts and allow her to get a rest before morning when her body would wake her up, whether it was a baking day or not.

"I've noticed she's been kind of moody since we got back from seeing her parents in Moose River. She's been under a lot of stress."

"Having to deal with the revelation that her brothers were trying to kill her pa for the clan—that kind of stress?" They both sipped their drinks, thinking about it. "Yeah," Terry agreed. "I think we can give her a little bit of latitude for that one."

Erin watched K9 chewing on his biscuit. Orange Blossom was

creeping closer, watching for his opportunity to steal what was left of the treat or to lick up the crumbs from the floor and K9's face.

"Do you want something to eat?" she offered Terry. "I can make a sandwich or rewarm some pasta."

"No, I'm fine. I'll eat when we get up in the morning."

"Nothing? A cookie?"

He smiled, the adorable dimple in his cheek making its appearance. "I can't very well say no to a cookie."

Erin got up and went to the fridge to see what was in the freezer. "We've been making a lot of sugar cookies cut out in Easter shapes. Do you want one of those?"

"Sure. Got a bunny?"

"We've got bunnies, eggs, lilies, lambs..."

"You'd better give me an assortment so I can do a quality check," Terry suggested, smiling, the dimple even more prominent. *Officer Handsome* Vic was fond of calling him.

Erin defrosted several Easter cut-out cookies for him. Terry tested them seriously, gazing out the window.

"There must be a security light out. The backyard shouldn't be that dark."

Erin looked, then nodded. "You're right. If someone other than Vic had been out there, I wouldn't have been able to tell who it was. Someone should check into that." She gave him a wry smile. He would, of course, check to see which of the bulbs was out and replace it. He was very determined to see that Erin was as safe as possible, especially when he was on shift and she was home alone.

Things had happened in the past. They didn't want a repeat.

CHAPTER 2

It was a bright, clear day, already warm when Erin got up in the morning, at a time which she would have considered late any other day of the week. But as Terry had said, all she had to worry about on Sunday was the ladies' tea after the Baptist ladies' church meetings. She didn't bake early Sunday morning; she either made something for the tea on Saturday or pulled something out of the freezer. It wasn't really the baking that the ladies came for, but the gossip session. A little fellowship after their services.

Erin's aunt, Clementine, had held the Sunday tea for many years when the storefront was a tea shop rather than a gluten-free bakery. Eventually, as her health had failed, she had been forced to shut down the business and the weekly get-together. After her death, a private investigator had managed to find Erin and told her that Clementine had left everything to her. They had been estranged for many years, since Erin had been put into foster care after her parents' death and had grown up mostly in Maine and on the eastern seaboard, nowhere near Clementine in Tennessee.

Erin rubbed her forehead and the bridge of her nose. She had been unable to kick the headache and knew that it was most likely tension. She should be relaxed now that she was back in Bald

Eagle Falls, but she'd been struggling with sleepless nights, and the fatigue that was building over the weeks never left her.

She wasn't actually sure how she had ended up moving from Tennessee to Maine as a child, when foster parents were not usually allowed to take children across state borders. But one of the early families that she had been with must have managed to get permission when the father's work transferred him north. Maybe they had been planning to adopt her at the time and some social worker had pulled out all the stops to try to make it work.

But Erin had never been adopted. A forever family had not been in the cards for her.

Erin set out the tray of cookies that she had set aside for the ladies' tea and turned to go back into the kitchen. Vic was coming out at the same time, her eyes down on her phone, and the two of them nearly collided.

"Whoa, I'm sorry," Vic apologized, shoving her phone into an apron pocket. "I wasn't watching where I was going. I thought you were still setting up."

Erin held Vic's arm to steady herself for a moment, then smiled and shrugged. "It's a wonder we don't do that more often."

Vic nodded vaguely. She looked at the small area at the front of the store with a couple of tables surrounded by chairs. "What else do you need? I've got the coffee perking and water heating in the boiler. Cookies. Plates." She laughed. "How about teacups?"

"That might be a good idea," Erin agreed. They were both so scattered it would be a wonder if the tea went off without some kind of snag. She hadn't used the checklist for the ladies' tea in a long time. Still, it was safely stored in a sheet protector in the operations binder, accessible to all employees. Maybe she ought to pull it out to make sure they hadn't forgotten anything. Like the tea.

Erin shook her head as she continued to gather the things they needed together. And she did flip open the binder to make sure they hadn't missed anything obvious. After the number of teas she and Vic had held, everything should be automatic. And usually, it was.

They weren't quite ready when the ladies started to come in the door. Erin focused on not running or appearing hurried as they arranged the final details. The best way to make people think that you were behind or unprofessional was by rushing. Instead, she carefully finished setting everything out, nodding to each of the women and addressing them by name. No one seemed to notice anything awry.

Once everyone had served themselves and was sipping tea and eating cookies—those who allowed themselves such indulgences—Erin took a deep breath and let it out slowly, trying to slow her breathing and heartbeat and to enjoy the moment. She had come to look forward to the ladies' teas, the final cap to her busy week, a time that was slower and allowed her to socialize and relax.

"We were mighty sorry to hear about your family troubles," Melissa told Vic, combing her dark brown curls away from her face with her fingers. Melissa always had the lowdown on the juiciest gossip, drawing from both doing part-time administrative work for the police department and from her relationship with Davis Plaint, in prison for the deaths of his brother and Bertie Braceling. Davis was the one, Erin suspected, who had passed on any word of Vic's "family troubles" to Melissa. Certainly, it hadn't come from Terry, who knew he couldn't rely upon anything he mentioned around Melissa remaining confidential. He wouldn't have passed any of Vic's private information on to her, and it wouldn't have been in the records of the Bald Eagle Falls police department because it had happened in Moose River.

"Well… thank you, I'm sure," Vic said hesitantly. It would be ungracious not to acknowledge and accept Melissa's condolences. Still, she didn't want to discuss any of the sordid details in front of the other ladies. And who knew how much Melissa had already told them? Vic wouldn't know until she started getting condolences from others as well.

"Yes, we were all sorry to hear," Lottie Sturm chimed in.

Her tone clearly indicated that she was holding something back. "But what could be expected from the Jackson clan?" or "We always knew you came from bad stock," or something along those lines. Lottie was one of the women who would never accept Vic for who she was. If she was polite to Vic, it was only because she knew Erin would eject her from the bakery if she weren't.

"How is your poor mother?" Melissa asked, oblivious to Vic's discomfort. "It must have been such a trial for her, your pa being so sick. I heard he was on his death bed."

Vic nodded reluctantly. "I'm sure she's doing better now that everything is back to normal. Pa was lucky to recover. It was pretty perilous for a while there."

Melissa gave a little gasp and covered her mouth in horror. But her eyes were dancing and it was obvious that she was enjoying the drama and having Vic as a captive audience.

"We were all praying for him," Cindy Prost chimed in. She was sitting beside her daughter, Bella, who was one of Erin's best employees. Even though Bella was still in high school, she had a good business mind. She was very responsible and often had ideas for Erin to try out to improve areas of her business. Cindy glanced sideways at Bella to make sure she heard and approved of this comment. Erin had her doubts that Cindy had prayed about anyone in Vic's family. Unless she was a closer relation than Erin thought. Many of the families in the area were related, and the Prosts and Jacksons had been around for long enough that Erin was sure the families' genealogies probably connected at several different points.

"We sure were," Bella agreed, and her words sounded genuine. She'd held down the fort while Vic and Erin had been in Moose River, and she had expressed her good wishes for Vic's father and the family several times. Erin never sensed the same insincerity in Bella as she did in Cindy.

Vic too sensed this and nodded real appreciation to Bella. "Thank you for that. It was miraculous that he survived."

Erin knew that sooner or later, one of the ladies was going to bring up Vic's brothers and their actions. She looked at Vic and cocked her head slightly, as if listening carefully.

"Vicky, would you mind getting the phone in my office? I can hear it ringing."

Vic stared at her for a moment in confusion. There was, after all, no phone in Erin's tiny, closet-sized office in the back. There was a wall phone just inside the kitchen doorway so that if a customer called, they could answer it from either the front or the back, but that was the only hard-wired phone in the bakery. Erin used her cell phone for everything else. Then understanding came into Vic's eyes, and she nodded and hurried into the back, out of the reach of the ladies' pointed questions and comments. If Erin needed a hand with anything in the front, she knew that Bella would jump in to help. Vic could hide out in the back and tidy away anything that had been left out in the kitchen.

The atmosphere in the bakery deflated as everyone watched their prime target retreat and disappear out of reach of their barbs. Lorrie Sturm gave Erin a glare, understanding that Erin had intentionally removed Vic from the line of fire.

"It was so kind of you to go to Moose River with Vic," Mary Lou commented. She took a sip of her tea. She had not taken any of the cookies, always mindful of her figure. "You are always looking for ways to help people."

Erin's face warmed at the compliment. She wasn't quite sure how to respond. It was true; she did the best she could to help those in need. But she was too modest to like having this brought to everyone else's attention. She shrugged and looked away. "Thank you."

∼

Conversations shifted and the focus moved away from Erin and Vic, since they would not indulge the women's interests. After draining a cup or two of tea, the ladies started looking at their watches and excusing themselves. Bella hovered as her mother made movements toward the front door.

"Can I help you clean up, Erin? We can wait for a few minutes."

"No, it's okay," Erin assured her. "There's not much to do. I'll see you next week."

"You sure?"

"I'm sure. Take care. Thanks for coming, Cindy," Erin raised her voice slightly to acknowledge Cindy's departure as well. Not a "see you soon," but more of a "don't let the door hit you on your way out."

Bella gave Erin a grin and scurried after her mother. Mary Lou was the last to leave, though usually she was one of the first, staying for just long enough to satisfy the others that she had made an effort.

"You can tell Vic that it's safe to come out now," Mary Lou said dryly. She patted her iron gray bob, though she didn't have a hair out of place.

Erin acknowledged this with a smile. "Vic! All clear!"

Vic poked her head out the door and looked around. She nodded at Mary Lou. "Sorry about that," she apologized, her cheeks growing pink. "It was a longer call than I expected."

Erin gave an unladylike snort. "Hopefully, by next week, they'll have moved on to other things. Or maybe you should give someone else the shift next week. They're bound to have something else to gossip about in two whole weeks."

"Maybe I will," Vic agreed.

Mary Lou gazed at Vic for a moment in silence. "I do wish you the best with your family," she said eventually. "I hope that… y'all will find some peace."

"Thanks." Vic blinked, her eyes swimming with tears. "I hope that too."

Mary Lou nodded once, smoothed invisible wrinkles on her pants, and left the bakery. Erin flipped the sign to Closed and locked the bolt on the door without a word, and they each moved quietly around each other to gather up the few things that needed to be put away.

"I swear, I thought things would be better this week," Erin sighed. "I thought that giving them a couple of weeks would head off any problems."

"Things must be too quiet in Bald Eagle Falls." Vic swiped at the corners of her eyes when she thought Erin wasn't looking. "We'll have to stir up some trouble!"

CHAPTER 3

There had been enough trouble in Bald Eagle Falls in the time that Erin had lived there. She was hoping to avoid any more. If she never had to deal with another dead body or family crisis, it would be a miracle.

"Terry and I are going into the city this afternoon. Did you want to go along?"

"I'm sure you and Officer Piper don't need a third wheel hanging around," Vic told her. "Willie is supposed to be picking me up anyway. I thought we'd try to hit a church service there and then go to a movie or the park or something. See what we feel like."

Vic didn't go to church in town because of their intolerance. She knew the kind of prejudice she would face if she tried going to the Baptist service as she was. They would welcome her only if she gave up her "sinful" ways and went as a boy. And there was no way she was doing that. She'd found an LGBT-friendly congregation in the city that she attended occasionally and hoped that God would understand her not attending in Bald Eagle Falls the rest of the time.

Not a believer herself, Erin found it hard to believe that any all-knowing god would insist that Vic go through the pain and dysphoria she would suffer if she forced herself to dress and act in a way that was not true to herself. But who was she to say? Other people could choose to believe what they wanted to. And hopefully, would allow Erin to *not* believe as she wished.

They heard a truck pull into the parking lot in the back of the bakery and the tap of the horn.

"There he is," Vic looked around the kitchen to make sure that they had completed the cleanup and everything would be ready for Monday morning. "All right, see you tonight. Or not. We might stay over in the city since I'm not on shift in the morning. We're taking Nilla."

Erin nodded. "Have a good time."

Vic hesitated for a moment, as if she would dispute it and say that she would not have a good time in the city. What was that all about? Then she just nodded and turned to the back door. "You too."

∽

Erin and Terry enjoyed themselves in the city and were back in good time so that Erin would have a chance to look over her planner notes for the upcoming week and have a bit of relaxing time before heading to bed. It wasn't always easy for them to sync up their schedules, with Erin working baker's hours and Terry doing shift work with the police department. Their sleep schedules were often off by hours. But they still tried to spend some time together every day, wherever they could fit it in.

Erin was sitting sideways on the couch with her feet resting against Terry's thigh as she wrote lists of things to do and he watched an old western on TV. With the way that Erin was turned, she could see through the kitchen window on the back of the house. She was surprised to see headlights as a vehicle pulled onto the gravel pad.

Terry sensed her gaze or attention shift and looked at her face to see what she was looking at.

"Vic home?"

Erin nodded. "I thought they would end up staying in the city tonight. Vic had said that they might."

"Maybe Willie had other plans."

"Maybe." Erin hoped that Vic hadn't been too disappointed, whatever it was that had kept them from staying.

She pretended to herself that she wasn't still watching out the window, spying on Vic. She just happened to be watching as a shadowy figure stepped out of the passenger side of the extended cab of Willie's truck, and then Vic crossed in front of the headlights as she marched purposefully toward the stairs up the side of the garage to her loft apartment, Nilla running to keep up.

Erin's stomach was tight. By the speed and jerkiness of Vic's gait and the fact that Willie did not get out of the truck to follow her, she guessed that they'd had an argument and Willie would not be going in that night.

"What's wrong?" Terry asked, looking at Erin and not turning to look out the window.

"Looks like Vic is upset about something. Willie isn't getting out."

"Mmm." Terry still didn't look at the window. Erin didn't know how he could keep from indulging his curiosity and looking to see for himself.

"What does *that* mean?" she challenged.

Terry looked at her, surprised. "I didn't mean anything. Just acknowledging what you said."

"It sounded like... you weren't surprised."

"Why should I be surprised?" Terry asked carefully, trying to read her expression.

"They usually get along. It isn't like they're always fighting. And you know how Vic has been lately. It's a hard time for her."

Terry nodded. "So...?"

"It isn't necessarily Vic's fault if they're arguing."

"Didn't say it was."

"But you implied..." Erin trailed off, hearing herself and

knowing that she was pushing it too far. Terry hadn't said anything offensive. He hadn't criticized Vic or Willie or said they were always fighting or that Vic needed to get her head on straight if she wanted to keep her man.

It was Erin's own fears that bubbled up, always worried that arguments would lead to violence. Perhaps violence to each other, and perhaps to innocent bystanders.

She wasn't a foster child anymore. She didn't need to worry that the parents were going to explode and that terrible things would happen that were beyond her control.

It was just Vic and Willie. A few cross words or Vic spending the night by herself were not the end of the world. She and Willie would make up again the next day, once they'd both had a chance to cool off.

Lights went on in Vic's apartment over the garage, and only then did Willie shift the truck into reverse and pull back out of the parking pad.

Despite whatever they had said to each other or argued over, Willie had still stayed to make sure that Vic was safely inside before leaving.

∼

Erin kept looking over at Vic's dark apartment windows in the morning, expecting her to come down for a quick breakfast of tea and toast together. But she knew that Vic wasn't on the early-morning shift and that she had stayed up late the night before. Or at least, later than Erin had.

Erin had a difficult time sleeping after her usual wake-up time, even on days off. But Vic would have taken a sleeping pill and probably wouldn't be up for several more hours. Erin liked it when they worked the morning shift together. Still, sometimes one of them or the other needed a break, had an appointment to get to, or needed to cover someone else's afternoon shift.

After a good night's sleep, she was sure Vic would be feeling a lot better. A good sleep could do wonders for a person physically and emotionally. Erin wished that she could get a good night's sleep herself. She felt like she had been lagging behind for a couple of weeks now, almost since they had returned to Bald Eagle Falls.

She turned her attention to the orange cat winding around her ankles, making increasingly louder "feed me" noises. If she didn't take care of him, she was either going to trip over him and fall on her face, or Terry was going to wake up. Ever since his head injury, he'd had a harder time going to sleep when he wanted to and staying asleep. At one time, he'd been able to go to sleep within minutes of lying down, no matter what the time of day. His body and brain were so well-trained to be able to switch shifts as required. Bald Eagle Falls did not have a large enough contingent in the police department to have a designated day shift and night shift. They each did what they could.

"Shh, shh. You're going to wake up the whole neighborhood," Erin chided. "Come here and get your breakfast and quit being so loud."

She let K9 out to do his business in the dog run. Marshmallow waited patiently for her attention, as usual, and Erin grabbed some chopped vegetables from the fridge for him to supplement his rabbit pellets.

The toast popped, the kettle whistled, and there was just enough time for a quick breakfast before starting her morning's baking at Auntie Clem's.

CHAPTER 4

*E*rin was keeping an eye on the time, unable to stop thinking about Vic and whether she was still upset after the argument with Willie the night before. Maybe it had all blown over and there was nothing to worry about. But she wanted to know that her best friend was okay.

They always closed for an early lunch for the employees between the morning rush and the lunchtime rush. They couldn't go all day without eating, and it wasn't professional for an employee to be munching on a sandwich while trying to serve customers. Sometimes it was difficult to close and they ended up eating in shifts, but usually, there was a lull and they could close for half an hour to take a breather and some sustenance.

Vic showed up during Erin's lunch break just as expected. Bella had helped with the morning shift, and she sang out a hello to Vic when she showed up and grabbed her backpack. "See you tomorrow," she told Erin, waved to them both, and left.

Vic nodded to Erin. "Morning, sunshine."

Erin smiled. "Good morning. For a few more minutes. How are you doing?" She was careful to keep the question uninflected, as if it were just a routine question any old morning, and not that she had seen that Vic and Willie were fighting and was concerned about her.

Vic sighed. "Bit tired today. I guess we did too much yesterday. Wore myself out more than I expected."

Close up, Erin couldn't make out any shadows under Vic's eyes, but they did look a little puffy. Like she had been crying or was short on sleep. If there had been dark circles, Vic had carefully concealed them with makeup. Erin's stomach clenched and she had a little pain in her chest at the thought of her friend lying awake crying over whatever had happened with Willie.

But maybe she was just imagining it, seeing what she expected to see after Willie had dropped Vic off the night before and not stayed over. Maybe Vic had just been tired and ready for bed, and Willie had other things to do. Or he had to be somewhere early in the morning and didn't want to wake her up when he arose. Erin could have misinterpreted the whole thing.

But she didn't think so.

"What did you guys do yesterday?"

Vic busied herself in the kitchen after putting her purse in Erin's office. After tying on an apron, she drew a cup of coffee from the carafe and checked the counters and fridge and the checklist on the counter to see what needed to be done.

"Went to church. Picnic in the park. Some shopping and errands. Nothing earth-shattering."

"That sounds nice."

"How about you and Terry?"

"A movie. Thai food. Then back home to relax and make sure that everything was arranged for the week."

Vic nodded. She didn't give any indication that she had seen the lights in the house on when she had returned home. No comment on the fact that Willie hadn't stayed over or what his plans were for the day.

Erin chewed her sandwich slowly, watching Vic's preparations and hoping she would say something that would put Erin's worries to rest.

Mid-afternoon, Erin looked up when the bells over the door jingled and saw Officer Handsome in uniform, his trusty K9 companion at his side. She smiled.

"Terry!"

"How are you doing?" He leaned over the display case to give her a quick peck. "Having a good day?"

"Eww," Vic teased. "How unsanitary. We sell food here, you know. There's none of that going on."

Erin and Terry both smiled at the teasing, Erin's face getting a little warm and the dimple appearing in Terry's cheek. K9 sat down at his side, waiting patiently.

"Need a refill?" Erin offered.

Terry handed her his water bottle and she ducked into the kitchen for a moment to refill it. When she returned to the front, she saw both Adele and Beaver waiting to be served. She handed Terry his water bottle and got out a gluten-free dog biscuit for K9. Terry handed it to his furry sidekick, who crunched it happily.

"No excitement here," Erin advised Terry. "How is the rest of the town?"

"Mostly quiet." His glance to the side and vague reply told her that he'd had at least one call and hadn't just been quietly patrolling all day. But he wouldn't tell her much about what he'd been up to. She might get some details out of him over supper, but he would be extra-careful about what he said in front of others.

Terry stepped to the side, motioning for Adele to proceed with her order while he visited with Erin and waited for K9 to finish his snack.

Adele, stately with dark red hair, stepped up to the counter and indicated the hot cross rolls, one of Auntie Clem's Easter offerings. "A couple of those. They look very good. And do you have some day-old bread to get rid of?"

"Sure," Erin agreed. She had instituted a program where anyone who needed it could ask for what had been left over at the end of the day, goods that Erin wouldn't normally sell but would freeze and take into one of the homeless shelters or soup kitchens in the city if no one in Bald Eagle Falls had any need for them. But it was always preferable to feed their own indigent families before taking the surplus into the city. At first, no one had taken her up on the offer of "charity," but Adele clearly had a family she was helping to feed. Erin had no idea who they were. Her stated policy was "no questions asked," so she had to be satisfied with just knowing that she was helping someone who might otherwise have gone hungry. "How much do you need?"

"Three loaves, I think. And if you have any muffins or quick breads?"

"You bet," Erin agreed. She went back to the freezer to pull out several loaves and bags of muffins while Vic rang up Adele's purchase of sweet rolls. Adele usually went to the back door if she wasn't purchasing anything for herself, which was more discreet. But she apparently didn't mind Terry and Beaver seeing she was taking advantage of the free food program.

Erin boxed the goods while Adele was paying. "How has everything been in the woods? All quiet?"

Adele considered her answer. She shook her head slightly. "Someone has been camping out but, so far, I haven't been able to catch them at it."

"Oh." Erin didn't like to hear that. Terry had drilled into her how she could be held liable if someone squatting on her property came to harm or caused trouble so, despite her natural inclination to help people by allowing them to camp in her woods, she and Adele did the best they could to ensure that trespassers were quickly on their way and were not lighting fires or staying overnight. "Do you have any idea who?"

Adele shook her head. "Whoever it is hasn't lit any fires, or I would be on them in a wink. And I haven't seen any sign of a tent. But there have been a couple of places I've stumbled across where… it's obvious that someone has been there for a significant length of time, sleeping or waiting around."

Terry was listening with interest. "Whereabouts, exactly?"

Adele described the places the best she could, but it was difficult to describe more than the general area if there weren't any noteworthy landmarks.

"Maybe you could show me," Terry suggested. "If we're both keeping an eye out, then hopefully, we can find out who it is and put an end to it."

Adele's eyes flicked over to Erin to see if she approved of this course of action. Erin nodded. As much as she hated to kick out anyone in need, she didn't want to risk being sued if someone had an accident. Chances were it was not someone homeless and desperate, but maybe just a kid exploring or a couple of lovers seeking out a private place to spend some time together.

"Any indication of who it might be?" Terry asked. "Any litter or anything left behind?"

"No. Whoever it is, he's been pretty careful to remove any trace. But I can still see where the vegetation has been trampled or pressed down."

Terry nodded. "We'll see if we can find him... don't want anything going on in the woods that we don't know about."

"If you want to walk back with me, I'll show you where he has been."

Adele and Terry left together. Beaver stepped to the side to let them pass.

"And what would you like today?" Erin asked Beaver, forcing a smile as if she weren't concerned about anything.

Beaver, a tall, slim blond with a long nose and generous mouth, chewed her ever-present wad of gum while she looked at the items in the display case. Erin wondered how many calories she burned each day just chewing gum. The only time she wasn't chewing gum was when she was eating. And maybe while she slept, but Erin couldn't be sure of that.

"How 'bout some brownies and half a dozen of those pizza pretzels?" Beaver suggested eventually.

Erin smiled and nodded and proceeded to get them packaged up for her.

"How are you ladies today?" Beaver asked. She studied Erin and Vic carefully, chewing slowly.

"Good," Erin answered, keeping a smile on her face and focusing on the baked goods rather than meeting Beaver's eyes.

"Happy as a clam at high tide," Vic declared.

Erin glanced aside at her friend. Vic wasn't going to tell Beaver that there was anything wrong, but it niggled at Erin. Vic had not been happy since she'd gotten back from visiting her family in Moose River. Maybe she was just depressed after being around them and being reminded just how strong their objections to her choices were. Maybe because she was still worried about her father's recovery or if her mother could take care of everything by herself. And, Erin was sure, full of anger and disappointment and a dozen other feelings for her two oldest brothers. No one could expect her to be happy about everything that had happened.

Maybe that was why it bothered her so much to see Vic pretending that everything was all hunky-dory.

"How's your family?" Beaver prodded, looking at Vic.

Vic's expression didn't change, but her cheeks flushed. "Maybe I should ask you," she said. "You seem to know as much or more about them than I do."

Beaver chewed, looking at her. She didn't defend herself or offer any explanation or argument. As a federal agent, she probably knew a lot more than Vic did about Vic's father and brothers and the dealings of the Jackson clan, an organized crime syndicate. Who knew how much she had learned that she wasn't telling anyone?

Vic pressed her lips together at Beaver's lack of response. "How about Jeremy?" she asked. "How is he? I haven't heard much from him lately."

Jeremy was the youngest of Vic's big brothers, just a few years older than she was, the one she had been closest to growing up. He just happened to be Beaver's boyfriend. Despite their age difference—Beaver older than Jeremy by a number of years—they got along famously.

Erin couldn't help wondering what information Beaver might be getting from him about the Jackson family. Possibly information Jeremy didn't even realize he was giving her. She was a good investigator, and a few words here or there might be a treasure trove she could pass back on to the agency she worked for.

"Jeremy is fine." Beaver chomped a few times. "Finer than frog hair split four ways." She grinned widely at Vic.

Vic apparently was not amused by the colloquialism. She pounded the keys on the cash register, ringing up Beaver's purchase, and told her the total. Beaver paid without appearing to realize Vic was upset about anything. She nodded her thanks and was on her way.

Erin glanced over at Vic and didn't say anything.

"I'm sorry," Vic said tersely. "Sometimes, that woman riles me."

CHAPTER 5

*E*rin woke up and looked around, squinting into the darkness. She was disoriented, feeling like she'd been awakened out of a dream that she needed to finish. It wasn't time to get up and go to Auntie Clem's Bakery yet. She hadn't been awakened by Terry getting home; she was sure of that. Something else had made her wake up and was giving her an eerie, unsettled feeling.

She shifted around and found Orange Blossom cuddled against her, a nice warm, furry ball in the middle of the room that felt strangely cold and foreign to her.

She decided to get up. From past experience, the only way to shake the memories she sometimes woke up with of foster homes she had been in, of a feeling of menace or danger, was to get good and wide awake. Walk around, have something to eat. Turn on lots of lights. Watch TV. Once her brain finished waking up the rest of the way and was convinced that there was no danger, the shadows would subside again. She might be able to get back to sleep after that, and she might not. It really didn't matter, because she would not have a good, restful sleep if she tried to go back to sleep immediately after such an awakening.

Erin took a few deep breaths, then swung her legs over the side of the bed and stood up. Blossom made an inquiring meow and stretched, wanting to know what she was up to.

"Just need to get up for a while," Erin murmured to him. "Then maybe I'll come back."

Of course, the chances that he would stay on the bed when she walked into the kitchen were right about zero. There was no way he would turn down the chance of a possible treat. Especially an *extra* treat, at a time when he didn't usually get one. He lived in constant hopes of extra treats.

Erin turned on the living room lamp to its brightest setting, blindingly bright after sleep. She turned on the TV but didn't really pay any attention to what was on. She just wanted the background noise. There was no one in the house with her, but she could at least make it feel like there was. Not so empty and lonely.

As soon as she stepped onto the kitchen floor, Orange Blossom leaped off of the bed and came galloping down the hall. Erin laughed and turned on the kitchen light. She would give him a treat, because she was really happy for his company after such an unsettled awakening.

"Come on, Blossom. What do you want? You know it isn't dinner time," she teased.

He started meowing and making a funny yodeling noise that seemed to be reserved just for Erin. She opened the pantry and got out his treats, and sent a few skimming across the floor for him to chase. He still chased them like a kitten, which brightened her spirits. She was glad for the dusty, skinny little kitty that had shown up at Auntie Clem's when she had first moved there. Where would she be without Orange Blossom?

"You're a lucky cat," she told Orange Blossom. "And I'm a lucky owner. We needed each other."

Orange Blossom purred his loud, rumbling purr, snuffling and crunching down the kitty treats and then looking around for more. Erin gave him a couple more and then put them away. She'd have to be careful not to give him too much to eat for his next meal or two. She didn't want his weight ballooning up because she had taken to feeding him at night to keep her own spirits up.

Erin put the kettle on and looked through the teas in the cupboard for something that would be nice and soothing and help her to relax for bed again, even if she didn't get back to sleep.

She caught a movement out the corner of her eye and turned toward it, then laughed at herself. It was just her own reflection on the glass of the window. It was too dark outside for her to see anything with so many lights on in the house.

It didn't look like there were any security lights on. She would have to get on Terry's case about replacing the ones that had burned out. Or to get out a ladder and replace them herself. It wasn't like she needed someone big and strong to change light bulbs for her. She wasn't helpless. She didn't need to fall back into splitting chores down the traditional lines. It was her house and she should be the one in charge of its upkeep. Fix the things that she could and hire someone to do whatever she couldn't. When Terry sold his house, they could talk about whether to put his name on the title and how they would manage tasks like maintenance.

Erin got closer to the window and squinted out, her face close to the window, trying to see if she could see anything at all in the backyard. There was a figure out there, and Erin's heart leaped to her throat before she recognized the general shape and gait as Willie Andrews. So he was back. He and Vic must have made up.

But he wasn't walking across the yard to the stairs that led to Vic's loft. He seemed to be adrift, not sticking to the path he would typically walk between his truck and the stairs as he came and went. He was pacing, Erin realized after a moment, his hand up to his ear. On the phone with someone. Maybe it was a call he needed privacy for, or he didn't want to wake Vic up with his conversation. So he was having it outside before going up.

She went to the back door and turned the porch light on. It wouldn't compensate completely for the security lights, but would at least give him a little light so that he wouldn't be standing out there in the dark.

Erin grimaced, remembering how turning the light on had surprised Vic so badly. Hopefully, it wouldn't affect Willie the same way. She wouldn't stick her head out the door and interfere with his phone call. She'd wait until he was finished talking, and then, seeing that she was up, he would probably come to the kitchen to at least say hello. She turned the bolt to unlock the door and went back to making her tea.

A few seconds later, Willie knocked on the door; a loud, abrupt pounding that was unusual for his normally calm demeanor. He tried the handle and thrust the door open. He still held the phone to his ear, and Erin wondered if she had somehow messed up his call for him by turning on the light.

"Erin, what are you doing up?" Sweat trickled down the temples of Willie's darkly stained face, even though the weather had cooled since Erin had been out last. He was older than Erin, considerably older than Vic. He did not enter.

"I woke up. I couldn't sleep."

"Pull the kitchen blind down."

Erin frowned at him. "What?"

"Pull down the kitchen blind and stay away from the window." He gave her a stern look that told her not to argue with him.

The burglar alarm started to beep a warning, and normally Willie would have keyed in the disarm code so that it wouldn't start blaring, but this time he didn't. "Keep that on and lock the door." He withdrew, pulling the door shut again.

Erin's intestines were tying themselves into knots. She held her hands over her stomach, trying to convince herself that she wasn't going to be sick. For a few moments, she just stood there, frozen, at a loss for what to do. But his words sank in and she obeyed him mechanically, bolting the door again, walking to the kitchen window and pulling down the blind that she never used.

What was going on? What was wrong?

CHAPTER 6

The kettle started to whistle, and Erin stared at it, not sure what to do. Willie had told her to stay away from the windows, but that didn't mean she couldn't go past the one that she had just pulled the blind over to get her boiling water, did it? Whoever might be out there that Willie was worried about would not be able to see in to tell where she was or what she was doing now that the blind was down. Would they? Or would her shadow on the blind give away her position?

Willie must think that she was in danger. Why else would he tell her to lock the door and keep the burglar alarm on? He would normally step into the kitchen to say hello and inquire after her. Despite his rough appearance, Willie was a gentleman, always kind and concerned for her health and safety.

Erin tiptoed across the kitchen to her singing teakettle and shakily poured it into her waiting teacup. Should she sit at the table? Was that too close to the kitchen window? Or should she go into the living room? There were bigger windows in there and she would have to pull the heavy curtains across. Why couldn't Willie have told her exactly what was going on so that she could make an informed decision?

But she knew why he hadn't. He was busy on the phone with

someone else and had only had a moment to spare to talk to her. Close the blinds. Stay away from the windows. Lock the door and keep the burglar alarm armed.

An intruder. Someone who might be close to the house, maybe trying to peer in her windows even now. Someone who might be dangerous.

One name came immediately to mind and Erin tried to push it away. She didn't know what was going on, but she wasn't going to jump to any conclusions.

A siren started in the distance, getting louder as it moved toward the house. She wouldn't have long to think about what to do. Soon the police would be there to tell her that she was safe and what she should do to stay that way.

Orange Blossom yowled, looking at her and wondering why she was standing around with her teacup like a statue.

"Hey, Blossom," Erin said to him softly. "It's okay. Everything is all right. I'm just going to…"

He rubbed against the pantry door, prompting her to get him more treats. Like he hadn't had enough already. He would be as fat as a pig if she kept feeding him in the middle of the night. He yowled again, a long, ululating call to get her to pay attention to him.

"Shh. You know better than that. We're trying not to attract attention here."

The pantry was a reasonable size and, of course, had no windows, only shelves, and a door that shut. If she were in the pantry, no one would be able to see her from anywhere outside the house. Erin could just wait there until she received the all-clear from Terry.

Erin tiptoed again, making her way across the kitchen to the pantry. She was half-expecting someone to bang on the door or throw a brick through the window, but the only thing she could hear was the siren that got louder and louder as the police car approached. Orange Blossom put his ears back and shook his head. Erin slipped into the pantry casually, as if she were just inventorying her ingredients. It was perfectly natural that she would be counting cans of soup in the middle of the night, wasn't it? They said to count sheep, but she didn't have any sheep...

There was another siren approaching from a distance away, a slightly different direction. The two sirens together were discordant, making Erin wince and want to cover her ears. But she had her teacup in one hand and didn't want to put it down. Besides, she was counting...

The sirens cut off as the cars pulled up to the house, first the one, and then, a few seconds later, the other. Erin took a deep breath and let it out. The silence was deafening after the building wails of the sirens. But now it was over and she was safe.

She still couldn't relax her body. Her stomach hurt and all of her muscles were stiff, tensed in readiness. She waited for the sound of shots being fired. Of shouts and crashes and breaking glass. There weren't any. She could hear loud male voices, but couldn't make out what they were saying. There were no screams or sounds of anyone in distress, no one being chased from her yard off into the darkness of the night.

Eventually, there was a knock on the front door. Erin stayed where she was. The polite thing would be to answer the door. That was what a normal person would do. But Erin was frozen. She was away from the windows and doors and didn't want to expose herself. Willie had said to stay away from the windows.

There was another knock, more voices, and then she heard a key in the lock of the front door. Terry opened the door slowly and sent K9 in ahead of him. K9 went immediately to Erin and sat down in front of the open pantry door. Terry followed.

"Erin? Are you okay?" He held out his arms for her and Erin stepped into them, carefully holding her teacup so that it wouldn't splash and scald him. He rubbed her back, then pulled away slightly to look at her face and assess the situation. "Are you all right?"

Erin nodded. She tried to swallow the lump in her throat.

"Come on out of there, to the table. Sit down. Is that tea fresh? Let's get some sugar in there."

"I don't take sugar," Erin protested as he sat her down at the table.

"Tonight, you do. Good for shock."

"What happened?"

"We'll talk about that. Once I'm sure that you're okay and you've told me what you saw and heard." He sat down across from her.

"Nothing. I just got up… Willie was outside. I thought I'd make some tea. I turned on the light for him." Erin was aware that she was getting the steps out of order, babbling to him. But she wanted to know what he had to tell her. "He said to close the blind and stay inside… so I did."

"That's good. I'm glad you listened to him. That's it? You didn't see anyone else outside? Hear anything?"

Erin shook her head. "No. Unless I heard something in my sleep. I don't know what woke me up. I think it was a dream."

"Maybe," Terry said neutrally.

"What happened? What's going on out there? Did Willie see a prowler?"

"No. Maybe. We're still trying to sort that out. There will be an investigation. We won't have the answers tonight."

Then it couldn't be something as simple as someone looking in windows or even breaking into cars at night. A crime like that, and they would have immediate answers. "What, then? Was somebody hurt? What did Willie see?"

"We will be interviewing him about it. We need to talk to both of you separately, in case you saw or heard anything important. Keep your stories from influencing each other."

"But I didn't see or hear anything. I only saw Willie out there," Erin motioned, moving her hand back and forth as if to follow his movements. "Talking on his phone. I guess he must have been talking to the dispatcher? I don't know. Then you came. That's all I know."

"And that's just fine. It's okay. A nice, uncomplicated account." She looked at him, waiting for the explanation.

"Well…" Terry let out a long sigh. He took her hands in the middle of the table. "Willie called to report a dead body."

Erin stared at him blankly. The words entered her brain and didn't register because they didn't make any sense. A dead body? Whose dead body?

The only other person who should have been in the yard was…

Erin gasped and leaped to her feet, trying to run to the back door. Terry caught her and held her still.

"It's okay, it's okay. You don't want to see, Erin, just leave it to us."

Erin squeezed his strong arms as hard as she could, trying to steady herself. "Tell me it wasn't Vic."

CHAPTER 7

Terry pulled Erin against himself and held her tight. "No. No, Erin. Not Vic."

Tears of relief sprang to Erin's eyes and she started to sob. She smacked him on the chest with her open palm. "Don't scare me like that! You scared me to death!"

"I'm sorry. I didn't mean to make you think that anything had happened to Vic. I'm so sorry, Erin. It's okay. It wasn't Vic."

Erin was waiting for him to say, "It wasn't anyone we know," but he didn't. Which meant that it was someone they did know. Erin started to shake violently.

Terry took her back to her chair and sat her down. He picked up the teacup and took it to the counter to add a couple of spoonfuls of sugar to it. He gave it a brisk stir and brought it back to her.

"Drink that. We don't talk any more until you have at least half of that."

Erin breathed in the scent of the chamomile lemongrass blend and brought it up to her lips. The first couple of sips were so sweet she could barely get them down. That was how Reg liked her tea, Erin thought inconsequentially. She hated anything the least bit bitter and loaded up her tea with sugar until that was practically all it was. Sugar water, like she would put in a hummingbird feeder.

But Erin drank it anyway. As much as she could. It wasn't quite half, but she'd given it her best effort. Terry, sitting across from her once more, nodded.

"The body was... Theresa."

Erin gasped. "Crazy Theresa?"

He nodded. "Crazy Theresa."

Erin breathed out in a huff, almost a laugh. "Well, hallelujah."

Terry looked surprised at this reaction.

Erin shrugged, spreading her arms wide. "I can't say that I'm sorry to hear it. The thought of her always being in our lives, causing trouble and then disappearing like a ghost... Any loss of life is terrible, but... I'm not going to miss Crazy Theresa."

Terry nodded, a very small movement. "I must confess to a feeling of profound relief when I found out that she was dead." He looked down at the table and squeezed one of her hands. He had suffered much more at Theresa's hand than Erin had. While Theresa had attacked each of them, it was Terry who had ended up in the hospital with a head injury and all of the problems that went with that, from insomnia and migraines to mood changes and irritability. It hadn't been fun for either one of them.

Erin breathed in and out slowly, feeling the same sense of relief in knowing that she would never bother either of them or Vic again.

Erin turned and looked at the window abruptly, even though she already knew that the blind was down and she wouldn't be able to see anything.

"What?" Terry asked.

"Vic. Where is Vic? Does she know?"

"We're trying to track her down right now."

The words didn't make any sense to Erin. "What do you mean... trying to track her down?"

"Willie says she is out. She's not answering the door. Didn't tell

Willie that she was going out or where she would be. Not answering her phone."

Erin put her hand over her pounding heart. "Did something happen to her? Where is she? She couldn't have been kidnapped, could she?"

"Don't jump to conclusions. There are plenty of places around Bald Eagle Falls where a cell phone won't work."

"She and Willie were fighting last night…"

"Which would explain her not telling him where she was going today. She didn't tell you her plans? The two of you are always so involved in each other's lives…"

"No." Erin thought back, trying to catalog all of the conversations she'd had with Vic over the past few days. Had Vic mentioned anywhere that she had been planning to go? It didn't make sense for her to be gone in the middle of the night. "I don't know where she would have gone."

"I'm sure she'll show up."

Erin worried it over in her mind. It was easy for Terry to say that Vic would be fine. But he didn't know that.

"Was everything okay in her apartment…? There wasn't any sign that… Theresa hadn't gotten in there, had she?"

"We haven't been able to get in there to find out."

"Willie has a key."

"Willie isn't giving it up. He says it is Vic's apartment and he can't let someone in there without her permission. Even the police."

Or especially the police. Willie didn't exactly have a long-standing relationship of trust with law enforcement. While he and Terry got along most of the time and the police department occasionally called on Willie for his services, there was definitely a breach between them. Willie had a history.

"But what if she's in there hurt? If she and Theresa—what kind of a bullet was Theresa killed with? Have you ruled out Vic's gun?"

Terry leaned forward slightly. "What kind of bullet was she killed with?"

"Yes!"

He was silent and Erin tried to figure out what was going through his head. Had she said something wrong?

"How do you know Theresa was shot?"

Erin stared at him, processing the question. No, he hadn't told her that Theresa had been shot. He hadn't said anything about how she had died. Just that her body had been found. It could have been a natural death or an animal attack for all Erin knew.

"I guess… I just assumed that was the only way anyone would be able to kill her. She's so fast and strong, and carries a knife and a gun and who knows what else. I just can't see… how else she could have been killed."

Terry nodded.

"And it wasn't Vic?" Erin asked tentatively. "It wasn't the kind of gun that she carries?"

She had seen the small gun that Vic had a concealed carry permit for. Vic was determined to be able to protect herself if she was ever attacked or her apartment burgled. But she hadn't pulled it on Theresa on either of the last two occasions they had seen her on. Whether she forgot about it in the heat of the moment, froze up, or couldn't bring herself to threaten her old friend, Erin didn't know. Had Theresa made a fatal choice in confronting Vic a third time?

"We don't know anything yet," Terry said. "We'll have to wait for the Medical Examiner on that question. But… I don't think she was shot with Vic's gun."

Erin let out her breath. "Good." Her mind circled back around to her earlier concern. "You have to make sure that Vic isn't in her apartment, hurt, or…"

"Willie says that he checked. She's not there."

That didn't do much to allay the anxiety that Erin was feeling. She took another sip of the too-sweet tea, hoping that it would calm her mind. She needed something to do with her hands other than biting her nails.

"You could let me into her apartment," Terry suggested. "You're her landlord. You have a key."

But Willie was right to worry about Vic's privacy. The police had been in her apartment once before, and she had *not* been happy about it. Erin knew that as a landlord, she could enter the premises in an emergency without giving Vic notice, but letting the police in without a warrant was completely different.

"I don't think that's a good idea."

"We need to check on her welfare."

"But Willie already told you that she's not there."

"Willie is a suspect."

Erin caught her breath. A suspect? In Crazy Theresa's death?

Of course he was. Theresa had been obsessed with Vic. With getting back together even though they had both moved in different directions in their lives. Maybe Vic represented a happier time for Theresa. Maybe it was the only good relationship she'd ever had. If Theresa had come around looking for Vic again, Willie would probably be fully justified in shooting her. Theresa wasn't exactly well known for her calm and reasonable approach.

Not Crazy Theresa.

"If Willie was protecting Vic, then why would he lie about her being in the apartment? Especially if she was hurt?"

Terry shrugged. "Let's just say that he cannot always be taken at his word, and I would like to verify everything he says. We have to be careful of appearances. We can't give people the impression that we are giving Willie preferential treatment because he is a friend."

Erin considered Willie a friend, but she wasn't sure that Terry ever had. There had been too many cases where his suspicions had landed on Willie as a suspect.

"Why don't I go check? Will you take my word for it that Vic isn't there, or am I a suspect too? Maybe you think this is something that Willie and I cooked up together."

"You know that isn't true." Terry's mouth turned down. He was clearly hurt by her words.

Erin took a deep breath and blew it out in a stream. "Sorry. I'm scared. And Willie *is* a friend. I don't like him being treated like a suspect."

"You know I have to. Even if you don't like it. Even if Vic pops me in the nose for it. I have certain responsibilities. If I don't take them seriously, I'll end up in trouble. And I'll be off the case."

Erin nodded.

"If you would check Vic's apartment, I would appreciate it," Terry said. "I'll take your word for it."

Erin nodded. She stood up to go to the door.

"Wait a moment." Terry stopped her. "Let me take care of things out there. Wait until I come get you."

Erin did as she was told and waited as he went outside to talk to the sheriff and whoever else was there to process the scene. It was a few minutes before he came back inside.

"Okay. Are you feeling all right now? If you're faint or unsteady, you're not going up that flight of stairs."

Erin had been on her feet while she was waiting for him, and the shakiness had passed. "Yes, I'm fine."

"We can wait if you're not."

"No. If Vic was hurt, I would want to know right away."

She caught the look that Terry gave her.

"And I don't think there is anything wrong. I don't think Willie would look the other way if she was hurt. He'd want to get her treated as soon as possible."

"You're probably right. And if she was hiding out there waiting for the police to leave because she's the one who killed Theresa?"

Erin stopped beside him and looked into his eyes. "Is that why you want me to go in there? To see if Vic is hiding from you? You said you wanted to check on her welfare."

"I do. That's exactly what I need."

"So if she is in there, hiding out, you wouldn't need to talk to her."

"Of course we need to talk to her. Someone she knew was

killed in her front yard. She needs to make a statement. Tell us what she knows."

"And me too? Because I know Theresa and she was killed in my backyard?"

"You've given me your statement already. You were sleeping. You didn't hear anything. When you got up, Willie was already there, on the phone."

Erin examined his summary from every angle, trying to see if he could trap her in some way with her own words. But she didn't see how he could. It was the bare-bones truth. She didn't have anything to hide.

Erin walked past Terry and out the door. She looked at the stairs that ran along the outside of the garage, across the yard. She could just focus on the stairs and nothing else. Block everything else.

As it turned out, she couldn't keep her gaze from straying over to where Theresa's body lay. But apparently, part of the reason Terry had gone back out to the yard before allowing Erin out was to ensure that the body was covered so she wouldn't have to see it.

"Thank you," she breathed, even though Terry was still back in the house, waiting for her to perform her task.

CHAPTER 8

Erin gave a brief nod to the sheriff and the other law enforcement officers who had gathered in her yard to investigate and made a beeline for the stairs. She climbed up them, maybe a bit faster than she normally would have, because she found herself out of breath when she reached the top. She paused for a moment to catch her breath. Eventually, there were no other excuses to stall, and she inserted her key into the lock.

Feeling awkward about just walking into Vic's space when she wasn't there, Erin knocked first. Unnecessary, of course, since Willie had said that Vic wasn't there, but Erin just didn't feel like she could walk in without at least knocking first. It was just common courtesy.

"Vic?" she called tentatively as she opened the door. "Are you home?"

There was no response. Vic's apartment was dark and quiet. Erin fumbled for the light switch and turned it on.

Her eyes roamed over the interior of the apartment, looking for anything that was out of place. There was no blood. Nothing to suggest that the apartment had been burgled or that there had been a fight. It looked pretty much like it did all the time. Except that Vic wasn't there.

There was a high-pitched whine, and Erin crouched down to look inside Nilla's kennel. The fluffy white dog sat there watching her and gave another whine.

"Hey, Nilla. It's okay. Where's Vicky, huh? Do you know where she went?"

Vic usually took the dog with her wherever she could. She didn't like leaving him at the apartment, especially in his kennel.

But Nilla didn't have any answers for Erin. Erin took a quick look around the apartment to ensure that Vic was not in the bathtub or on the floor beside the bed, and then left. The more she stayed and talked to Nilla, the more he would whine and fuss. Without her there, he would go back to sleep until Vic got home.

Erin left the apartment, turning to lock the door after her. She descended the stairs again, aware that all eyes were on her. She felt suddenly conspicuous in her pink pajamas. Luckily, she didn't trip.

She shook her head. "She's not there."

~

A death investigation was always stressful. Erin didn't want to hear all of the details, yet she was curious. She knew that when she went back to Auntie Clem's Bakery the next morning, everyone would be there to ask about the latest death. Auntie Clem's was always busiest when there was some extra-juicy gossip or shocking news. Erin couldn't exactly plan crimes to boost her sales, but she sometimes wondered what she could do to mimic the boost she got after something tragic happened. So far, she hadn't found any sale campaign that could rival it.

And Erin was worried about Vic. Each of the law enforcement officers that she had talked to assured her that there was nothing to indicate that anything had happened to Vic, and they were sure she would show up at any time, safe and sound.

But how could anyone be sure without knowing why she was gone in the first place?

It had been almost an hour since Erin had woken up so

abruptly when Vic finally did get home. She drove up in Erin's yellow Volkswagen Beetle—which Erin had not even noticed was missing from the garage and had not given Vic permission to take. Erin had insisted on raising the kitchen blind again, so she saw Vic's pale and pinched expression when she emerged from the garage, looking around anxiously at all of the police activity.

She couldn't hear what Vic was saying, but could hear her tone, and was pretty sure that it was along the lines of "What's going on?" or "What's wrong?"

When they wouldn't let her walk through the backyard, she circled around to the front. Erin hurried to open the door before she got there.

Vic grabbed Erin and pulled her close, mirroring the relief that Erin had felt when Terry assured her that it wasn't Vic who had been killed. They just clutched each other for a few minutes before Vic finally drew back and wiped at her leaking eyes.

"I thought… it was you," Vic blubbered.

"Yeah. And I thought it was you," Erin agreed. She pulled Vic over to the couch, where they both sat down. Vic pulled a few tissues from the box on a nearby shelf and mopped her eyes and face.

"Who, then? What happened?" Vic demanded. She could see Terry in the kitchen, where he'd been keeping Erin company and asking the occasional question as they waited for Vic to show up. Vic looked back at Erin. She swallowed hard, her lips pressed into a thin line. "Willie? Is he okay?"

"Willie's fine. It was…" Erin caught one of Vic's hands and held it. "It was Theresa, Vic."

"Theresa? Oh… thank goodness." She gave a long sigh. "Thank goodness for that. But… where's Willie?" She cleared her throat. "Exactly what happened?"

"Willie is the one who found the body and called it in. No one is really sure what happened yet, how she got there."

"And where is he…?"

Erin looked in Terry's direction. "Taken to the police department offices to make a statement, I guess."

"Why couldn't he just make a statement here? Why would he have to go in for that?" Vic raised her voice, aiming the questions at Terry. "Why are the police treating him like a suspect?"

Terry gave a little sigh and approached them so that Vic wouldn't have to yell across the house at him and they could keep the conversation civil.

"If you found a body, you would have to make a statement too," he said calmly. "You know that."

"You didn't answer my question."

"You asked several questions."

"Why are you treating him like a suspect? If he called you to report it, what have you got on him?"

"We don't *have* anything on him. We're just following the proper protocols for interviewing a witness."

"Like heck!"

Terry looked at her, brows up.

"If it was Erin who had walked back there and tripped over a body, you're telling me that she would be over at the police department right now underneath your heat lamps?"

"Erin has had to do the same thing in the past," Terry reminded her.

"Every time?"

He shifted his feet uncomfortably.

"But you've got Willie over there now. And I *know* he didn't volunteer to go to the police department."

Erin looked back at Terry, wondering how he would respond to this allegation. It was true that Willie had resisted any attempts to interview him in the past. He would exercise his rights and insist that he didn't have to talk to them unless they arrested him.

So, what had changed this time?

"Willie is not under arrest," Terry said calmly. "He's not being detained in any way. He's making a voluntary statement about what happened here tonight. He can leave at any time and I'm sure he'll be in touch with you soon."

Terry *didn't* say that Willie would be back soon. And he didn't tell Vic to just go home and relax and wait for him there. Was the apartment off-limits?

Vic snorted. She pulled out her phone and unlocked it. Tapping her way through a few screens, she thumbed a quick message to Willie and pressed *send*. She looked at Terry.

"If he's not being detained, then he'll get right back to me, won't he?"

"I'm sure he will," Terry agreed.

In a moment, Vic's phone lit up, and she quickly swiped to answer the call. "I'm home," she said, though she had undoubtedly already told him that in her text. "Are you okay?"

Erin couldn't hear what Willie answered, his voice calm and not raised loudly enough for her to make anything out.

"Can you come back here?"

Vic listened to his answer, biting her lip.

"Well… don't be long, okay? I need you here."

He said something reassuring, Erin assumed, and Vic tapped to end the call.

"He's all right?" Terry asked in a neutral tone.

"So he says."

"And he can leave any time."

"He said he needed to stay a little longer." Vic's words were slightly sullen, slightly accusatory. But Terry wasn't at the police department offices. He wasn't the one who was keeping Willie away from her. She could complain all she liked, but nothing Terry did was going to change things.

Vic put her phone down and dabbed at her eyes a little bit more. "So, you're okay?" she asked, looking at Erin.

"Yeah. I didn't have any idea what was going on. Just got up and saw Willie in the backyard talking on his phone."

"What was he doing here? He came to see me?" Vic shook her head. "He didn't call to say he was coming over."

"He said that he'd tried to call you but couldn't get you," Erin told her. She didn't know whether Willie had called her before or after finding Theresa's body, or maybe even both, but that didn't really matter. "I guess you must have been out of range or something...?"

"Cell phones." Vic shrugged. "The one time they don't work is when you really need them to."

It felt that way sometimes.

"Where were you tonight, Miss Victoria?" Terry inquired. "You're not usually out this late. Were you... *expecting* company?"

"Don't 'Miss Victoria' me. You're always formal when you're acting like a cop. I don't need a cop right now. I just need my friends around me."

"I'm just wondering what happened. You're not usually out this time of night."

"I couldn't sleep. Decided to go for a drive." Another casual shrug, as if this were something she did all the time. "Get out, look at the stars. Reconnect with nature."

"In the middle of the night?"

"You can't see the stars in the middle of the day, *Officer Piper*."

"No, I didn't mean that. I have a hard time envisioning you just wandering around town, 'reconnecting.'"

"Well, I wasn't wandering around town. You can see the stars better away from the lights in the town. Out where it's really dark."

"And last time I checked, you don't have a driver's license."

Vic rolled her eyes. "I can drive. Been driving a tractor since I was seven."

She didn't say that she *did* have a driver's license. And since Erin had rarely known her to drive, Erin suspected that Terry was right. But he wasn't likely to ticket her for it when she had come home to a dead body and the police all over the yard.

CHAPTER 9

*E*rin had known that she would not get much sleep before going to Auntie Clem's in the morning. But despite Terry's repeated suggestions, she did not call in any of her other workers, but went ahead with the shift that she had planned on. She gave Vic the option of arranging for a sub herself if she wanted to, but Vic was of the same mind. She wasn't going to get to sleep either way. She might as well have something to keep her busy rather than sitting around with nothing to do, focused on what had happened and all of her questions and worries about it. She would have to answer all of the townspeople's curious questions sooner or later anyway; she might as well get it over with quickly. And the bakery might as well benefit from everyone's morbid curiosity.

So, tired as they were, they prepared for the day with some nice strong coffee, girded up their loins, and headed in to Auntie Clem's to get started on the baking that would need to be ready by the time people came in to gawk and ask questions.

Vic yawned, mixing chocolate chip cookie dough in the big machine. "I can't really believe that Theresa is dead, can you?"

Erin nodded her agreement. "She was so… so strong, so much of a force. It doesn't seem possible that she could be stopped by a bullet. Like she should have been able to dodge it and keep on going. She was so skilled…"

"Even the best soldier can be taken down by a bullet," Vic said with a shrug. "But yeah… it seems like after all of the trouble she has caused, it would take more to get rid of her. It should have taken more people, and it should have taken longer, with her fighting to the end. Right?"

Erin agreed. "Or maybe a silver bullet or stake through the heart." She started filling loaf pans with banana bread batter. "I'd like to get started on marshmallow eggs today. Think we'll have time to do that?"

"I don't know. I haven't done them before and it's going to be pretty busy today."

"Yeah. It will be for sure. We'll see whether there are any lulls."

"Might not be best to set your heart on it today."

"I won't. We can make some more cut-outs. We'll have time for that."

"Can we make some of them into sandwich cookies?" Vic suggested. "That's always fun."

"Good idea. Jam or icing for filling?"

"Some of each?"

Vic really was just a kid at heart. Erin smiled and wrote a few notes on the fridge whiteboard to keep them on track for the day.

"Who do you think will be first in this morning?" Erin asked, recapping the marker.

"Are you taking bets?"

"No, I can't afford to lose!"

"Melissa's got to be here early. Because she'll want to tell everything she knows. Make sure that everyone remembers that she works at the police department and has all of the inside scoop."

"Yes."

"Charley will be the last to know because she won't even wake up until noon," Vic offered with a grin.

"She could have heard before going to sleep."

"I doubt it."

"She doesn't *always* sleep until noon."

"No, sometimes she's later," Vic laughed.

Erin shook her head. Charley was Erin's half-sister, and she certainly hadn't inherited any early bird genes. There might be some similarity in their faces, but waking up early was not something they had in common. Erin tried to make allowances, because Charley was younger. But she really didn't believe that age had anything to do with it. Charley was just Charley. She wasn't a morning person.

"Well…" Vic looked at the clock on the wall. "I guess it's time to start filling the display case. We can't open late today!"

~

Vic was right, and Melissa was waiting in the small crowd outside of Auntie Clem's front door when Erin flipped the sign to Open and turned the bolt. They all poured in, trying to act casual, as if they were always there at that time. While Auntie Clem's definitely had a morning rush, it was only that full when there was something important to gossip about.

Melissa didn't try to pretend that she didn't know about the previous night's events. She was, after all, "with the police department." She clutched at Erin's arm and asked in a concerned tone whether she was okay, and if she really thought that she should be there working after the dreadful night she had been through.

"I'm fine," Erin reassured her, smiling. "I don't think the mixers count as 'heavy machinery,' so we can muddle through the day even though we are tired."

"You can't have gotten very much sleep last night. Did you get any at all?"

"Not much. But I got a couple of hours in before the body was discovered, and I did doze off for a while this morning when I was sitting on the couch." Erin rubbed at a crick in her neck. Not the best way to sleep.

The other customers pressed forward at the mention of a body being discovered, wanting all of the details. Erin returned to the other side of the display case to start filling orders. She felt better with a physical barrier between her and the curious customers. She didn't want them all grabbing at her to express their condolences as Melissa had.

"I hear it was Willie Andrews," one of the older ladies declared. "I never have understood why that one is not in prison. All you have to do is look at him to see that he's a ne'er-do-well."

Erin didn't look at Vic. People knew that she and Willie were together, even if they pretended not to. "Willie has always been very helpful to me. I don't know why you would think that of him."

But she did know why. Much of it was Willie's appearance, his skin stained and dirty looking because of the mining and the processing that he did of his own raw ores. No matter how hard he scrubbed at his skin, it would never look clean. And there was also the fact that he didn't work a single job with regular hours, but instead worked several smaller jobs intermittently, as he pleased. So people never saw him as "employed."

And then, of course, there was the fact that he had also come from a clan—the Dysons rather than the Jacksons—and had been a soldier with them for several years. He didn't talk about what he had done during that time, but Erin guessed he had done any number of things that might have landed him in prison if he had been caught. And that was what people remembered about him.

"I'm sure he did it." Mrs. Mans insisted. "He's just that kind."

Erin shut her eyes and gave her head a little shake. "What would you like today?"

"Oh, yes." Now it was time for Mrs. Mans to pay the piper for her curiosity. She couldn't very well admit that she had only come into the bakery to gossip. "Well, those hot cross rolls look so nice and springy. I remember my mother making just that recipe."

Erin didn't bother to remind her that all of Erin's goods were gluten-free, many of them her own recipes, and even if they looked like the same ones as Mrs. Mans's mother used to make, they were undoubtedly not. "A dozen?" she asked.

Mrs. Mans opened her mouth, hesitating. She probably hadn't been planning to take a whole dozen. But put on the spot in front of her acquaintances, people she wanted to impress, she was backed into a corner. "Yes. A dozen would be just perfect. We're having the grandchildren over spring break, so I should have something nice for them."

Erin nodded her agreement and assembled a box to arrange them in. "Maybe the grandchildren would like some cookies too."

"Yes… I suppose they would. Those Easter cookies look a real treat."

Erin added those to the order too. She glanced sideways at Vic, wondering whether she should push it and suggest that Mrs. Mans get something else as well. She would pay dearly for her comments about Willie!

Vic suppressed a smirk, but ended up snorting as she tried to keep a straight face. Erin decided that Mrs. Mans probably had all she needed for her grandchildren's visit and didn't press for her to buy anything else. Vic rang up the total and Erin looked to the next person in line.

Mary Lou smiled at her and did not ask anything about what had happened the night before or how they were feeling that morning. She touched her gray helmet of hair to make sure that nothing was out of place. "Just… a few slices of the banana bread," she said, pointing. She glanced around. "You haven't seen Joshua this morning, have you?"

Joshua, her younger son, had been going through a difficult time lately. Erin hoped that he would be able to get through it, to get back to school again and stay focused on his goals. He wanted to be an investigative reporter, so he really needed to get his high school diploma, at least. She didn't know what other qualifications reporters were expected to have. Joshua had a few articles published with the Bald Eagle Falls weekly paper, which was a good start. Still, Erin didn't suppose there was much competition trying to get into the weekly. They pulled a lot of their material from the bigger papers in the area and didn't have much exclusive content. The more prominent papers would probably want reporters with a degree of some sort.

"No, I haven't seen him, but I'll keep my eyes open."

Erin tried not to be concerned that Mary Lou didn't know where Joshua was the first thing in the morning. Had he left during the night? It was not that long since he had been abducted in the middle of the night. Erin was sure Mary Lou was probably having kittens over his not being home that morning, despite her neatly-turned-out, calm and confident appearance.

"I'd appreciate that. I'm sure he's fine. You didn't see him last night?"

"Last night? Why would—no. I didn't see him last night." Of course, the intrepid reporter might have followed the sirens to find out what the disturbance was. Erin hadn't noticed Joshua around, but that didn't mean that he wasn't there, standing somewhere out of the way, making his notes and watching the police, gleaning everything he could from some vantage point. She hadn't been looking for him.

Mary Lou nodded, taking her banana bread and giving Vic exact change. "Have him call me if you happen to see him. You know how *men* are. Never thinking about who will be worrying about them."

"I will."

"Thank you." Mary Lou nodded and left.

∼

Eventually, the morning rush trickled off, but there were still more people than usual coming into the bakery to prepare for their Easter celebrations. Erin knew that it wasn't a coincidence. They kept the baked goods flowing and kept the gossip to a minimum, expressing their distress over a dead body showing up in the yard but not giving in to any of the speculations on what had happened.

Erin knew what most of the gossips were going to say. Like Mrs. Mans, they would suspect Willie. He had, after all, been the one to find the body. He was in a relationship with Vic. And he had previously been in the Dyson clan and was suspected of being involved in all kinds of other nefarious dealings. People were not going to give up on a target like that.

CHAPTER 10

Midmorning after school had started, Erin looked up to see Mrs. Foster coming in with her two youngest children. Little Traci, who had been a babe in arms when Erin had first moved into town and was now a going concern, and Alan, the baby they had been blessed with most recently—finally, a brother for Peter, who was one of Erin's favorite customers. But Peter was in school, as were the oldest two girls.

"Good morning, Mrs. Foster. It's good to see you today!"

Mrs. Foster nodded at Erin's greeting and waited while the customer ahead of her made his selections, trying to keep Traci quiet and under control, which was a bit of a challenge. Alan was also fussing in the sling. Erin knew that he was colicky, maybe reacting to something in Mrs. Foster's milk that upset his stomach. She was having to be very careful with what she ate, tracking what she consumed and trying to match his behaviors and symptoms with what she was eating. Something almost impossible to do if he was reacting to multiple different foods. Eliminating one thing at a time would not work.

When Mrs. Foster reached the counter, Erin could see that she was exhausted. There were fine lines extending out from her eyes and creased into her forehead. She had shadows under her eyes, and her face had taken on a stretched-thin quality.

"Is Alan keeping you up?" Erin asked sympathetically. Mrs. Foster had a lot to do, with five children under the age of ten. She couldn't just deal with Alan's colic. She needed to take care of all of the others too. As much as Peter tried to help, and he was a very responsible child, he couldn't take all of the pressure off of her. Erin didn't know what Mr. Foster did for a living, but he was often working and didn't seem to have much to do with parenting and childcare.

Many of the ladies in town, even the young ones, still seemed to believe that childcare was a woman's work and didn't expect their husbands to co-parent. Erin supposed that traditional values were still deeply entrenched in the Bible belt. She wasn't sure why religion should dictate something like women's roles in the home. Didn't their god expect men to be equal partners with their wives? To ease their burdens so that they weren't as worn out as Mrs. Foster?

"I'm worn slap out," Mrs. Foster admitted. She continued to thump Alan on the back and tried to redirect Traci so that she didn't get fingerprints all over the display case.

"Don't you worry about that," Erin told her. "They wipe right off. What cookie do you want today for kid's club, Traci?"

Traci pressed her nose against the glass. "Want the lamb," she said eventually, pointing to the sugar cookies. Erin reached in to pick up the one closest to Traci, which resulted in a shriek of protest from the little girl. "No, no!"

Erin stopped and looked at her through the glass. "Which one?"

Mrs. Foster tried to tell Traci that they were all the same, but Traci clearly had her heart set on a specific one.

"There!" Traci insisted, tapping on the glass, tears starting down her cheeks. "No… no… that one!"

Erin eventually managed to pick out the particular lamb that Traci wanted and handed it to her. Traci didn't bite into it immediately, but held the lamb cradled in her hands, looking at it with wide eyes.

Mrs. Foster rolled her eyes and shook her head at Erin. "I don't know if it makes things better or worse to cater to her whims," she sighed. "I want her to be flexible and to be grateful for what she gets, but if I don't indulge her… she'll pout and be a terror the rest of the day. And"— another sigh—"I want her to grow up to be a strong woman who is not afraid to express her opinion. Not a mousy little thing who lets everyone else run over her wants and needs."

Erin wondered where Mrs. Foster put herself on that spectrum. Was she a woman who got what she wanted, or who always capitulated to someone else? Or somewhere in the middle?

"I don't know how you can make those decisions. I'm afraid I wouldn't be a very good parent," Erin told her. "I would be so worried about making the wrong choice."

"It's scary, knowing that you are shaping your children's lives. A wrong decision could lead them on to… the wrong paths and a much more difficult life. Of course, it would be one thing if you could just tell them what to do and they would do it. But kids don't work that way."

"No, they don't," Vic chimed in, laughing.

"I have been so spoiled with the older children. Peter, in particular. The girls always look to him as a leader and try to mimic what he does, which is great. But between Alan's colic and Little Miss here…"

Erin nodded understandingly. "What can we get you today?"

Mrs. Foster ran through a long list of what she would want for the week's groceries and the upcoming Easter feast. While Erin started to pull together a box for her, Mrs. Foster turned around to make sure that there was no one behind her before venturing, "Have you had a lot of business today? When I heard about what was found, I thought that maybe today wasn't the best day to come. I know how the women around here gossip and I don't want the kids to overhear these things."

"It was a pretty busy morning," Erin agreed. "But it has quieted down for a little bit now. You picked a good time."

Mrs. Foster nodded. She didn't ask about the discovery, but the silence hung heavily in the air.

"We don't really know anything yet," Erin offered. "The police have only begun their investigation."

"But they must have their suspicions. Directions they are investigating."

Erin glanced over at Vic. "Yes. I'm sure they do."

"They're looking at Willie Andrews," Vic said. "But he didn't do it. He was just the one to discover the—to make the discovery." Looking at Traci, Vic reworded her answer quickly.

"You don't think he had anything to do with it?" Mrs. Foster sounded doubtful.

"No. I *know* he didn't."

Erin didn't say anything. She expected Vic to defend Willie, but she didn't know how Vic could be certain. She hadn't been there. Could she really say that she knew one hundred percent that it was not Willie? There was no niggling doubt at the back of her brain?

Erin and Terry both knew that Willie had been looking for Theresa ever since she had slipped through their fingers the first time. Willie blamed himself for not having searched Theresa thoroughly before tying her up. She'd had a knife and had cut through the heavy twine that held her bound while they went out to the outbuildings looking for some sign of Jack Ward and Terry.

Willie had made several extended trips out of town, not telling anyone where he was going. Erin knew that those had been attempts to track Theresa or confirm how reliable a sighting had been. He had certainly worked harder on finding Theresa than law enforcement in Moose River had seemed to. Of course, Erin didn't know everything that went on behind the scenes. Still, Jack Ward had always seemed pretty casual about it, assuring Erin that Theresa would show up sooner or later on her own.

And Theresa had. That was the problem. She could show up

anywhere at any time, and they all knew she was dangerous. She had nearly killed Jack and Terry. She'd had her hands around Erin's throat. She was suspected of having killed a lot of people for the clan. She had as much as admitted to having poisoned her parents. Erin didn't think it was a good idea to just wait for someone like that to reappear and sow more carnage. Willie had the right idea about tracking her down.

It was the next step she was troubled by. What would Willie have done if he had tracked down Theresa? Or if he *had* run into her in the backyard on his way to see Vic? She doubted if Willie had ever intended to turn Theresa over to the authorities. There was too much of a danger that they wouldn't have enough to charge her or she would be released on bail, or she would find a way to escape. And then she would be back in their lives again, appearing out of the blue at the most inconvenient times, threatening to ruin Vic's life or end it altogether.

Willie would not have trusted the authorities to keep Theresa in prison for the rest of her life.

Willie would have put a permanent end to the threat.

CHAPTER 11

*E*rin and Vic took an early lunch, as usual. Business would pick up at noon, then wane, and then pick up again as the school kids were getting out and parents were figuring out what to make for dinner. Erin anticipated that the after-school crowd would be just as ravenous for more details of the investigation as the morning crowd. Maybe even more so, after going most of the day without hearing anything new. The police department wasn't going to break anything that fast.

Erin tried to be normal and casual over lunch. Like it was just any other day. She had her sandwich in one hand and laid out her planner and held a pen in the other as she looked over her notes for the day. But she couldn't concentrate on the everyday running of Auntie Clem's when Theresa's death and Willie's possible complicity in it hung over their heads. And Vic had to be feeling twice as stressed as Erin.

"So… did you get any sleep after Willie got home last night?" Erin asked, endeavoring to keep her tone light. Just normal curiosity, wondering how her friend had fared during the night.

"He was in so late and I was already in bed. I took a pill, figured it was the only way I was going to get any sleep, but…"

Vic shook her head. "I dunno. It didn't work. They've always worked before, and I thought I would just pop it and fall asleep."

"But you didn't go back to sleep at all?"

"Kind of dozed, in and out a few times, but I could still hear everything going on in the apartment and my brain was trying to answer all of these questions… I just couldn't." Vic rubbed her forehead and then cupped her hands over her eyes for a moment, trying to wipe the sleep away without rubbing the makeup that concealed the shadows.

"And you and Willie are okay?"

Vic flashed her a look. "Who said we're not okay?"

"No one. I just wondered… after the other day, you know, it seemed like the two of you might be arguing." Erin shrugged. "Maybe not, and it's none of my business if you were or weren't. I just want my friends to be happy."

"We're fine."

Erin had another bite of her sandwich and pretended to be going over something important in her planner. She hoped Vic would volunteer more information. What she and Willie had been arguing about or that they had made up before Theresa's death. Or just that they had put their differences aside for a day, both needing the comfort of the other's arms around them.

She stifled a sigh.

Vic looked at her again but didn't elaborate.

∼

Charley arrived after the lunch rush to help with the end-of-day work and after-school rush.

"Your favorite sister is here!" Charley announced herself.

Erin smiled and shook her head. She was tired and worn thin, but Charley had probably just gotten out of bed and was chipper.

"How do you know you're my favorite sister?" she teased.

"Because I'm your only sister."

Erin shook her head. "I've had lots of foster sisters. It might actually be pretty hard to decide…" she teased.

"Well, your favorite biological sister, then," Charley conceded, shrugging. "What do you want me to work on?"

"There's a list of what we want to start on for tomorrow on the counter. Actually,"—Erin changed plans midstream—"why don't I start on the batters, and you take the front for a while? I'm so tired I can barely smile."

Charley nodded, slipping her apron on and tying it behind her. "Sure, no trouble." She held up a hand to stop Erin before she retreated to the kitchen. "Did I overhear someone on the street say that you stumbled over another body?"

Charley turned to Vic and rolled her eyes dramatically about her crazy sister.

"No, it wasn't me; it was Willie," Erin protested. "I was sleeping."

"Sure you were. One day it's all going to catch up to you, sis."

Erin shook her head and walked into the kitchen. She hoped that Vic didn't feel like she was being thrown to the wolves. Charley wasn't the most sensitive person and tended to "tell it like it is." Hopefully, Charley would behave herself and if she got too impertinent, Vic wouldn't have any qualms about putting her in her place. They knew each other well enough now that Vic shouldn't be worried about offending Charley.

She started to mix her base bread recipe in the big mixer and let her mind wander. Charley was the only biological sister that Erin had. With both of her parents dead now, there was no chance of there ever being another. Unless another child had been born before Erin. Or if her dad had fathered children that she didn't know about. But she wasn't even going to go there. There *was* a whole boatload of foster siblings.

She didn't have a hope of remembering all of them. There were a few special ones she had spent more time with or had developed a better relationship with. Carolyn, Erin's inspiration to become a gluten-free baker. Reg Rawlins, a wild and colorful character, who had always gotten Erin into trouble.

Erin's phone rang and she slipped her earbuds in so that she would be able to hear the caller over the noise of the kitchen equipment and still have her hands free to work while they talked.

"Hello?"

"Erin? It's Reg."

Erin laughed. "Isn't that funny? I was just thinking about you."

"I know," Reg agreed. "I can hear you!"

"Uh…" Erin wasn't sure how to respond to this suggestion. Reg had been treated for psychosis in the past. The doctors disagreed on whether her problem was schizophrenia or something else. Erin had found that it was best not to challenge Reg's delusions, but just to take them in stride the best she could. "So, how are you doing? I haven't heard much from you lately."

Not that Erin ever called to check up on Reg. She didn't want to get pulled into any of Reg's scams, and even more than that, she didn't want to know where Reg was calling from in case Terry or someone else asked. It was better to not know than to have to lie about it.

"Yeah, sorry, I was on a vacation," Reg declared. "Well, not really a vacation, but it was a trip…"

"A vacation would be nice," Erin said brightly, not wanting to know what kind of a trip Reg was talking about. "We went on a cruise to Alaska once. I told you about that, right?"

"A cruise," Reg breathed. "I'd love to get out there on the ocean. But… well… things don't always turn out like we expect, do they?"

"No, that's true." Erin's Alaskan cruise certainly hadn't turned out as expected. She had been planning on something that would help her to relax and renew herself. She hadn't anticipated the seasickness or everything that had happened while they were on board. It was like a bad dream. "So…" Erin searched for a safe topic of discussion, one that wouldn't be controversial or trigger Reg's delusions. "Are you doing anything for Easter? Sounds like we're going to have some nice weather here."

"Yes," Reg's voice got a little higher, sounding excited. "We have this Ostara community thing, and spring equinox, and the ma—the games."

"The games?" Erin tried to imagine what kind of games Reg would be interested in. She doubted Reg had taken up chess or checkers lately. Last she'd heard, Reg was somewhere in Florida. Maybe she was cheating retirees out of their savings playing canasta.

"The games are… something like the Olympics, only not between different countries. There are a bunch of different teams, and they compete for medals. Kind of… extreme sports. I've never been to it before, but it sounds like it will be really good."

Erin nodded. "That's cool. You're really getting into the local color?"

"It's not like anywhere I've lived before."

They had both grown up on the northeastern seaboard. Florida was probably as much of a shock to Reg's system as Tennessee had been to Erin's.

"I know what you mean!" Erin agreed.

"Is everything okay, Erin?"

Erin turned on a second mixer. She frowned at the concern in Reg's voice. "Sorry, I hope that isn't too noisy. Yeah, I'm okay. Why?"

"I just… had a feeling that maybe something is wrong. Are you and that handsome cop still together?"

"Terry. Yes, we are. How about you and…" Erin searched for a name, trying to remember the latest man Reg might have mentioned. But when Reg told Erin about a guy, it was usually because she was mad at him. Which Erin supposed might be a cover for liking someone. Or she might be mad because she liked him and he had done something to disappoint her.

"I'm not with anyone right now," Reg dismissed. "I don't need any man in my life making things more complicated."

"Oh... okay, then." Erin shrugged it off. Apparently that topic wasn't going anywhere either, and the mixers were making conversation even more difficult. "I should probably let you go. As you can hear, I have a bunch going on right now," she said apologetically. "I need to get everything ready for tomorrow."

"Okay. Take care of yourself. You'll be careful, won't you? Especially around the water? Or alone in the woods?" Reg said worriedly.

Paranoia now too? "Uh... sure. Of course. You used to always get after me for playing it too safe, you remember that? I'm not a big risk-taker," she reassured.

"Yeah... I guess I'll talk to you later, then. If you need something... give me a call...?"

"I will," Erin agreed. She said goodbye and reluctantly terminated the call. She stared blankly at one of the mixers for a few minutes, mesmerized by the metallic shine and the hypnotic whir. She tried to make sense of the conversation with Reg, but could make neither heads nor tails of it.

Hopefully, Reg was all right and not in the midst of a breakdown. In all the time that Erin and Reg had lived in the same household, Reg had never been completely symptom-free, as far as Erin knew. She'd been able to keep her symptoms hidden from foster parents and case workers for a while, but Erin had seen Reg when the adults were gone and she stopped masking them.

Erin hoped Reg had friends in Florida who would help her through whatever was going on.

CHAPTER 12

"*E*rin, there's someone out here to see you!" Charley stood in the kitchen doorway, gesturing to the front.

Erin straightened up and arched her back, trying to work out the kinks. "Who is it?"

"A couple of kids. I'll take over here. What are you working on?"

Erin pointed out the various different batters she had been in the process of preparing. Charley had been helping out for long enough that she seemed to grasp all of the details right away. She picked up the recipe book, where all of their regular recipes were printed and stored in sheet protectors. "I'm on it."

Erin took a quick look around to make sure that she hadn't forgotten to tell Charley anything, then returned to the front of the store. She saw Harold, one of the teenage boys from the school. He had been friendly with her and helped her out in the past, and had continued to come to Auntie Clem's even when a number of the townspeople had blacklisted Erin for a time, unhappy with her role in solving a series of thefts before Christmas. Harold and his family had stood by her through a lonely time.

"Harold, so nice to see you. What can I get you today?"

"Some granola bars?" Harold suggested. He looked into the display case. "And... one of those brownies?"

"Sure." Erin nodded. She picked out a few granola bars for him and packaged up one of the gooey double-fudge brownies. "Don't ruin your supper!"

"Maybe this *is* my supper."

"It better not be. That's no way for a budding basketball star to fuel up."

Harold chuckled. He wasn't really into any organized sports. He just played some pick-up basketball and skill drills with his friends at school. He didn't play for any of the school teams.

"I heard what happened," Harold ventured. "I hope... is everything okay? That must have been scary for you."

Erin thought about the discovery of Theresa's body in comparison with some of the other things that had happened to her in Bald Eagle Falls. "Actually... it wasn't so bad," she said. "I wasn't the one who found it. Her. And I didn't see her. So it was just..."

"Just a corpse in your backyard."

Erin laughed. "You make it sound a lot worse than it is!" Erin wondered how much she dared to say to Harold. He was not one of the children whose parents had been up in arms about her talking to their son, But they might not support her bakery or her friendship with Harold if she gave him any graphic details or anything that might upset him or give him nightmares. "The lady whose body was found... she wasn't a friend. She was a very dangerous person. So however it was that she died..."

"Someone did you a favor?" Harold suggested.

"I wouldn't want to put it that bluntly. But... I am relieved to know that she won't ever be coming after me."

"Can I quote you on that?"

Erin looked past Harold in confusion. She hadn't taken a good look at any of the other customers who were waiting to be served. She always tried to keep her focus on the customer she was serving. She had taken all of the lanky figures for Harold's basketball buddies, but the young man who had spoken was not one of Harold's friends.

Joshua Cox.

Joshua's older brother, Campbell, had been a big sports star at the school. Joshua had initially followed in his footsteps, but found that he didn't have the same skill level as Campbell did and that he didn't have the interest and energy to pursue a career in sports. The Cox family had been through a series of tragedies and, while the boys had tried to weather the storm, they had both eventually run out of steam, unable to keep up with the school's expectations of them. Campbell had dropped out. Joshua was still enrolled at the school, but he had put his education on hold for a semester as he recovered from being kidnapped.

Erin sincerely hoped that he would go back to school in the fall.

Joshua stood there with his pencil and open notepad, waiting for Erin's response to his question.

"What?"

"Can I quote you as saying that you were relieved to know that Theresa Franklin would not be coming after you?"

"Mmm..." Erin looked at Vic to see what she thought of this. It was the truth and, surely, most people would be able to understand that it was better to not have a murderer terrorizing her. But the allegations against Theresa hadn't been proven in a court of law, and people in Bald Eagle Falls who might be related to her might take offense. "I don't think you'd better quote me on that. I didn't even see you standing there; I didn't intend to give a quote to the press."

Joshua stepped to the side so that she could see him better. Still somewhat paler and skinnier than he had been before his kidnapping. Erin had noticed that Mary Lou had reduced the amount that she was buying from Auntie Clem's Bakery. Was that because Joshua was not eating as much?

Maybe he had just finished a growth spurt.

"What *can* the two of you tell me about the body of Theresa Franklin being found in your yard?" Joshua asked.

"I imagine you know all of the basics already," Erin said slowly. "There really isn't much that we can add. I didn't even see it. Her. And Vic wasn't there." Erin looked over at Vic.

"Not that it's anyone's business," Vic said firmly.

"You knew her too, right?" Joshua persisted. "She used to be your friend."

Vic wasn't in any position to argue. Especially not if Joshua managed to get his hands on a picture of the two of them together. Vic looked considerably different from the way she did now, but people would still know it was her.

"A long time ago," Vic admitted.

"Less than five years," Joshua countered.

"Yes. But would you want me throwing a relationship back in your face that you're having now, a few years from now?"

"I don't really have any relationships," Joshua said, his face getting red.

"Yeah. And anything I had back then, it wasn't serious either. It was just… experimenting. Figuring out who we were and where we wanted to go in life. And that wasn't with her."

"Why was she at your house? Did she still want that relationship?"

Vic gave Erin a warning glance. They both knew that Theresa did, in fact, want a relationship. But that information wasn't widely known and Vic didn't want Erin spreading it around.

"I never saw her," Vic told Joshua with a shrug. "I wasn't home. So I can't tell you why she was there."

Joshua looked dissatisfied with this answer. He considered it seriously, probably recognizing that she was holding back. "So… where were you when Willie Andrews found the body?"

"That's none of your business."

Joshua shrugged, looking a little embarrassed at his own question.

Harold, finished making his purchase, turned around to face

Joshua. "Leave them alone, man. It's not like they did anything wrong. Miss Victoria can't help it if some psycho is stalking her."

"I'm just trying to get the story. For the paper."

Erin was surprised to hear Harold confronting Joshua. She knew how much he looked up to the Cox boys. "Maybe we should just leave the investigating up to the police," she told them reasonably.

Joshua snorted. Erin looked away, her face heating up. Yes, she had involved herself in a lot of police matters since she had moved to Bald Eagle Falls, but that wasn't the same. Most of the time, she found herself in the middle of things by accident. The few times that she had intentionally tried to solve a case, it was when her friends had been suspects, and she had to help them out…

That wasn't the same as investigating for a newspaper story. But she couldn't bring herself to try to explain that difference to Josh. He was right; she was being hypocritical by telling him he should stay out of it when she had put herself in the midst of an investigation so many times before.

"Can't I get comments from either one of you?" Joshua pressed. "Anything? What did you think of Theresa Franklin?"

Erin pressed her lips together and shook her head. It probably wouldn't go over well, especially with the church ladies, if she were to express her real feelings.

But if they were honest, they would have to admit that it was true; it was better that Theresa was dead.

"Sorry. I don't really have any comment."

After Erin had dealt with the other schoolboys and they were gone, she gave a long, exasperated sigh. "I suppose I'm going to come off looking like some bloodthirsty vigilante in Joshua's article."

Beaver had been behind the boys and stood looking into the display case, chomping on her gum. "You didn't say anything that isn't true. Life will be a lot easier for you without Crazy Theresa Franklin around."

CHAPTER 13

*E*rin expected that Terry would have a long day at work. Whenever there was a homicide or other major crime to be investigated, she could count on his putting in long hours to try to break the case. The police department did not have a big staff, and Terry was the most qualified.

Vic had gone straight home to her loft apartment, informing Erin through wide yawns that she was going to go straight to bed for a nap. It didn't sound like a bad idea. Still, Erin suspected that if she took a nap early in the evening, then either she wouldn't be able to wake up after that until one o'clock in the morning, or she would sneak in a nap and then not be able to get to sleep again at bedtime. Either way, she didn't relish another poor night's sleep, so she was determined to stay up until it was either her regular bedtime or she couldn't stay on her feet any longer.

She made a light supper for herself and petted and fed the animals, then opened up one of Clementine's journals and read through it on the couch. Mostly, Clementine's journals were pretty routine. Gossip about friends, events going on around town, any special events or holidays coming up that she was preparing for. Routine, everyday kind of stuff.

But that was the kind of life Clementine had led. Safe and

routine and pretty uneventful. She certainly hadn't had Erin's knack for running into trouble. But people did confide in her, and she kept their confidences—but wrote them down in her journal. Erin did occasionally find out something about a Bald Eagle Falls resident that she wouldn't otherwise have known. Usually, they were parents or grandparents of people she knew, but sometimes they were senior customers of Auntie Clem's.

There was a knock on the door. Erin hadn't heard anyone coming up the walk, so she was startled. But it wasn't a loud, insistent knock, so she didn't panic. She went to the door and checked the peephole, then opened the door to Willie.

"Hey." She smiled at him. "Vic is at the loft, I think. She was going to lie down."

"Yeah. I'll head over there in a few minutes." He continued to stand on her step expectantly.

Erin nodded and stepped back, letting him in. Willie didn't usually approach her alone. She hoped it didn't mean that there was something wrong between him and Vic. Or that he was worried about Vic. Of course, he had every reason to be. All of the recent drama in her family, topped off with the killing of a former lover right outside her door? It would have been enough to upset anyone.

"Pull up a chair," Erin invited. "Make yourself comfy."

She wondered if she should make some tea, but discounted it. Willie wasn't a big tea drinker. And Erin didn't want to make coffee or open a bottle of wine. Coffee would keep her up and wine might make the conversation between her and Willie look like something far more intimate than it was. Erin had once been somewhat interested in Willie. Intrigued by him, at the very least but, when Officer Piper had started showing her more attention and Vic had shown an interest in Willie, Erin had put any such thoughts out of her mind.

Willie sighed and didn't look particularly comfortable in the upholstered chair that he selected. "How are you doing, Erin?"

"I'm fine." Erin shrugged, surprised at the question.

"I didn't get a chance to talk to you last night about what I found... I'm sorry about being so abrupt with you."

"No, that's fine. I wasn't offended. You were just doing what anyone would have expected you to. Calling the police and keeping everyone safe in case the killer was still around."

Willie looked at her, his gaze piercing. "Is that what you think?"

"Yes...?" It became a question. What else would Erin have thought? That was exactly what had happened.

"You don't think I had anything to do with it."

The thought had floated around in the back of Erin's brain, but she hadn't given it any heed. Maybe Willie had caught Theresa hanging around Vic's door. Maybe he had been defending Vic, keeping her safe from Theresa. If that were the case, though, then surely he would have just said so. Anyone with half a brain could understand that it was self-defense. Or whatever you called defending someone else under the law. Justified.

But in truth, she hadn't heard Willie's story. She had only assumed that she knew what he had told the police. But if Willie had been claiming self-defense, then wouldn't Terry have asked her questions about that? Whether she had seen the two of them fighting, had heard any yelling, or whether Willie had told Erin he had killed her.

"Did you have something to do with it? Other than finding the body?"

"No."

Erin shrugged.

He continued to look at her as if he expected more.

"The police kept you for a long time," Erin observed.

"Yeah. They were full of questions. Did Terry talk to you about it?"

"You know he doesn't talk about police stuff at home. He'd get in trouble if he told me stuff about active investigations. He's always really careful."

"What have you heard? Between what you saw last night and

all of the gossip at the bakery, and whatever Terry *didn't* tell you, you must have a pretty good picture of what happened."

Erin shifted uncomfortably. She picked up Clementine's journal and fiddled with the cover. "I don't really know what happened last night. And you don't want to hear the gossip."

"Everyone thinks that I did it."

"Well… a lot of them are suspicious. But those are just prejudices. It doesn't mean that you did anything. Just that they're making assumptions. I don't think that." She paused, thinking about it. "Unless you tell me that's what happened."

Could he have had a confrontation with Theresa? Come back to see Vic and found a stalker in the yard? Maybe it was the two of them arguing or a physical altercation that had woken Erin up in the middle of the night.

Willie didn't say one way or the other. He didn't say that he had just found Theresa's body there, and he didn't say that he'd done it. She knew that he had been trying to track Theresa's movements for some time. He'd never said what he'd planned to do if he found her. And Erin had never asked.

If Willie had told the police that he'd killed her, then he would have been in jail. Even with a claim of self-defense, they would still arrest him and then let a jury decide whether he had been justified or not.

Erin shook her head, thinking about it. As obvious as it would be to suspect Willie, the one who had reported the killing and had a motive for killing her, the pieces just didn't fit.

Willie knew of caves and mines where Theresa's body would never be found. If he had killed her, then the easiest thing would have been to take her body to one of those horrific holes in the ground and deposit it there. Theresa was on the run, wanted on several charges, so no one would be surprised not to see her for a while, and the longer it went before people really started questioning, the harder it would be to establish where and when she had been killed, and therefore establishing who could have killed her became a more and more impossible task.

Willie couldn't have killed her; it just didn't make any sense.

"Do you know who did it?" Erin asked.

Willie frowned. He shook his head at her as if he couldn't believe the question. "Don't be so naive, Erin."

Erin looked toward the back of the house as if she could see through the walls. "Vic? It wasn't her." She shook her head. Willie's eyebrows pressed toward each other, a deep crease between them. "Terry already said that it wasn't a gun the same size as Vic's. And I've seen them both together, Willie. Twice now. Vic never made a move to threaten or attack Theresa. You were there when we went to Theresa's house. Vic never even reached for her gun."

"No," Willie agreed, nodding.

"She wouldn't do it. When we saw Theresa in Moose River in the coffee shop, she was threatening, but Vic never responded. I don't think she could. She might talk tough, but I don't know if she could shoot someone she knew personally, and was close to, like Theresa. They knew each other once, and Vic feels sorry for her, despite all of the stuff she's done. Vic knows that... events can shape people. She could have ended up where Theresa did, if she'd stayed with her family. She was that close."

Willie's brows remained furrowed.

"She wasn't even here," Erin reminded him. "She wasn't home." Erin bit her lip, thinking about it. "Do you know where she was?"

"Do you?" Willie countered.

"No." Erin smoothed her thumb down the clean edges of the journal pages. "She didn't say, and I didn't think it would be right for me to ask. If she didn't volunteer anything..."

Willie nodded.

"Are the two of you okay?" Erin asked him. "I know that you sort of... had a disagreement over something. Not that Vicky said anything, she didn't. I just want to make sure that you're okay."

"We're fine. Both of us tend to get... excited about things sometimes. Have opinions."

Erin nodded, smiling. "That's what I told Vic before. The two of you are both so passionate. You're going to bump heads sometimes."

"I don't know if passionate is necessarily the right word. Opinionated. Bullheaded."

"You're not always going to agree on everything."

"No. We're not. But we're still okay."

"Good. Are you going over there tonight?"

Willie looked in the direction of Vic's apartment. "Yes. That's the plan. If she'll let me in."

"She will," Erin assured him. "Won't she?"

"We haven't really had a good talk. I was so late getting back last night, and she was asleep. So I didn't stay; I just went home." He scratched the back of his head. "In retrospect, I probably should have woken her up and talked with her. But knowing that she'd been up most of the night, I didn't have the heart. And… she hasn't called me today."

Ouch.

Vic had said that she needed Willie, and he hadn't talked to her when he'd finally gotten back from the police department offices. It was no great surprise that she'd given him the silent treatment for the day. And maybe it would not be surprising if she refused to let him into the loft and kept the silence going for a few days. This wasn't just a broken date, after all.

Erin looked Willie over critically.

"What?" Willie demanded, palms up in query.

"I don't see any flowers. Chocolate. Where's your peace offering?"

"Uh…"

"You've got to have a peace offering."

"I… didn't think of it."

"Well, it's a good thing you came here first, then." Erin considered. "We can put together a box of cookies, at least."

Willie humbly let Erin lead the way into the kitchen to help him prepare something to take to Vic.

CHAPTER 14

*E*rin tried not to pay too much attention to Willie's trek across the yard and up the stairs to Vic's loft. But it was sort of hard not to see it, right outside her kitchen window. And while, like the night before, she could not see any details or hear the words exchanged between them, she couldn't help noticing that Willie didn't come back down the stairs again, which meant that Vic had allowed him in. Maybe the cookies had done the trick.

She was asleep when Terry got home. Or at least pretending to herself that she was asleep. She might have fallen asleep for a few minutes, but she felt like she hadn't stopped tossing and turning all night.

Terry slipped into the room silently to change out of his uniform. She could hear K9 shake himself, dog tags jingling, and then settle into his kennel to sleep.

"How was your day?" Erin murmured.

"What? You know, you're not supposed to be awake at this time of night."

"I know." Erin flipped over to face him as he changed. "But I want to hear about your day."

"Mmm. Not much I can tell you. You know that."

"There must be stuff that you are releasing to the public. To the media."

"Well, I suppose..." He sat on the edge of the bed to take off his socks. "Theresa Franklin, known to be involved in a criminal organization..."

"Crazy Theresa, part of the Jackson clan," Erin clarified.

Terry smiled. "Was found to be DOA by officers responding to a call."

"By Willie Andrews."

"We're not going to release that part."

"Why not? Everyone already knows."

"Because you have to be careful what names you give the media. If they twist things around and Willie sues for defamation, we don't want to be in the line of fire."

"You can't even say that he found her?"

Terry shook his head. "We won't."

"Do you have... time of death? When will the autopsy be done?"

"Tomorrow, if we're lucky. We won't have results of all of the testing right away, but cause and manner of death are pretty clear."

"She was shot?"

"Uh... I can't say that."

"You can't say that she was shot?"

Terry turned to look at her, then away as he continued to get ready for bed. "I can't say that."

"What about when? Do you have to wait for the medical examiner for that?"

"From the physical evidence and timeline that we have, within forty minutes of when Willie called."

"Oh!" Erin was surprised. "That's a really narrow window. How did you figure that out? Especially if the autopsy hasn't been done yet."

"Her phone activity."

"Oh." Erin's heart started beating faster and her stomach clenched into a tight knot. "Oh, boy."

"Oh, boy," wasn't what she was thinking, though. The words in her head were a lot more colorful than that.

Terry folded his clothes and put them close to the bed as usual. He put on a t-shirt and lay down facing her. He didn't kiss her or put his arms around her to pull her close. Erin stared at him in the dimness of the room, then closed her eyes to shut him out.

"Erin."

She put her hand over her eyes.

"Erin, do you have something you want to tell me?"

Erin didn't know what the point was now. She hadn't been thinking about Theresa's phone. Somehow she had told herself that it had been lost or stolen when Theresa died. And the police wouldn't know her unlock code to be able to check the call history. But they had everything already.

Erin moaned.

"You've been in touch with Theresa," Terry stated.

"No," Erin objected. "She called me. I never called her."

He was silent, waiting. Erin's heart pumped hard. She wasn't going to go back to sleep. She would be a wreck at Auntie Clem's.

"Why didn't you tell me that you were in contact with her?" Terry's voice was very calm and quiet. Like he didn't want to spook a wild animal. Or like he was talking to a child who was in big trouble.

"I wasn't in contact with her."

"Why didn't you tell me she had called you?"

"What difference would that make? You wouldn't be able to tell from her calls to me where she was calling from. You wouldn't have been able to get any closer."

"We could have. With her phone number, we could have found out who else she was in contact with. What cell towers her phone was pinging off of. Maybe even be able to trace her exact GPS location. You know all of that. You didn't even let us try."

"I didn't think she was in town. I thought she was probably far away and just trying to get me worked up over nothing."

"You still could have given me that information so that we could try."

"I guess. I just… I didn't want to talk to her or to have to deal with her calls. I just hung up. I thought that if I just ignored her and didn't yell and react to what she was saying, she would just give up and stop calling." Erin shrugged, feeling his eyes on her in the dark and squirming uncomfortably. "That's what they always said about bullies at school or in foster care. Just ignore them and they'll stop."

"We're not talking about a six-year-old echoing everything you say. This is a dangerous criminal. Someone who could do a lot of damage. Who *has* done a lot of damage."

Terry's hand went to his forehead. He rubbed the spot that Theresa had slammed into a table to knock him out. It had taken his brain a lot longer to heal than the stitches. His skin was unmarked now, but Erin could still remember, and so could Terry.

He was recovered now.

Mostly.

Erin didn't know if he would always be susceptible to migraines if he got too tired. Or to the mood swings and anxiety that had plagued him. He had it under better control now, but was not one hundred percent, not to where he had been before it had happened. Erin could see it in his eyes and hear it in his voice, even when he managed to control his facial expression and behavior.

"I should have told you," she admitted.

But she hadn't. How could she torment him whenever she heard anything from Theresa? It would have been cruel to keep bringing her up, to make Terry think she was there in Bald Eagle Falls, watching their every move. He was Theresa's victim far more than Erin was. It wouldn't have been fair to involve him. And it wouldn't have been fair to go to the sheriff and keep it from Terry.

What other options were there?

Terry wormed his fingers under Erin's pillow to grasp her hand. He squeezed it gently. Big, strong hands compared to hers. She should have just been able to pass her burdens over to him. But that wasn't the way it had been.

"Tell me about it now," he urged. "Start at the beginning."

At the beginning?

"I don't know… I guess when we came home from Moose River after seeing Vic's pa. Theresa started calling me, texting me, sending little recordings of herself that would disappear after I opened them. I didn't know what to do. Like I said… I thought if I just ignored them… I figured that was what you would tell me to do if I told you about them."

"Maybe I would have. But at least we would have gotten her number. It would have been a starting point for tracking her down."

"I guess. I didn't think about it that way."

"Did you tell anyone? Vic?"

"No." Erin's voice was a hoarse whisper, sounding foreign to her own ears. "Nobody."

"You didn't even tell Vic that Theresa was harassing you?"

"No, of course not! I would have upset her. She might have done something stupid."

"Something stupid?" Terry answered his own question. "Like hunting her down and shooting her."

Erin sniffled. She tried to keep the tears from flooding down her cheeks, even though it was dark and he wouldn't be able to see them. She swallowed, but it didn't get rid of the hard lump in her throat.

"Erin…" Terry's other hand found Erin's hair and stroked it back. "Vic didn't shoot Theresa."

"I know."

"Do you? Vic *did not* shoot Theresa."

Erin nodded. "But you think Willie did."

Terry didn't say anything for a while. As if he were trying to work his way through each possible answer and see the consequences of each. Like a master chess player, visualizing all of the options and the moves that they would prompt.

"I think that Willie had something to do with it, yes," he said eventually. "That's what makes the most sense. And if he would talk to us about it, describe what was happening, how he reacted… he might be able to plead it down to manslaughter. This is the South; we understand about protecting our womenfolk. But he needs to come forward and to be honest and open about it."

"What if he didn't do it?" Erin couldn't remember any of her arguments from earlier in the evening, the reasons she gave herself that Willie couldn't have been the one who had killed Theresa. "What if it was someone else?"

"We are investigating it. If it was someone else, we will find out."

Erin wished that she had the confidence that they would work it out on their own. Terry and the others in the police department were professionals. They'd been trained and they would do the best that they could. But too many times, they had missed key pieces of information that would have helped them to unravel the crime that had been committed.

She knew she should stay out of it and just nod and say that she knew Terry would figure it all out in the end. But she was afraid that they were looking to convict Willie Andrews, not to chase down the truth.

Erin rubbed her eyes. "Did Vic give you a statement?"

"No. Does she have something to report?"

Erin shrugged. "I don't know. I didn't ask her anything about it. She didn't say that she knew anything about it. About Willie or anything else. I just hoped… that she might have told you something… about where she was when it happened… or if she knew something else."

"So far, she hasn't said anything or made herself available for an interview. I would really like to hear where she took off to and why. And no, I do not believe the story about going out stargazing when she had trouble sleeping."

Erin grimaced. That hadn't rung true to her either. If Vic had been an avid astronomer, always following the planets and stars with her telescope, it would have been believable. But Erin wasn't aware of any interest Vic had in the heavens. It was just an excuse to explain where she had been while they were waiting for her to return home.

CHAPTER 15

*E*rin moved around the kitchen like a zombie. She had known that she was going to have trouble in the morning. Barely any sleep for two nights in a row. It made it harder than ever to get up at the usual time and to start her usual morning rituals. Terry muttered something as she got out of bed, probably telling her to stay put and just call someone in to sub for her for once. But Erin couldn't stay in bed any longer and her head was whirling with all of the scenarios that had been chasing through her mind since the time that Theresa's body had been discovered. She needed to get up and have something to do. She couldn't stay in bed any longer.

As the coffee started to dribble into the carafe, she saw the security lights go on in the backyard. Someone had apparently gotten around to fixing them. It hadn't been Erin. Terry? Or Willie? Either one of them had good reason for wanting the yard to be well lit, though it was somewhat akin to closing the barn door after the horse was gone.

Erin wasn't worried about it being a prowler at that time of the morning. Any self-respecting burglar would be in bed. Even the birds were not up yet.

She saw Vic walking down the steps from the loft. That wasn't surprising. It was their usual routine to have a bit of tea and toast before starting at Auntie Clem's together. Vic wasn't always on the morning shift, but Erin almost always was, and she and Vic worked together well.

What was surprising was that Willie was there with Vic. Erin wasn't exactly surprised that Willie was awake; Vic had told her before that Willie was a light sleeper. But he didn't usually come down at the same time as Vic. He either went back to sleep or went off in his truck to his own work, whatever that might be on the day in question.

But Willie walked Vic all the way to the back door, then came in with her. Maybe he was worried after what had happened to Theresa. He wouldn't be if he were the one who had killed her. Only if it had been someone else and he thought that there might be a danger to Vic as well.

Did he think it was something to do with the clan? A hit taken out by the Dysons? A vendetta against the Jackson clan?

"Hi Vic, hi Willie," Erin tried to keep her voice as light and casual as possible. As if Willie came in with Vic every day. Or regularly enough that it didn't immediately jump out as something abnormal.

"Mornin', sunshine," Vic greeted.

Willie nodded and grunted.

Erin felt like Willie's grunt was a more honest representation of their morning moods than Vic's "sunshine." But they had to make the best of things.

Vic looked over at the coffee machine. "Caffeine! I'll have some of that."

Willie chuckled as he sat down at the table. "Bringing out the hard stuff, eh Erin? I take it you didn't sleep well?"

"No. I was still pretty restless last night... you would think that I would sleep like a log after the night before, but... my brain just wouldn't settle down."

He nodded his understanding. Erin studied Vic, wondering how much sleep she had gotten and if she'd been able to get it without a sleeping pill. They had both been unsettled since coming back from Moose River. Things had not gone as smoothly as they normally did. Everything seemed harder. Erin thought that for her, a lot of it was the result of Theresa's harassment campaign. Her calls and messages would drive Erin up the wall, making her hypervigilant, sure that something bad was going to happen at any moment. Feeling herself being watched. Telling herself that Theresa wasn't in town, but never really believing it.

The messages would trickle off and she would think that Theresa had moved on and would not be bothering her anymore. And then they would start up again. The cycle of the harassment and never knowing when it would hit was worse than constant harassment would have been.

Vic was skimming through her social networks or emails on her phone while they waited for the coffee to finish. She stopped in her scrolling.

"Our church in the city is having a special Easter program."

Erin nodded, not really paying any attention. The comment was obviously aimed at Willie rather than her. Checking to see if he would make the time to attend the Easter program with her.

"That's what you said," Willie responded, sounding irritated.

"I was telling Erin."

Erin looked at Vic, confused. Willie raised an eyebrow, also surprised by this declaration.

"I thought you might want to come to the Easter program," Vic said. "You and Terry could both come. All of us could go together."

Erin shook her head. Vic knew that she didn't go to church. Didn't believe in any higher power in the universe or any faith or organized religion. She believed in what she could see and hear and smell and taste. Not some myth she'd learned at the knee of a foster mother.

"You went to the Christmas thing with Terry," Vic said, as if that explained her invitation. "That was really cool, and Terry appreciated that you went with him. I just thought... maybe you would like to attend an Easter program with him too."

"No... there were a lot of negative consequences to me going to the Christmas thing with Terry. I don't really want a repeat."

"Negative consequences?" Willie repeated. "What do you mean?"

Willie wasn't very religious either, as far as Erin could tell. But men seemed to be extended more understanding for sporadic church attendance than women.

"I mean... people either thought that I was a hypocrite for going when I said I was an atheist, or they thought I was going to convert. You wouldn't believe all of the invitations I've had to church services and prayer circles and fellowships... they thought that I was... ripe for the picking, I guess. Because I'd shown some interest by going to the Christmas candlelight service."

"When you only went for Terry," Willie said. "Just to support him in how he would normally spend Christmas Eve."

Erin nodded. At the time, it had seemed like the perfect Christmas gift for him. From her heart. Supporting him in his beliefs and traditions, just as he had never challenged her non-belief or insisted that she had to convert to Christianity if she wanted anything to do with him.

"Yeah. But I guess it made a lot of people mad... especially after everything that happened at the school. People didn't want to see me anywhere. But especially not inside a church, somewhere... sacred to them."

"I didn't even know all that." Vic went to the coffee machine and filled a mug for each of them. "I mean, I heard some whisperings, people wondering what was going on with you, but I didn't know it was that bad."

Just like people knew not to run Vic down in front of Erin, they had probably learned not to badmouth Erin in front of Vic either.

"It's fine. It was... an experiment. And now I know how it would turn out... I don't need to do it again."

"It would be different coming to our congregation in the city," Vic pointed out. "They don't know you. Don't know anything about whether you're an atheist or a Christian. You would just be a visitor, coming in for a nice Easter service. They would welcome you and wouldn't be talking behind your back."

"No." Erin shook her head. "Thanks for the invite, but I'm not interested. You can tell Terry; maybe he'll want to go with you."

"He's not going to go without you."

Erin chewed on her lip. That was a problem. She didn't want to change Terry. She didn't want to take away his traditions and his faith. But just by the fact that she wouldn't go to church, she would change his attitude toward it and keep him from going.

"I don't know… I guess we'll have to talk about it."

Vic nodded. "No pressure. Just if you want to. I'm not trying to twist your arm."

"I know. Thanks."

Willie looked at his watch. "Well, we'd probably better get going."

"Are you… taking us today?"

Willie nodded. "Just to be safe."

Erin took a couple more swallows of her coffee. She wasn't going to be able to finish it before going to Auntie Clem's, but that was probably a good thing. She knew it would keep her hyped up for much of the day. She welcomed the boost in energy and focus, but knew it wasn't good for her body and didn't want to crash afterward.

"Do you really think we're in any danger?" Erin asked. "From who?"

"We don't know who killed Theresa," Willie said reasonably. "And there have been some strangers in town… Now, I'm not one to be suspicious of people just because they are new in the area but, considering the circumstances, I think it is wise to be careful."

Strangers in town? Erin was surprised. That was something that she should have noticed. Usually, she was aware of people as they walked by on the street or if she saw them in one of the Bald

Eagle Falls restaurants. Had she been so wrapped up in her own challenges that she hadn't paid any attention to what was going on around her?

"There's nothing to worry about," Vic assured Erin. "Willie's just being careful."

"Well... Theresa was killed outside the house." Erin put her mug into the sink. She would deal with dishes later.

"But think about it. Theresa was the one who was a threat. So whoever killed her isn't."

"The enemy of my enemy..."

"Exactly," Vic agreed, nodding her head. "The enemy of my enemy is my friend."

"That doesn't always hold," Willie warned. "When you're dealing with factions like the clans, the threats may come from several different directions. There is no guarantee that just because someone killed Theresa, they wouldn't hurt you too."

CHAPTER 16

"I'm heading over to The Book Nook with the book club treats," Erin informed Bella and Vic as she headed out with a tray full of goodies.

"Say hi for me," Vic told her, and Erin nodded in agreement.

The Book Nook was just across the street, and it was a nice day out. Erin didn't feel like she had to hurry to find shelter from the sun or to put on a jacket because it was too cool. It was just comfortable.

They had been supplying treats for the book club almost since Erin had first opened Auntie Clem's. It was a great way to keep the bakery in people's minds and to convince those who wouldn't have thought to try gluten-free baking that it could be delicious. Once they'd had a few cookies or pastries, they no longer feared the unknown, and it was perfectly natural to stop by the bakery the next time they were having a dinner party.

Erin balanced the tray while she opened the door to The Book Nook.

"Delivery!" she sang out.

Naomi straightened from behind a bookshelf to look over it at Erin. "Oh, cookies!"

"We've got cookies!" Erin agreed. She took the tray over to the counter, where Naomi usually stashed them until the book club began.

"Those cut-outs are adorable."

"And we made some of them into sandwich cookies. They were a lot of fun."

"The ladies will love them." Naomi finished shelving or rearranging the books at waist level and came around the shelves toward Erin. "So, how are you? I heard about your excitement…"

"It's crazy." Erin shook her head. "I don't know what to think. I had no idea that Theresa was in town, and then she is killed right in my yard. I guess I owe a 'thank you' to whoever did it. Who knows what she was planning to do, lurking around the place."

"Whoever it was?"

Erin whipped around in surprise at the voice behind her. Melissa was in the children's section, a Dr. Seuss book in her hand.

"What?"

"Whoever it was? You know who it was," Melissa said in a self-assured voice. "It was Willie."

"No, I don't know that," Erin said, her cheeks getting warm. "I know that Willie was the one who found the body and called it in. It doesn't make sense that he would do that if he was the one who had killed her."

"Why? Because he would have left it for you to discover?"

Erin shuddered at the thought. Willie knew how it had affected her to be the first one on the scene to discover a body in the past. He wouldn't do that to her. "No. He wouldn't have left it there at all. Why would he? There are all kinds of places he could hide a body."

"Unless someone had already seen him," Melissa pointed out. "There's no point in trying to destroy the evidence if someone has already seen it. Then you've got to work with what you have."

Erin rolled her eyes. She hadn't heard anything that would indicate that there had been any witnesses. If there were, then surely they would have stepped forward already and everybody would know about it. Melissa was just looking for ways to make Willie look guilty. To cause drama.

"It wasn't Willie," Erin reiterated.

"Then it was Vic."

"Vic couldn't have done anything to hurt her," Erin declared. "I've seen them together before, and Vic wouldn't do anything to hurt her. No matter what she was threatening. That's just the way Vic is."

"I've heard she carries a gun," Naomi said in a whisper.

"She doesn't just carry one," Melissa reminded them. "She shot Alton Summers."

"Yes… but shooting an intruder is not the same as shooting someone you know."

"Anyway, Theresa wasn't shot," Melissa said.

Erin was glad that she'd already put the tray of cookies down. She looked at Melissa in shock. "What do you mean, she wasn't shot?"

Melissa laughed, her dark curls bouncing. "What could I mean? It's pretty obvious. Theresa wasn't shot."

"But Terry said…" Erin thought back, trying to replay the scene in her mind. She had talked to him about Vic's gun, making sure that it couldn't possibly have been Vic that had shot Theresa. He had confirmed that it hadn't been Vic. But he hadn't said she was shot. Erin had just assumed from the start. Theresa was a violent person. She carried a gun. Naturally, the way to kill her would have been with a gun.

"Then what killed her?"

Melissa raised her brows. "I probably shouldn't be giving you any information you don't already have."

Now she stopped leaking information?

"Melissa…"

Melissa put the book in her hand back on the shelf. "And she wasn't killed in your yard."

"My yard, Vic's; we share it."

"No. She wasn't killed outside. She was killed inside."

"Inside... where?"

Erin was afraid to know the answer.

"The police are still trying to get a warrant so that they can match carpet fibers and hairs found on the body with the scene."

Erin's spirits rose. She felt like a weight had been taken off her shoulders. Theresa hadn't been killed in her yard! She had just been dumped there. Someone wanted to implicate one of them in the murder. So, to throw suspicions on them, they had dumped Theresa's body, hoping it would look enough like Theresa had been killed there that the police would focus their inquiry on Erin, Vic, or Willie. It had been a set-up.

"That's good news."

"Is it?" Melissa cocked her head.

"Yes, that's excellent news."

Melissa didn't respond.

"Well... I hope it all gets straightened out," Naomi told Erin. "It must be horrifying to know that something like that happened right in your own backyard."

Except it hadn't. It had happened somewhere else.

That was very good news.

"At least the police have a good list of names to start with," Melissa offered, smiling.

"They do?" Erin didn't like that smile. Melissa clearly knew something that she knew was going to make a splash and get her more attention.

Melissa nodded. "All of the people who Theresa was calling and messaging on her phone."

Erin's heart took a nosedive. She should have guessed. Terry had already mentioned that they had found Erin's name and number on Theresa's phone and could see Theresa's calls to her. Why wouldn't the same be true for everyone else she had been in contact with?

She swallowed. "Are there a lot of names?"

Melissa's brows peaked, letting Erin know that yes, she knew that Erin's name was on the list, but she wasn't going to say so in front of Naomi. And if Melissa knew that Erin's name was on the list, she must know the other names too.

"She was in contact with a lot of people," Melissa confirmed.

"But… not all of those people will be suspects, will they?"

"It will depend on who has an alibi and who had the opportunity to kill her."

Erin cleared her throat. And did the group of people who had the opportunity to kill Theresa include Erin herself? Terry said that there was a window of approximately forty minutes. Erin had been home for the forty minutes before Willie had found Theresa's body. If Theresa was killed indoors instead of out, she could have been killed in Erin's house and then dragged outside. But what motive would Erin have to kill her? Of course, she didn't like being harassed. She wanted Theresa out of her life. What would Erin have done if Theresa had shown up at her door? She certainly would not have let Theresa in, but Theresa was armed and bigger and stronger than Erin was. She had been trained by the clan. Erin had no doubt that Theresa would not have had a problem getting past Erin's door.

But of course, the fiber analysis would verify that Theresa hadn't been killed in Erin's house. So would any blood evidence, since they would not find any of Theresa's blood in Erin's house. Even if Terry suspected Erin of somehow being involved in Theresa's death—and Erin was sure he would not—the evidence would prove that Theresa had never been in Erin's house.

CHAPTER 17

*E*rin headed back to Auntie Clem's, her mind whirling with this new information. She wasn't quite sure how to process it all. It was not her job to figure out who had killed Theresa, but she wanted to protect herself and her friends. She didn't want anyone to be unjustly accused of killing Theresa, even if they had done the world a favor by doing so. The law wouldn't necessarily take the same view as those who actually knew Theresa Franklin and the kind of person she was.

A man watched from the other side as she crossed the street. Erin looked at him a couple of times, trying to place him. Not someone that she knew from Bald Eagle Falls. Usually, she could place most of the faces she saw. Even if she didn't know them personally, she had seen them before, associated them with a particular family or group. More often than not, she knew their names and something about them.

Willie had said that there were some strangers in town, and Erin had been surprised that she hadn't noticed them. Here, then, was one of them. A man in his forties or fifties, dark hair, a mustache, scowling as if she had done something to offend him. But she was sure he wasn't actually mad at her. He probably wasn't even looking at her as he seemed to be, but just across the street at something behind her or at his own dark thoughts. No point in getting paranoid and thinking that everyone was out to get her.

But he did turn his head to look at her as she stepped up onto the curb and headed toward Auntie Clem's. Erin looked openly at him, making it clear that she saw him watching her and wanted to know why.

Most people would have looked away at that point, but he didn't. He continued to watch her as she entered the bakery. Once inside, Erin could no longer see him. She waited for a moment to see if he would follow her inside. Maybe he had mistaken her for someone else. Maybe he needed directions. But he didn't come after her. She *was* just being paranoid. He didn't know who she was or care that she had gone into the bakery. He'd probably just had a bad day and wasn't even aware that he was scowling at the whole world.

"Everything okay?" Vic asked, cocking her head at Erin.

"Yeah. There was just this guy outside… I don't know who he is. Looked like he was watching me, but maybe not. I'm probably just imagining things."

Vic looked out the glass door, but she wouldn't be able to see him either. She shrugged. "It's probably nothing."

Erin agreed. "Just getting paranoid after everything that has happened."

"Probably. How was Naomi?"

"Seemed good… we didn't really talk. Melissa was over there…"

"Oh," Vic drew the word out long. "Looking like the cat that got the cream, I suppose. Full of news of the investigation into Theresa's death."

Erin nodded. "I'm sure she doesn't realize how she seems to others…"

"A lot of the others seem to encourage her… interests. I think she's quite aware of the position of power she holds when she knows things that no one else does. Or that she's not supposed to be talking about. It makes her feel good."

"I suppose." Erin slid in behind the counter and started rearranging the goods in the display case, tidying up and evaluating what she should take out or refill before the after-school rush. "I just wish she'd find another hobby."

Vic snorted. "Testify!"

They were both silent for a few minutes. Erin could hear Bella in the kitchen, talking on the phone as she ran a couple of mixers.

"That said... did she have anything interesting to divulge?" Vic asked curiously.

Erin hesitated. She didn't like to gossip. But what had happened affected Vic just as much or more than it affected Erin. It was also in her own yard, right outside her own door. But in addition to that, her boyfriend was being investigated or accused of having killed Theresa. And Theresa was Vic's ex-girlfriend, someone she had grown up with and who she still had some feelings toward. Not romantic feelings, but pity for the abuse she had been exposed to as a child, regret over the way that things had not worked out between them and that Theresa had not been able to escape her family and the designs of the Jackson clan as Vic had. Theresa had stayed behind, had jumped into working with the clan with both feet, and now... barely more than a teenager, her life had come to a violent end.

Vic had a right to know everything Erin did. If the police department wanted to keep things confidential, then they should start with fixing the leaks they knew existed, and the biggest one, gushing like a fire hose, was Melissa.

"I didn't talk to her for long. There were just a couple of things..."

Vic nodded eagerly.

But at that moment, Bella came out of the kitchen with questions about Erin's plans for the next day and what she should work on next. Erin gave Vic an apologetic look as she headed back into the kitchen with Bella. "I'll tell you about it later..."

∽

"Is Willie going to be around tonight?" Erin asked Vic as they tidied up at the end of the day.

"No, said he had some stuff to do. What about Terry?"

"He's wrapped up in this case. Do you want to go out for dinner? I don't want to make anything, but I want something other than canned soup or frozen dinners."

"Sure," Vic agreed. "That would be great. I'm in the same position." She looked at the time on the wall clock. "Willie is going to pick us up and drop us at home, and I need to take Nilla out for a few minutes. Then I'm all yours."

That would give Erin a chance to feed her beasties and give them some attention before going off for supper as well. "Perfect. It's a date."

It wasn't until they were getting into the yellow bug that Erin remembered Vic borrowing it the night that Theresa was killed. She'd never told Vic *not* to take the car. Vic knew where the spare keys were, but they'd never discussed whether Vic *could* take it. One of the top considerations being the fact that Erin didn't think Vic had a driver's license. While she trusted Vic's driving skills, she didn't want the car getting impounded because Vic got stopped for driving without a license.

Erin looked at the gas gauge and the odometer, but they were not noticeably different from what she remembered from the last time she'd driven. Not that she paid close attention to those things. As long as there was enough gas to get around and she wasn't due for an oil change, she took little notice of either.

Vic pulled her seatbelt across to buckle it and paused, apparently noticing Erin checking the gauges. "Uh... yeah. I should have asked before I borrowed it. But I figured you were asleep and didn't want to wake you up."

Erin nodded. She still wasn't sure what to say about allowing Vic to take the car—or not.

"I could give you some gas money," Vic suggested.

"No... it's fine. But we should talk about it later." Erin chewed on the inside of her lip. She didn't want to tell Vic not to take the vehicle, but... maybe she could offer to drive Vic wherever she needed to go. If it had been an emergency, she would have been happy to drive Vic, even if it were the middle of the night. But to go stargazing?

Erin had a feeling that was just a cover story. Whatever had prompted Vic to borrow the car without permission, it hadn't been an overwhelming desire to see the stars outside of the town limits.

"Okay," Vic agreed.

"Later," Erin repeated. "I just want to kick back and enjoy the meal tonight."

Vic looked a little happier at that. "Me too." She clicked her seatbelt into place. "What did you want tonight?"

"I'm kind of in the mood for Chinese."

"Sure. Fine with me."

CHAPTER 18

They looked around at the restaurant while waiting to be seated. Vic spotted Jeremy sitting by himself and waved. Vic went over to talk to him, then motioned Erin over.

"Are we joining you?" Erin asked Jeremy.

He motioned to the empty seats. "Looks like I'm on my own tonight. Some company would be great."

Erin and Vic sat down with him.

"Beaver out of town today?" Erin asked.

"Busy. I don't know for sure where she is," Jeremy answered with a shrug. The time that she spent with him was sporadic. As far as Erin could tell, it didn't follow any particular pattern. Beaver's job was not a predictable nine-to-five office job. She joined Jeremy when she could, and otherwise was gone, maybe across the state and maybe across the country, none of them had any way of knowing. Erin didn't even know for sure what agency she was with. If Terry knew, he hadn't told her. Erin's suspicions fell on the DEA, but Beaver wasn't telling.

A waitress came over, and they discussed what they wanted and placed their order. They all ate there often enough to know what they liked best. The waitress filled their water glasses and left them alone again.

"So… you were going to tell me about Melissa," Vic reminded Erin, leaning forward with her elbows on the table. "I need to know what she said."

"Oh, right."

Jeremy leaned forward as well. "Is this about your newest corpse?"

"It's not *my* corpse," Erin insisted. "I wasn't even the one who found her."

"Well, she was on your property, and they say possession is nine-tenths of the law…"

"She is not *my* corpse!"

"Leave her alone, Jer," Vic told him, slapping him lightly on the arm. "Quit being such a tease. He's only joking, Erin. You know that."

"It's just that…" Erin trailed off. Of course Jeremy was only teasing her. But after all of the police investigations she had been through and the suspicious eyes and fingers that had been pointed at her, she wanted to make sure it was understood that she hadn't had anything to do with the body of Theresa Franklin being found on her property. Somebody else was to blame for that.

Vic nodded and patted Erin's arm. "It's okay."

Erin nodded.

"So, what did you find out?"

"Melissa said that Theresa wasn't shot."

Vic nodded but looked unsurprised by this.

"You already knew that?" Erin asked.

"Willie found the body. So, yeah, of course I asked if she was shot or how she was killed."

"How did he say she was killed?"

"He wasn't sure. It was dark, and you can't always tell just by looking at someone. How did Melissa say?"

"She wouldn't tell me that."

"Okay… what else, then? That was it? That she wasn't shot?"

"No. She also said that Theresa wasn't killed outside. There was evidence on her body to indicate that she had been killed inside and moved outside. So that's good! It means that someone dumped her on our property to divert suspicion. Once the police figure out where she was actually killed, they'll know that it wasn't Willie."

Vic nodded slowly, but she didn't look convinced.

"What are you worried about?" Erin asked. "That's good news."

"Yeah... I'm just waiting for the other shoe to drop. Until we know *where* she was killed... I don't know if it helps or hurts."

"Anything that places her somewhere other than our yard is good."

"I suppose so," Vic nodded.

"They don't have any idea where she might have been moved from?" Jeremy asked.

"I don't know. Melissa said they are trying to get warrants, so I guess they have some idea of places to look. Maybe her hotel or wherever she was staying? Maybe her car? I didn't see any strange cars parked nearby, so who knows where that is." She sighed and smiled. "At least it's not in the parking lot of Auntie Clem's."

That had happened before, and it had not made for a fun day for Erin.

"Anything else?" Vic asked.

"I guess they have Theresa's phone, and they're getting information off of it. Who she's been talking and texting with."

Vic picked up her glass of water for a sip. Her face was even paler than usual. Erin remembered how she had felt when Terry told her that he knew she had been in communication with Theresa before she was killed. That heavy pain in her chest returned as she thought about it. Now she knew that she hadn't been the only one Theresa had been in contact with. But that didn't mean that they wouldn't be looking at her. They just had a wider net to cast, that was all.

"Vic..."

Jeremy looked from Erin to Vic and back again. "What?" He shook his head, not sure what he was missing.

Vic looked at Erin but didn't say anything.

"Had she been bugging you too?" Erin asked.

Vic's cheeks flushed pink. She took a couple more swallows of water. Jeremy's brows drew down as he studied her.

"Bugging you?" he repeated. "Are you telling me that she was calling you and you didn't even tell me?"

"Why would I tell you?" Vic demanded. "What could you have done about it?"

"I could have tracked her down and put a stop to it," Jeremy said, his voice tight and cold. "I would have."

"There were already other people trying to track her down. It's not as easy as you think. Willie's been looking for her ever since Terry and Jack Ward were injured before Christmas. And you know he has good contacts in... the criminal world. How would you have been able to find her if Willie couldn't?"

"Well, it looks like Willie eventually did," Jeremy pointed out.

"Willie isn't the one who killed her."

"I'll bet he wishes that he was. I wish *I* was."

"Don't say that," Vic snapped. "You think I would want both of you under suspicion? Or in prison? I don't want anyone I know to have had anything to do with this. I don't want any of you going to prison. I just want my life to go back to..." Vic shook her head, not finishing the statement.

Not back to the way they were before Theresa was killed, because she had been harassing Vic. Not back to the way they were when Theresa was on the run and they had no idea where she was and were constantly looking over their shoulders. Not the way that they were before Vic had come to Bald Eagle Falls.

She just wanted a place where she could be herself and not have to worry about Crazy Theresa Franklin and what she would do next.

The waitress brought their food to the table. For a few minutes, they were occupied with passing the dishes around to serve themselves and finding room to put them all in the middle of the table once everyone had their initial helpings.

Erin took a couple of bites of her chicken, savoring the sweet and spicy flavors.

"Was she bugging me *too*?" Vic asked suddenly.

Erin looked at her, not understanding at first.

"You asked me if Theresa was bugging me too. *Too*, as in, I wasn't the only one."

Erin shrugged and didn't look up from her food. "Melissa said that there were others."

"That's not what you meant."

"She was obviously calling other people too," Erin pointed out.

"Yes. Were you one of them?"

With the question put to her so directly, Erin couldn't avoid it. She couldn't lie to Vic's face. She'd never been able to pull it off like Reg could. Reg could tell the wildest stories and never flinch, never give any sign that she wasn't telling the absolute truth.

"Erin?" Vic prodded.

Erin nodded. "Yeah. She was calling me too."

"Why didn't you tell me?" Vic demanded.

"Why didn't *you* tell *me*?"

Vic sat there with her mouth hanging open. "Oh."

"Yeah. If you didn't tell me, why would I tell you?"

"Well, maybe because she was my friend once, so maybe I could get her to leave you alone if I asked."

"Did she leave you alone when you asked her to?"

Vic sighed. "No."

"I didn't tell you because I thought you already had enough to worry about and had been through enough crap."

Vic chuckled. "Well… yeah. That's exactly why I didn't tell you."

Erin shook her head and had some fried rice.

"How about you, Jeremy?" Vic asked her brother. "You get any calls from Crazy Theresa?"

Jeremy had been laughing at the two of them, each trying to spare the other's feelings. At Vic's question, he just looked at her.

Vic's laughter died away. She stared at Jeremy in disbelief. "Why would she be calling you?"

Jeremy cleared his throat. "People like that... she wanted to hurt you and to do as much damage as she could to your support network. Spreading lies, trying to break friendships or family connections..."

"What lies?"

"I don't know." He looked up at the ceiling, away from Vic. "That you were cutting all ties with the clan and wished that I hadn't come to Bald Eagle Falls. That you thought I was weak. A sissy. Whatever she could think of. And it could be opposites on different days. That you were still part of the clan. That you despised me for being part of the clan. You know Theresa. Whatever vile vomit she could think of."

It was a pretty good description of the communications Erin had received from Theresa as well. Bizarre, off-the-wall accusations and stories. Little digs that hurt her and wild speculations that made no sense at all.

Vic nodded slowly, but there was a crease between her eyebrows. "You didn't tell me either. I thought... that I was alone. That she was only targeting me. This is crazy."

They all nodded. *Crazy Theresa* echoing in their heads.

"And do you think..." Vic looked at Erin, and Erin knew by her expression what the question was before she even opened her mouth. "Willie? Do you think she was in contact with him too?"

"Seems like she was targeting anyone close to you... so I guess so, probably."

"And *he* never told me." There was anger in Vic's voice.

"None of us told you. Because we love you and didn't want to put that burden on you," Erin told her. "If she was talking to Willie, he did the same thing. He tried to keep it from you so that you wouldn't feel worried and responsible for it all."

"But he's supposed to be my partner. He's supposed to tell me important stuff like that. *Relationship* stuff."

Erin wondered again what they had been arguing about

recently. More secrets? Mysterious phone calls and messages? Erin had found it hard to keep Vic from finding out that Theresa was calling her. She would have to make up a reason for a call, brush off a text message, make sure that she never left her phone lying around where Vic could spot a message from Theresa on the notification screen.

It had not been easy to keep Vic from finding out.

CHAPTER 19

They continued to turn these new revelations over in their minds. Erin was glad that there was food to distract them. She would really have loved to just eat and not to worry about everything that had happened and how what Theresa had done had affected their lives and relationships. And what the long-lasting effects of her death were going to be.

"Maybe it was an accidental death," she suggested. "Or natural. Melissa didn't say what it was, so she probably doesn't know. Maybe it's something that they won't know until the Medical Examiner does the autopsy. But maybe she just... had a heart attack or took a drug overdose. Maybe there isn't anyone responsible for her death."

"Then how was her body moved after she died?" Vic challenged. "Or rather—why? Why would anyone move her if she just died accidentally? Someone was trying to cover it up. To throw suspicion on us. On one of us."

Erin had to admit that the accidental or natural death angle did not look promising. It would have been nice, though.

Jeremy swore. Erin looked across the table at him, then followed his eyes across the restaurant to the bar. A blond figure she recognized was just sitting down on one of the bar stools, talking to the man next to her.

Beaver.

If Beaver was in town and able to take a dinner break, why wasn't she with Jeremy? Why would she be there with another man?

Erin looked at Jeremy. "Did you know she was going to be here tonight?"

"No. Do you think I would have set something like this up?"

"Did she know you were going to be here?"

He shook his head. "I just decided. I didn't feel like making anything but still wanted something nice. So, I came here…"

Erin nodded. Just like she and Vic had decided to do.

Why was Beaver meeting with someone in town when she knew that she could be seen there by Jeremy or someone else who would tell him that she had been there?

The man that she was talking to was young. Probably closer to Jeremy's age than to Beaver's. Like Jeremy, he had long, shaggy blond hair. But that was where the resemblance ended. Jeremy was usually smiling or laughing. Cheerful and laid back, there was not a lot that got him upset or angry. He took his challenges in stride, and even when he had been shot on his job at the farm, he had been upbeat and had returned once he was able. He brushed off most of the problems he and Vic had with their family, preferring not to talk about the clan or internal family issues like physical and emotional abuse.

The man Beaver was with was morose, with a long, narrow face. He brushed his hair out of his eyes and where Jeremy would have been laughing and animated, he looked depressed. Maybe hungover or in the grips of some drug-induced haze. He leaned on the bar with one elbow as they talked, head hanging down, looking like he might collapse at any moment due to the weight of the world on his shoulders.

Beaver looked as she always did. Casual, loose, her graceful movements looking lazy and effortless, like she just flowed from one place to another. She chewed vigorously on a wad of gum, even though they were at a restaurant. She would undoubtedly have to throw it out to eat her dinner or to have a drink with the man, if that was what she was there for.

"Do you know him?" she asked Jeremy. "Did she tell you who she was meeting with or mention anyone lately?"

Jeremy shook his head. "She doesn't talk to me about the job. I have no idea who she's talking to or what she's working on. Sometimes I get a whiff—something that she asks me, usually—but then it's gone again."

It would be challenging to have a relationship with someone who was working undercover, who couldn't tell you what they were involved with on a daily basis. Too many secrets were bad for a relationship. Erin should know. Between Terry's confidentiality about his work as a law enforcement officer, Erin preferring to keep as much of her past as possible confined to the past, and her recent attempts to keep anyone from finding out about Theresa's calls and messages, she felt like their whole relationship was teetering on the edge. Like the only things they could talk about were the animals and anything she read in the paper. And there wasn't a lot of exciting news happening in Bald Eagle Falls. Most of the articles that made it to the weekly were not local, but were pulled from the bigger news syndicate feeds.

Beaver leaned in close to the young man, very intent on the conversation. Whatever was going on, she was very involved in the conversation.

"I'm sure it's just work," she told Jeremy.

His jaw was clenched. He tried to answer casually, keeping his usual smile firmly pinned in place. "Yeah, of course. If she didn't have work, she would have come home to me. We could have ordered something in. Or come here together."

"She's really devoted to her job."

"Uh-huh."

Erin looked at Vic, hoping that she would say something that would distract Jeremy from his concern or anger toward Beaver.

"Who else do you think might have wanted to kill Theresa?" Vic asked. "There must be a whole lineup of people who would have wanted something to happen to her."

Jeremy looked away from Beaver. He blinked at Vic, considering. "I thought you didn't want to talk about it."

"I never said that."

"Well, maybe not, but I got the feeling…"

Vic shook her head, her expression grim and determined. "What's there to hide now? We should get it all out in the open. We're not going to figure anything out with everyone hiding what we know. We have to pool our information."

Erin bit her tongue and didn't ask Vic when she had decided she was taking on the case. Usually, Vic was the one warning Erin to back off and leave the investigating to the police.

"Well…" Jeremy forced himself to turn his head toward Vic and Erin and not be distracted by whatever his girlfriend was doing with the stranger at the bar. "Assuming that it was not one of us or Willie…"

"It wasn't," Vic agreed, her voice firm.

"Willie is a really good suspect, you know," Jeremy said. "We all know that he was looking for Theresa. And I'm not so sure he ever intended to turn her in to the cops if he found her."

"It wasn't Willie," Vic repeated.

Besides, if it was, the police would prove it soon enough. They didn't need to help that process along.

"There is the whole Dyson clan. Theresa was working with the Jackson clan, so anyone in the Dysons could have had motive to kill her."

Vic nodded. "I don't know a lot of the players, other than the old guys like Pa." She didn't go as far as to point out that Jeremy had been working with the Jackson clan until relatively recently, so he would probably know most of the possible players from the Dysons. But the question was clearly there.

"You know a couple of others," Jeremy said. "Willie and Charley."

"Neither of them are with the Dysons anymore," Erin said quickly, heading off Vic's reaction to this suggestion. "Willie hasn't been in years."

"Maybe, maybe not. Just because he says he hasn't been, that doesn't mean he's completely separated from them. Seems to me he still has a finger in a lot of pies."

Erin glanced at Vic. Jeremy hadn't been around when Charley's boyfriend in the Dysons had been murdered and she had been arrested for it. That was when they had found out that Willie had once been in the Dyson clan and still had some dealings with at least Nelson Dyson. Something to do with computers and security equipment, but Erin didn't know all of the details.

Vic gave no sign that she remembered any of this. She just glared at Jeremy. "Willie is not in the Dyson clan. That ended a long time ago."

He looked at her for a minute, then his eyes slid away.

"Besides everyone in the Dyson clan, I imagine there are a few of the Jackson clan that wanted her out of the picture too."

"Why would they?" Vic challenged.

"Well, you did, didn't you? Just because she was part of the clan, that didn't mean she got along with everyone. In fact, I doubt if she got along with anyone. She was pretty much a lone wolf. And a crazy one at that. Putting a tiger on a leash doesn't make it a house cat."

It was probably an apt comparison, from what Erin had seen.

"Including her own family," Erin agreed. "Did she have anyone other than her parents?"

Vic shook her head. "No brothers or sisters. But she's a Jackson. She has cousins in the clan. Like Biggles. I don't know how close any of them were."

"But you can bet that if she killed her parents, some of the other Jacksons would be upset about it," Erin pointed out.

Vic nodded her agreement. She scratched the back of her neck. "So, who else?"

"Dysons, Jacksons, that's not enough?" Jeremy asked, laughing. "You and me. Anyone else that she was harassing"

"What about law enforcement?" Erin suggested. "Jack Ward and his police department."

"Terry and the Bald Eagle Falls police department," Jeremy added.

Erin didn't like him putting Terry and the police department into the same basket as all of the other law enforcement officers. But yes, Theresa had nearly killed Terry. Had set him and the rest of the police department up for Bo Biggles' death. The Bald Eagle Falls police had just as much reason to want her dead as those in Moose River. Although, she didn't know what other things Theresa might have done to put herself in their crosshairs. If she was a contract killer for the Jackson clan, she might have taken out policemen or their loved ones or some local politician that Erin hadn't ever heard of. There could be a dozen reasons that they wanted to take her off the street permanently.

"Whatever other law enforcement agencies are trying to shut down the Jacksons. FBI, DEA, whatever."

Jeremy and Vic nodded.

"Anyone else?" Vic asked.

Erin opened her mouth to answer and then closed it again.

Vic looked at her, raising her brows. "What were you going to say?"

"Nothing. I think we have it all covered."

Vic and Jeremy both shook their heads. "No. You thought of someone else. Who was it?"

Erin shrugged uncomfortably. "Your brothers," she said reluctantly. "Daniel and Joseph. She kind of... played them for fools and left them holding the bag."

Vic grimaced.

"But they're in jail," Jeremy pointed out. "They can't do much from there."

"They can still communicate with the clan. Have visitors. Send letters. Phone calls. They might be monitored, but there are ways around that."

Vic and Jeremy looked at each other.

"I suppose," Vic sighed. "Daniel and Joseph. They could have set something up. But we kind of already covered them when we said the Jackson clan. We just… happen to know a couple of the Jackson clan who have a personal vendetta."

They were silent while they thought through the different names. It was turning out to be a pretty long list. And that was a good thing because the longer the list of potential suspects was, the better the chances that they could defend Willie with an alternate theory of the crime.

CHAPTER 20

It had been a stressful dinner, despite the fact that they were trying to relax and pamper themselves. Erin couldn't help looking at Beaver, watching to see what she would do next, still trying to figure out whether she was there for a social evening or something to do with work. Of course she would never know. Beaver would never confide in her. And what looked like a romantic interlude could still be one hundred percent about work. Beaver had confessed to being involved with informants or subjects of investigation before. She would do whatever she needed to do to get her man.

But Beaver hadn't done anything remotely intimate while talking to the morose man at the bar. No kisses or hand-holding, no touch or leaning in that might be construed as romantic interest. It probably was just a business meeting. Something that Beaver would never tell them about.

When they separated, Jeremy went to his apartment, looking disgruntled and out of sorts. But he did his best to put on his usual jocular attitude and bid them farewell. Erin and Vic went back to the house together. Erin didn't know whether to suggest they stay together, or if Vic needed some space to think things through. She didn't move after turning the car engine off and looked at Vic.

"I don't really want to be alone," Vic confessed, looking up at the ceiling. "But poor Nilla has been home alone all day. I need to spend some time with him, give him some socialization other than just taking him for a quick pee."

Erin nodded. "Of course! Well…" she considered, "maybe it's time to try introducing him to the others."

"To the others? Orange Blossom and Marshmallow? Do you think he's ready?"

"He's been a lot better lately. You've got him trained pretty well. And he's good with K9."

"But a cat and a rabbit are quite a bit different than a big German shepherd. I know that K9 can take care of himself if Nilla tries to be aggressive with him. But Orange Blossom and Marshmallow… I don't know."

"Do you think Orange Blossom can't take care of himself? He's bigger than Nilla."

Vic chuckled. "I suppose, like barn cats on the farm. And cats and dogs get along together all the time, right? I mean… a lot of people have both, and they don't kill each other. They don't have to grow up together to get along, do they?"

Erin shook her head. "I've never had pets of my own, other than Blossom and Marshmallow… but I've seen cats and dogs that get along together just fine. I don't think they have to be babies to make friends."

"Well… I guess what's the worst that could happen? I'll keep Nilla on leash and Blossom will hiss at him and either run away or defend his territory. Blossom puts up with K9."

Puts up with was accurate. Erin had hoped that the two of them might become friends, but the closest Orange Blossom got to making friends with the dog was licking biscuit crumbs off of his face. And once K9 was licked clean, he was back to treating K9 like an enemy invader again.

But he had never scratched or bitten K9, and K9 hadn't ever been aggressive toward him. K9 would, Erin suspected, be quite happy to be friends with Orange Blossom if the cat had been open to the idea. He got along with Marshmallow and had never done anything to make Erin think that he might bite or chase him if she happened to be out of the room for too long.

"I think we should do it," she encouraged Vic. "Introduce them. We've been talking about it for a while, and Nilla has been really good. Like you said, he's alone all day when you work. If we can get him and Orange Blossom to make friends, or at least tolerate each other, maybe Nilla can stay over sometimes when we're both out and not be lonely."

"Let's not get ahead of ourselves," Vic warned. "We'd better make sure they can get along with each other first."

"I'll go prepare my guys. You bring Nilla over when you're ready. Maybe take him for a quick walk before you come over to burn off some of his energy."

"Good idea." Vic opened her door and got out of the car. "I'll see you in a bit."

∽

Although Erin had said that she would prepare Orange Blossom and Marshmallow for the visit, there wasn't really much she could do to make sure that they were ready to handle it. She gave them each treats and talked to them, trying to make sure that the atmosphere was as soothing as possible. She told them that Nilla would be coming over but, of course, she didn't expect them to understand that part. She sat down and flipped through Clementine's journal again, but she couldn't concentrate on it. It seemed like Clementine wrote the same thing every day. The weather. How she was feeling. How sales went at the tea shop. Maybe a thing or two that passed for news in Bald Eagle Falls. An engagement, wedding, birth, or death.

But was any of it really newsworthy? Anything that Erin wanted to know a generation later? That the younger generation after her would be interested in? Clementine had spent a lot of time writing in those journals. While they had helped Erin to solve a couple of mysteries, she figured that was probably the limit of their usefulness.

That didn't mean that she didn't appreciate Clementine. She especially appreciated her aunt leaving her tea shop and house to Erin. But Erin was finding it difficult to connect anything else in Clementine's life with her own. They lived in two such different worlds. If she were on a TV show, she would open the journal now and find something in it that would help Erin to figure out who had killed Theresa. Or at least a direction to point the police in that would lead them away from Willie. Erin flipped a few pages, but couldn't find anything that suggested a course of action.

Sunny weather. Rain. Obituary. Sale of lemon balm tea. Engagement. Another obituary.

Toward the end of her life, Clementine wrote a lot more about deaths than in the early journals. Of course. Her friends were getting older and were falling victim to the flu, pneumonia, falls and broken hips, and other ailments common among the elderly. Until Clementine, too, had started to fail and had been forced to close her business and live out her last couple of years at home, without the distraction and productive feelings that her business had given her.

Everyone's lives ended sooner or later. Whether they faded out like Clementine or died suddenly by violence like Theresa.

A quick knock at the door roused Erin from her dark thoughts. She smiled and put the journal aside as Vic opened the door and walked in with Nilla.

Orange Blossom had been lying curled up next to Erin, purring happily away. His head shot up and his ears pointed into the kitchen. He jumped down from the couch and marched over to the kitchen doorway.

"It's okay, Blossom," Erin soothed. "It's just Nilla."

The cat sniffed the air and watched the little dog's approach with big black eyes.

"Now you be nice, Orange Blossom," Vic told him. "This little guy's name is Nilla. You know he's my dog. You've smelled him on my clothes before."

The big orange cat put his ears back and growled a warning. As Vic continued to approach with Nilla on the leash, Orange Blossom arched his back and puffed out his fur. He hissed and growled again.

Nilla was panting and, at Blossom's growl, he gave a sharp yap. Vic tugged on the leash. "Shh, Nilla. No barking."

Nilla looked back at Vic and resumed panting. He was doing very well not to continue barking at the cat. When Vic had first gotten him, he had been a terror—barking, running around wildly, and destroying everything. But Vic had been working hard with him, training him to heel and to obey commands. Trying to get him more used to men, who he seemed to hate. He had an uneasy truce with Willie, but Erin thought that was just because Willie was so much bigger than Nilla and didn't back down. If Nilla could have terrorized him, it would have been another story. Nilla tended to think he was a much larger, more dangerous dog than he really was, but he hadn't been able to back Willie down.

"Just keep him there for a minute," Erin suggested. "Let's see if Blossom will settle down and get used to him being here."

"Sit, Nilla."

Nilla sat and panted, watching the cat with eager eyes. Erin could see that he wanted to play. He was sure that Orange Blossom was there to play with him, and he was eager to see what kind of fun the fluffed-out orange cat had in mind.

Orange Blossom growled a couple more times, then subsided and just watched Nilla. Not too bad.

"Who wants treats?" Erin asked in her usual pet singsong.

Orange Blossom's ears flicked. He turned his head and looked at her. Not responding as he usually did to the offer of a treat, but he was still aware of it. Marshmallow had been lying at Erin's feet, watching the dog and cat with some interest, but no concern. Erin had watched some internet videos of pet rabbits and dogs interacting, so she wasn't that surprised by Marshmallow not responding like a prey animal. The dog was too small to do him any real harm. If he got too close or did something Marshmallow didn't like, he would get a kick from two powerful back legs in his face.

Erin got up and went into the kitchen. Marshmallow followed her, watching Nilla with a side gaze, as rabbits do. Erin got out a couple of small carrot pieces and offered them to him. Nilla quivered, looking up at Vic mournfully. He wanted to at least go sniff those carrots to see if they were something good to eat. The rabbit was eating them; he wanted to know if he could eat them too.

"Good boy," Vic told him. "You can go see."

Nilla jumped to his feet and ran toward Marshmallow. Marshmallow's back feet gave a loud thump on the floor, and he turned, keeping Nilla in his side view, ignoring his carrots for the moment.

Nilla rushed forward and smelled them, pushing them around for a minute with his nose before looking at Erin in disappointment.

"Do you want a treat?" Erin offered. "Want a cookie?"

Nilla immediately sat down, then raised his front paws to beg.

"Oh, look how nicely you ask," Erin crooned. She went to the cookie jar and selected a broken gluten-free dog biscuit for Nilla. "Here you go, boy. How do you like that?"

Nilla took the piece of biscuit from her fingers and chowed down. Marshmallow went back to gnawing on his carrot pieces. Erin looked over at Orange Blossom. He was still crouched in the same place, watching Nilla eat his cookie.

"You don't want a treat?" Erin asked.

He flicked his ears again and gave her more attention this time. He didn't get up and go to the pantry where his treats were stored, but he did let out one meow.

"Yeah. You want a treat?"

CUT OUT COOKIE

He meowed again, and finally stood up, walking mostly sideways to the pantry door, his gaze alternating between Erin and Nilla. There was no reason for him to look at Marshmallow. While they were good friends, Orange Blossom already knew that he didn't like rabbit food.

Nilla munched on his cookie and whined, watching Orange Blossom walk over to the pantry door. Erin got out a couple of treats for Orange Blossom and skimmed them across the floor for him to chase.

Nilla gave a sharp bark and dashed after them, ignoring Vic's shout of alarm and command for him to stop.

It was too late. He'd already eaten Orange Blossom's treats.

The cat sat there looking at him with an angry stare that should have melted him. Nilla shifted his paws, looking at the cat, and whined slightly.

"No, Nilla," Vic told him sharply. "That was Orange Blossom's treat. Yours is here." She tapped the floor with her fingernail beside the abandoned dog biscuit. Before Nilla decided to go back to eat it, Orange Blossom was crawling low to the floor, sneaking up on it. Orange Blossom began to eat, trying to crunch the biscuit into smaller pieces that he could eat. Erin laughed. She went over to him and picked him up, pulling him away from the biscuit. Blossom gave a yowl of protest.

"Let's try this again," Erin said. She put Orange Blossom down close to the pantry. Vic let Nilla return to his cookie. "Keep his leash short," Erin warned, and she dropped a couple of treats for Blossom, giving them a little flick to move them a few inches across the floor. Not close enough for Nilla to go after. He looked up from his biscuit, eyeing the cat treats, then continued to eat his own food.

Orange Blossom ate his treats, then watched Nilla. Erin could see him pondering whether to try getting the cookie away from Nilla or if he should simply lick up the crumbs from the floor and the dog's face as he did when K9 had a biscuit.

Erin put down a couple more treats and flicked them to

Orange Blossom. He attacked them with vigor. She wondered if he were showing off for Nilla. Showing him just how much of a hunter he was. Erin flicked another one that took him closer to Nilla. Nilla tried to lunge for it, but Vic held him back.

Orange Blossom darted forward and ate it, then sat there a foot away from Nilla and started to wash.

CHAPTER 21

Vic had decided that the animals had probably seen enough of each other for one day and taken Nilla home. Erin sat back down, with her planner this time, and looked through her lists, checking things off and planning for the next few days. What would the next generation say if they read her planner long after she was gone? While they might find one or two items to be of interest, she didn't imagine that they would be any more enthralling than Clementine's daily reports on the weather. They certainly wouldn't have any idea that she had been involved in solving any crimes around Bald Eagle Falls. Erin was writing down her plans for Auntie Clem's and the things she needed to do around the house, not about what had happened the last few days and the discussions she and Vic and Jeremy had shared over dinner, speculating on who would make a good suspect and might have been involved in Theresa's death.

So far, she couldn't even say murder. She hadn't heard that the police had the medical examiner's report back yet. There was still the chance that he could come back and say that it had been an accident.

But there was no way that Theresa had just keeled over and fallen dead in her backyard. Erin had no doubt that it had been homicide. Not only that, but someone had tried to frame Erin, Vic, or Willie for Theresa's death.

But none of that was in her planner. Maybe she should start keeping memoirs of her cases, like Sherlock Holmes's Watson. That, at least, would be something that would be interesting to the next generation or two to read.

Erin heard a door slam out on the street and turned her head to look out the window to see which of the neighbors had just gotten home. But it was Terry's truck, and Terry himself was walking up the sidewalk with K9. Erin didn't jump up to answer the door, since he had a key and the burglar alarm code. Still, she put her planner aside, wondering what he was doing home so soon.

Was he sick? He might have come down with a migraine after all of the time he'd been putting in at the police department lately. They knew that overwork or stress or lack of sleep could trigger a migraine.

Maybe he'd just stopped by to check in on her while he was on patrol, like he did when he stopped by the bakery in the afternoon.

Terry's key turned in the lock and he opened the door. He let K9 in ahead of him, tapped the door code into the burglar alarm, and shut it again behind him.

"What's wrong?" Erin asked, taking in the lines of fatigue around his eyes and mouth. He had done too much. Or he'd gotten bad news. Maybe he'd had to arrest Willie and wasn't happy about it. Though he'd tried to pin a crime on Willie before and had not succeeded. She thought he would be pleased if he could finally prove that Willie had done something wrong. After so many near misses, he would like to show that he'd been right about what kind of a person Willie was all along.

"Nothing is wrong," Terry assured her.

"Why are you home so early? Is everything okay?"

He sat down on one of the chairs across from her, but didn't relax. He held himself rigid, like a statue. Unyielding. "There have been some... developments."

Erin didn't like the sound of that. She searched his face for some hint of what the developments had been. Just how bad the news was.

"What is it?"

K9 made a long, tired noise and lay down on the floor beside Terry's chair.

"For starters... I'm off the case."

She didn't have to ask which case. "Why? What happened?"

"There have been issues from the start. Even though it isn't my official residence, everyone knows that I spend most of my time at your house. So there is automatically a conflict with a dead body showing up there. I did my best to convince the sheriff and everyone else that I didn't really have a conflict. I was pursuing a vigorous investigation. There were clear suspects. And we didn't really use the yard; it was more for Vic's use."

He grimaced, knowing that he and Erin used the backyard just as much as Vic. Using the dog run, walking across to the garage, where Erin's yellow bug was kept. Erin doing her tai chi practice outside as long as the weather cooperated. Sometimes visiting on the porch and enjoying a cool evening breeze. Whenever Adele came from the woods to the house, she cut through the yard.

A tiny fib to try to hold on to the case. But eventually, they had decided that Terry was too close to the case to work on it.

"Well, I'm sorry they kicked you off of it."

"That's not the full story."

"Oh, sorry. What else, then?"

"Today, someone called to say that they had seen a uniformed police officer over here around the time that Theresa was killed."

At first, Erin thought nothing of it. Of course Terry came and went in his uniform all the time. That was perfectly normal and the neighbors were used to seeing him coming and going.

But when Theresa's body had been discovered and Willie had made his call to the police to report it, Terry had been on patrol.

Not home with her. She frowned, rubbing the space between her eyebrows where a headache was starting to form.

"Where were you then, do you know? What part of town were you in?"

"About that time, I was looking into some vandalism at the community center. Graffiti, illegal dumping, some other minor trouble."

"So that would be on your log. They would know that you weren't here."

"They know that's where I said I was. But I didn't talk to anyone while I was over there. There are no independent witnesses. I could have been somewhere else."

"They don't really think that, do they?"

"No… but an accusation has been made, and they have to respond to it. They're going to have a look at my GPS but, of course, there is the argument that I might have left the truck at the community center and walked here."

Erin tried to think of how long it would take Terry to walk from the community center to the house. Not that long. Ten minutes at a brisk pace. Shorter if he ran. But he wouldn't have run; that would attract attention. People were used to seeing Terry patrolling Bald Eagle Falls on foot as well as in his truck. No one would have thought anything of his walking anywhere in town. Running was a different story.

"And the time of death…?"

"Time of death doesn't help me. Even though it's narrow, I can't prove that I wasn't here during that window. Unless they can find someone who happened to see me somewhere else."

Erin nodded slowly. That was a problem. But Bald Eagle Falls was a small place. Someone might have seen him when he'd been at the community center. They just didn't know yet that it was an important piece of evidence.

"They can canvass people who live close to the community center," she suggested.

"They may. I'm not sure how hard they will work at trying to prove that I was not here around the time of the murder. They really didn't want me in on the case from the start. And the sheriff says he's been getting a lot of pressure to call in the FBI instead of investigating it ourselves."

"Why? What could they do that you can't?"

"I don't know if they could do anything we can't. But they have social and emotional distance. They can say that they are unbiased. And since she was a member of an organized crime organization, they have resources allocated for that. It wouldn't come out of our budget."

"The mayor is trying to cut costs?"

Terry shrugged. "I can't say for sure that the pressure is coming from him, or that it is because of the money. That's just… my own personal speculation."

"Well, it's stupid. But…" Erin sighed. "Maybe it is best if someone else is investigating it."

"You too?" Terry looked taken aback. "Why do you say that? You know I didn't have anything to do with it."

"Of course," Erin agreed. "But maybe it's better if you aren't investigating our friends. I know you aren't going to show Willie any favoritism, but it's better for us—for me and you—if we don't have to justify it to Vic and Willie. This isn't exactly the first time that you've investigated him for a crime. It… causes a rift."

Terry rubbed his chin, the sandpaper-like noise setting Erin's teeth on edge. "Has it caused tensions between you and Vic? I guess I knew it could, but I have to ignore that kind of thing when there is a crime to be investigated."

"Exactly. And sometimes… it is a problem. We all try to separate what you do from our friendships, but… that doesn't stop people from being angry."

Terry nodded slowly. "Makes sense. I don't like to cause problems, but it is a small town. Just by working where I live, it's going to cause some discomfort."

"Who was the witness that said you were here? Do you know?

And how can the police department say it was definitely you? You're not the only one in town who wears a uniform."

"It was an anonymous call to a tip line, so I don't have any way of tracing it back. If I was allowed to do such a thing. But I have my suspicions." He didn't voice what his suspicions were. But who would want him off the case? Erin could see where his mind would go. "And I was the only law enforcement officer on duty that night, so…"

"But someone else could have put on their uniform and been around here."

"Why would anyone do that?" Terry asked, bemused.

"I don't know… if they were up to no good, then a police uniform would be a good way to lurk around without looking suspicious. Make people think that you had legitimate business."

"You think that one of the others planned to kill Theresa? In your backyard?"

Erin raised her brows. "*Not* in my backyard, from what I hear."

"Okay, not in your backyard. But someone—another cop—planned to kill her, and then dumped her body in your yard. Is that what you're suggesting?"

Erin tried to picture Tom Banks creeping around, killing Theresa and dumping her body. There was no way that the part-time officer would have done that. He was fine for giving tickets, investigating routine break-ins, and other small-time crimes, but the bigger stuff was always given to Terry or Stayner.

Sheriff Wilmot… possible, but unlikely. He was crusty but kind. He did what was needed in Bald Eagle Falls to keep law and order, but she didn't see him as a violent man.

Stayner. Now, Stayner was another story. Young, impulsive, still learning the ropes. His behavior varied widely between bullying and unexpectedly thoughtful gestures. He was loud and brash and tended to leap into things rather than thinking them through. He was certainly the kind of guy she could see killing

Theresa on impulse and then trying to clean up after himself by dumping her body in Erin's yard.

But she didn't tell Terry that. "There's also the Moose River police department. One of them could have tracked Theresa here and intended to arrest her on the outstanding warrants. Or it could have been a costume, not a legitimate police uniform. Or even somebody who was mistaken and took another outfit as a police uniform. A security guard, utility worker, something like that. And they might not have had anything to do with Theresa's death."

"You're right, of course… but I can't help thinking that it was a false call that was made just to get me off the case. And maybe the rest of the department too."

CHAPTER 22

There wasn't much that Erin could do to help Terry feel better about being kicked off the case. Except to do what she usually did—make him something to eat.

While she pulled a small supper together for him, she entertained him with the story of Nilla coming over to meet Orange Blossom and Marshmallow.

Blossom seemed to know that he was being talked about and wound around Erin's legs, meowing in protest either of Nilla coming over or of the way that Erin was telling the story. Terry chuckled.

"You're going to have to make friends with the dogs," he told Blossom. "They've got you surrounded."

"I think he'll get along with Nilla better than K9," Erin said. "He's smaller and not as threatening. Blossom can bully him."

"We'll see. From what I've seen of cats and dogs, it's not the size of the dog in the fight but the fight in the dog."

"I've heard that before, you know."

"I didn't claim to have made it up."

Erin removed the dish from the microwave and put it in front of Terry. There was a loud knock on the front door, making her jump. She looked at the clock on the wall. "Who would be coming at this time of night?"

Terry looked at the food, then got to his feet. "Let me check. I don't like you answering the door this late."

Erin thought that she should protest, remind Terry that she was a grown woman perfectly capable of answering her own door no matter what time of night it was. But she'd had late-night visitors in the past. Visitors that Terry would be much more equipped to handle than Erin was. She was happy to let him be the macho protector and ensure that there wasn't an ax murderer at the front door.

Terry strode across the living room to the front door, not bothering to look out the living room window or check the peephole before turning the locks on the front door and pulling it open.

Stayner stood there, as straight and stiff in his uniform as if he himself had been starched, expression stony. He didn't smile at Terry or greet him by name. He handed a folded piece of paper to Terry.

"Search warrant," he explained. "If we could get the two of you to sit on the sofa here while we conduct the search."

Terry stared at him, unmoving.

"You know how this is done," Stayner said in a tough-guy voice. "Step aside, please."

Terry reached for the burglar alarm pad, an unexpected movement that made Stayner jump and reach for his sidearm.

"Need to disarm this," Terry advised, as the panel began to beep steadily. "If you don't disarm it within thirty seconds of the door opening, it's going to make a heck of a racket."

Stayner relaxed and watched Terry punch in the security code and disarm it. "Thank you. And now, if the two of you would please sit down."

Terry strode back toward the kitchen. "We'll be in here. We were just sitting down to eat."

He didn't look back at his fellow officer. Stayner stared after him for a moment, then decided to let it go. He was mellowing out. When he'd first started at Bald Eagle Falls a few months ago, Erin was sure that he would have made a huge big deal over them choosing to sit in the kitchen instead of the living room. Probably would have arrested them both and held them at gunpoint until someone could take them into the police department offices.

Terry sat down and took a couple of bites of his dinner. Erin watched him, her eyes wide.

"Did you know that they were coming?"

He didn't appear to be surprised by the search. Terry looked back over his shoulder at the door as Sheriff Wilmot and Tom Banks entered. The whole gang was there to perform the search.

"Please be sure to shut the door tight," Erin told Tom as he swung the door partway closed behind him so that it met the jamb but didn't latch. "We have animals."

Tom gave a nod and pushed the door shut the rest of the way to engage the catch. He didn't look at Erin or meet her eyes. Terry turned around to face his dinner again, taking a couple more bites. He didn't look like he was enjoying it. Erin supposed that his mind was on other things and eating had just become a chore. Something to do while the other men in his department searched his house.

Well, Erin's house. But Terry lived there too, most of the time.

"Did you know?" Erin asked again.

Terry chewed, swallowed, and sighed. "I knew that we were working on warrants. I didn't know that they would be coming through tonight or that they would be served as soon as they got me out of the way."

"You knew they wanted a warrant for my house?"

He nodded, looking down at his plate. He clearly knew that her reaction to this news would not be pleasant.

"Who applied for those warrants?"

"We were all working on them."

"You drafted a warrant to search my house?"

"It's my job, Erin." He raised his eyes to look at her. "I don't think that you had anything to do with Theresa's death. But somebody killed her, and somebody moved her body. It was in the backyard of this house. So, yes… we needed a warrant to search your house. We need to establish where she was killed in order to move forward in the investigation."

"Not 'we' anymore."

"No," Terry growled. "I can no longer be involved in it."

"And not just because there was an anonymous tip about a policeman being seen in the area."

"No. I told you that was just part of it. I can't control where this investigation leads. I can't have anything to do with it. So… maybe that will help with your friendships with Vic and Willie." His words were tight, as if he could barely force them out through clenched teeth.

Erin knew that he was doing his best to do his job without letting it interfere with their relationship. Still, it was pretty hard to see his actions as anything other than a betrayal. She clenched her teeth together tightly to prevent herself from exploding. As a teen, this would be the point at which she started screaming at the top of her lungs, a tirade that would eventually end with her stomping off to her bedroom and slamming the door. Of course, as a foster kid, this presented several challenges, one of which was that she never had a room to herself. She couldn't actually shut the rest of the family out. There was rarely anywhere she could retreat for complete privacy, except maybe to a bathroom, and she couldn't stay there for long before others were knocking on the door asking her how much longer she was going to be in there.

With three law enforcement officers in her house performing a search, Erin had no way to have a private argument with Terry, even one that didn't include screaming and slamming doors. There was nowhere she could go to hide from them all. Not unless she went across the yard to Vic's loft. She glanced out the window in that direction. When she looked back at Terry, his lips were pressed tightly together. As if there were many things that he wanted to say too, but he knew he couldn't.

Either because his colleagues were searching the house or

because he couldn't say anything to Erin that might compromise the case.

"What about Vic's?" Erin asked.

"It will be searched," Terry confirmed.

"Is it all part of the same warrant?"

"Two separate warrants. Even though it is the same property, it is two separate residences, so we issue two warrants. Just to be sure there are no technicalities."

"You weren't allowed to tell me?"

He shook his head. "Of course not. Telling someone that their residence was going to be the subject of a search warrant wouldn't just get me taken off the case; it would get me fired."

Erin wasn't hungry, but she felt like she needed a reason to stay in the kitchen other than the fact that it was where the police wanted her to be. She needed a reason that suited her. She got up and put on the kettle to make some tea. Tea would give her something to do with her hands and mouth. It would calm her down and help her get ready for sleep.

How was she going to sleep with the police searching the house? How long would they be there? And when they left, how was she going to wind down enough that she'd be able to get to sleep?

While the kettle heated, Erin took out her phone and called Charley.

"Hey, sis," Charley greeted.

"Hi. Listen, Charley, could you call around and see who would be able to work the morning shift at Auntie Clem's? Vic and I aren't going to be able to get there."

Charley was silent for a moment. Erin had never asked her to do something like that before. She always insisted on being there herself unless she was on vacation. Even when she was on vacation, she did the employee scheduling herself.

"Sure, of course," Charley agreed eventually. "No problem. Is everything okay?"

"I'll have to talk to you about it later. I just know that with everything going on, we're not going to be able to make it. We've both been too short on sleep this week as it is."

"What's going on? Tell me you haven't been arrested."

Erin had to smile at that. "I haven't been arrested."

"Good. And Vic?"

"Nobody has been arrested."

"Are the cops there now?"

Erin nodded and sighed. "Yeah."

"I knew they were going to end up searching your houses and pulling you in for questioning. Are you okay? Do you want me to find you a lawyer?"

"No. Not yet. Hopefully, it won't come to that. But I don't know what else the police have in mind." She looked at Terry, raising one eyebrow. "I'm not getting very far in my interrogations."

Charley laughed. "Well, you keep at it, girl. He'll crack sooner or later. Call me tomorrow, okay? Let me know what's happening."

"I'll do my best. You have everyone's numbers, right?"

"Yes, you made me put them all in my phone."

"Good. I'll talk to you tomorrow, then."

Terry looked very serious as Erin hung up. "I've never seen you do that before."

Erin turned away from him to tend to the kettle as it started to whistle. "What, call Charley or make tea?"

Terry sputtered. "Well, of course I've seen you do that. I mean... canceling your shifts. Giving Charley that kind of responsibility. You're always such a control—you always want to be in control of Auntie Clem's and the employee schedules yourself."

"A control freak?" Erin asked, filling in what she thought he had intended to say before he cut himself off.

"No, that's not a nice way of putting it. A control freak would be someone... who was unreasonable. Who couldn't handle not being in charge of every little thing. You like things to be arranged the way you like them... but you don't have to control everything."

Nice save, Officer Piper.

Erin shrugged. "Well... maybe it's a sign of maturity. I'm getting practical in my old age. It's ridiculous to think that I can keep going in for the early shift without any sleep. I'm wrecked this week. What good is it going to do me to be at Auntie Clem's first thing in the morning every day if I chop off a finger and get blood in the muffins?"

Terry laughed loudly at that, surprised. Erin allowed herself a small smile. At least it helped to break the tension. And she did feel better knowing that the bakery would be taken care of no matter how late she got to sleep. It immediately reduced the pressure and helped her to breathe.

Charley and Bella would keep things running smoothly without Erin there.

Hopefully, it would only be for one day, and then things would get back on track again.

CHAPTER 23

After fiddling with her tea for a while, Erin sat down. She had a sip and gazed through the doorway at the living room. Stayner was on his hands and knees on the carpet, collecting some kind of sample. Did they really think that she had killed Theresa in the middle of her living room?

"Why are you searching here and Vic's?" she asked Terry. "Theresa could have been killed anywhere. You can't get warrants for everywhere."

"Well, that's one reason we're starting here. Because we have reason to suspect that Theresa could have been killed here or at Vic's. Bodies are not easy to move. The time of death window, calculated to be between when the last call was made on Theresa's phone to when Willie called the dispatcher, was very short. Getting a body out of the house, into a vehicle, driving across town, and getting the body out of the vehicle and into the yard… that's actually a pretty time-consuming process. It's not like putting a file box or shopping bag in your car to go home. The most likely scenario is that no one transported her body in their car. More likely that Theresa was killed right here, in one of these two residences."

"That's ridiculous. You know she wasn't killed in here. You

would know that; you live here. If there was blood on the carpet or something, you would know! You were here that night. You know there wasn't any indication that anyone had been killed here."

"I know. And I told you that I don't think you had anything to do with it."

He looked at her steadily. Erin shifted her position and had a sip from her cup, pulling her gaze away from Terry. She didn't want to be forced to meet his gaze. It was easier to talk if she didn't have to look him in the eye, with him watching to see whether she was lying or trying to hide something. Even though she knew that she was not.

"But logic dictates that it was likely to have been done in one of these two residences," Terry reiterated. "We had to get warrants for both. It would be bad police work to only search one, when either was an equal possibility."

"So… you think that Theresa was killed in Vic's apartment."

Terry shrugged. He was the one who looked away this time.

"But Vic wasn't even around. So that means… you think Willie killed her."

She already knew that Willie was the prime suspect. And they had spent plenty of time interviewing him. They didn't have enough evidence to arrest him, but they certainly had their suspicions.

"So you think that when you go over to Vic's—when *they* go over to Vic's—" she nodded at Stayner, "—that they're going to find evidence Theresa was killed in there."

"Yes."

"Then why didn't they search her place first? If they had warrants for both, but figured that hers was the murder site, then why not go to hers first?"

"Probably because of me."

"Because of you? But you said that you don't suspect me."

"No. But I am a suspect. And when I left the office today, knowing that the warrants were being signed, I could have come back here to destroy evidence."

Erin thought about this. "But wouldn't you have done that already? Why would you leave it until you knew the warrants were being signed?"

Terry smiled, but not in a way that made the dimple in his cheek appear. It was a tired, resigned smile. "Of course I would have. If I killed Theresa, I could have done a dozen different things by now to keep them from finding out. Evidence could have been lost or obscured. I could have arrested Willie the first night and kept the investigation focused on him, providing all the evidence they needed to show he was the killer. Anonymous tips could be called in—*other* anonymous tips. Trust me, if I killed Theresa, I would not have been sitting around on my butt waiting to be caught."

"No," Erin agreed, nodding slowly. She sipped her tea.

"Of course, if I had killed Theresa, I wouldn't have left her body in the backyard to be discovered by Willie."

"But bodies are hard to move," Erin said, repeating his previous explanation. "You might have set her down there while you went to get your truck and bring it around back. Or to get… a blanket to wrap it in or a wheelbarrow to move it more easily. And then Willie comes along and stumbles over it while you're making your preparations…"

Terry chuckled. "Yes, detective. All of that is possible. But there's one flaw in that theory."

Erin cocked her head, thinking it over. "What?"

"If Willie had found the body while I was making my evil plans, I would have stopped him before he could call the dispatcher. Told him to mind his own business and make himself scarce."

"And you think he would have?"

"Of course he would have. Do you think he would choose to report a dead body instead of just letting it disappear? You think he wanted to become a suspect?"

"Huh. No," Erin admitted.

Terry had pointed out at least once before that Willie had his own morality system, which didn't necessarily align with the law. Erin had to admit that staying off the police radar would have been a more attractive prospect for Willie than becoming the prime suspect in a murder investigation. Erin might have made the same choice herself. She knew what it was like to be the center of a murder investigation, and it wasn't nearly as much fun as the killers on the old *Columbo* movies made it look.

"How exactly was Theresa killed?"

Terry shook his head. "I can't give you information like that."

"Do you have the ME's report?"

"The preliminary report. Of course, tox screens and such will take longer, but we have the basics."

"I heard that she wasn't shot."

Terry nodded, but did not confirm or deny that conclusion.

"So, was she… cut or stabbed? She carried a gun and knife, so I thought that she would have had to have been shot."

"You're not going to find out from me, Erin."

"Well… was it something I could have done?"

"I told you, I never thought that you had anything to do with it."

"That doesn't answer my question."

Unless it did. Maybe he had known that Erin couldn't have killed Theresa.

"Oh… so maybe it was something I couldn't do?" Maybe something that needed more upper body strength than she had, or an attacker who was taller than Theresa. Or some technique that someone from one of the clans might have done that needed special training.

Terry didn't fill her in on the details. But Erin was sure to find out more. It would end up in the paper or be leaked by Melissa. Sooner or later, she would hear.

"I think we've got everything we need here," Sheriff Wilmot announced.

Erin looked at him. They hadn't even searched the kitchen or shone a black light to identify any blood evidence. How could they be finished already?

"Did you find what you were looking for?" she asked him.

Wilmot's face reddened. "Miss Price, nobody thinks that you had anything to do with this. But we have to cover all of our bases."

Pretty much the same thing as Terry had said.

"But you didn't even look for blood."

"Why would we—" Sheriff Wilmot cut himself off. He looked at Terry and shook his head. "I don't know how you can be around her and not give anything away."

Terry smiled slightly. "She doesn't make it easy."

"We have what we need here. Time to move on to the other residence. Miss Price, you are the landlord for Victoria Webster's unit over the garage?"

"Yes."

"We may need you to give us entrance to that unit if Miss Webster is not home."

"She is."

He looked across the yard at the loft apartment. The curtains were drawn and there was little light shining through the space between the panels. The apartment could have been occupied, or they might have just left a light on when going out.

"Thank you. I'll let you know if we need anything."

CHAPTER 24

Shortly after the police exited the kitchen to cross the yard to Vic's loft, Erin saw Vic and Willie traveling the reverse route to the house. Vic entered first, with Nilla in her arms, and whatever she had been planning to say froze on her lips when she saw Terry sitting there at the table with Erin.

"Oh. You're here."

Terry looked at her and didn't say anything. Willie stopped behind Vic and also glowered at Terry. "Officer Piper."

"Willie."

Erin looked from one to the other. "Terry is off the case," she informed Vic and Willie. "That's why he's here, instead of with them."

Vic walked the rest of the way into the kitchen and put Nilla down on the floor. He was on leash, so she let him explore the kitchen as they talked. "Is that good news or bad news?"

"I would have preferred to stay on it and wrap things up," Terry said. "But I realize it also causes problems for me to be investigating... friends."

"Acquaintances," Willie corrected. He didn't sit down, but looked around the kitchen as if looking for some way to escape.

Erin couldn't think of a more uncomfortable situation for him.

He knew he was the prime suspect in the case, and now he was closeted with the cop who had been investigating it while the rest of the police department searched Vic's apartment. Erin wondered if they also had a warrant for Willie's house. They wouldn't suspect Willie of killing Theresa at his house and then taking her body to Vic's yard. That wouldn't make any sense. But they might want to search his house for… whatever the weapon had been. Or whatever Willie had been wearing at the time, or other evidence that he'd been in contact with Theresa or that he'd known where she was.

But of course, they already had all of that. They knew what he had been wearing that night, even if they hadn't had a chance to test it for forensic evidence. They knew from Theresa's phone whether she had been in contact with Willie. Since she had been in contact with everyone else involved with Vic, Erin couldn't imagine that she wouldn't have been in contact with Willie. Making her crazy accusations and threats. Taunting and teasing him. Thinking that she was smart to be able to keep just out of his reach.

But had she?

Erin didn't like to think Willie could have been involved with Theresa's death, but it was a possibility. The police hadn't eliminated him as a suspect. He was the one who'd clearly had access to the body. He had a motive. He'd made no secret of the fact that he'd been searching for her for months.

What if Willie had managed to track and kill Theresa?

Erin still couldn't reconcile Willie dumping her body in the yard and calling the police. That didn't make any sense if he was the killer.

"Do you want some tea?" Erin offered. She felt suddenly exhausted. She didn't want to get up from the table to serve everyone, even though it was clearly the right thing for the hostess to do. But who dictated what was proper behavior when someone's house was being searched by the police? And when there was clear animosity between Willie and Terry?

Terry got up and put his dish in the sink. "I think I'll have a shower. Don't forget to tell Vic the arrangements for tomorrow."

He walked out of the room. K9's ears were pricked up and he turned his head to follow Terry's movements, but Terry did not call him, so he stayed where he was, comfortable lying on the kitchen floor watching Nilla explore the cracks and crevices.

No one said anything until water started running in the bathroom. There was no way that Terry could overhear them with the wall between them and the noise of the shower.

"What arrangements for tomorrow?" Vic asked, her eyes tired and worried.

"I told Charley to arrange for someone to take our shifts in the morning."

"Oh!" Vic looked relieved. "Well, that will be a nice break. That's probably a good idea. I don't know whether I'm going to get any sleep tonight." She looked back toward her apartment.

"I doubt they'll be very long," Erin said. "They were pretty quick here."

"They searched here too?" Willie raised his brows and looked around.

Erin nodded. "I guess that these are the two most likely places for Theresa to have been killed. That's one of the reasons that Terry couldn't stay on the case."

"I guess not, since he pretty much lives here," Willie agreed.

"Why else couldn't he stay on the case?" Vic asked.

"Someone called in a tip that a police officer was seen lurking around here at the time that Theresa was killed. And he was the only one on duty at the time."

Willie smirked. "An anonymous tip?"

"Yes."

"Well, that's one way to get a cop off of your back."

Erin was suddenly suspicious. "Was it you?"

He shook his head. "No, but it's a pretty good idea. *I* wouldn't put it past me."

Vic rolled her eyes and shook her head. "So does that mean

that Terry is going to be hanging around here now? Is he suspended or just off of the one case?"

"I… he didn't say. He just said that he was off the case. But I don't know for sure. He said, 'for starters,' but I don't think we ever got on to anything else. Then the rest of the police department showed up."

CHAPTER 25

Sheriff Wilmot didn't tell Erin anything except that they were finished, thanking her politely for allowing them to execute the searches. Erin wasn't sure what else she could have done. It wasn't like she had much choice in the matter. There were a few tense seconds when he turned to Willie and Vic, but he didn't tell them anything and didn't put either of them under arrest for Theresa's murder.

Erin could feel Terry behind her in the house. He had not reappeared when he was finished with his long shower, but retreated to the bedroom instead, staying out of the way of Erin and her friends. There was no point coming out when the sheriff confirmed that Vic and Willie were free to go back to the loft apartment. He was off the case, so Wilmot would not tell him what they had found in the course of either search. But Erin could still feel his presence, watching and listening from the other side of the house, wishing that he could be out there, part of the action, involved in solving the crime. Instead, he was banished, closed out from participating.

Even though Erin didn't like him investigating her friends or the antipathy that seemed to be growing between him and Willie, she felt bad for Terry. After seeing everyone off, she walked to the bedroom to talk with him.

"They're gone. It's just you and me now."

Dressed in light athletic pants and no shirt, Terry nodded. "Didn't take too long."

"No. I guess they knew what they were looking for."

"Yes. They did."

"What do you want to do?"

Terry raised one eyebrow. "What do I want to do?"

"I mean… it's just you and me now, and I don't have anywhere to be in the morning, so if you wanted to make popcorn and watch a movie, we could. Or if you have something else in mind…"

"I'm afraid… I won't be very good company tonight. I'm not in the best mood."

"I know you must be really disappointed in being kicked off the case. And not being able to take part in the search."

"The search—no. That would have been very awkward. I don't think I would have wanted to participate in the search anyway. But being taken off the case, like I'm biased or have my own agenda… yeah, that smarts. And they all know that it isn't true. That I would have put just as much time and energy into finding Theresa's killer and seeing that he's dealt with appropriately as I would have in any other case. They know that I wasn't involved in any way. That it's just someone's attempt to get me off the case. But there's nothing they can do about it. They have to deal with it as if it was a legitimate lead."

"What would help you to forget about it and relax?"

"Nothing."

Erin waited. There had to be one activity that would be better than another. Terry didn't suggest anything.

"Go for a walk?" Erin suggested, "Something physical? Do you need to work it out or to veg out and forget about it?"

He hesitated. "I don't want to disrupt your evening. And I know that you have to stick pretty close to your usual sleep schedule even if you aren't going to Auntie Clem's in the morning. Your body still wakes you up early."

"One day isn't going to make that big of a difference. If I don't get enough sleep, I'll have a nap in the afternoon." She didn't usually like taking naps. It tended to make her headachy and grumpy. But she could make one exception.

"Well… maybe a walk. I don't want to be out on the street where people can see us. I don't want to have to deal with questions and speculation."

"We do have these woods behind us. I happen to know that the owner would allow us to go out for a little jaunt and take advantage of them."

Terry shrugged. He still didn't seem very eager to go out. But his comment was the only indication she had of something that might help, and she wasn't going to just ignore it because he'd rather not mess up her sleep schedule for one night. Her schedule had already been disrupted by the search. Her brain wouldn't settle down for hours.

"Let's go, then. You'd better get a shirt on. Or are you going to go *á la* Hulk?"

Terry looked down at himself. "I would think that you'd be happy to take me out like this."

Erin smiled. "Sure, if you want. But you might get a little chilly."

He chuckled and went over to his drawer to find a t-shirt. They both got ready to go. K9 wandered around them, his dog tags jingling, unsure of this new behavior. His people didn't normally go out for a walk at night.

"Come on, pardner," Terry told him. "Go for a walk."

K9's tail swept back and forth. He went to the back door. Terry re-armed the burglar alarm, and they headed out, confusing K9 further by taking the back gate into the woods. Terry occasionally took him on walks through the woods, but only during the day.

They walked through the trees in silence at first. Erin's eyes adjusted to the dim lighting of the moon. She knew the woods fairly well now, unlike that first night when she had ventured out and come across Adele doing her nighttime rituals. It was different in the silvery moonlight, not quite as familiar, but she didn't trip or stumble on the rough pathways too many times. Terry kept Erin's hand on his right arm to help guide her along. K9 stayed close, but occasionally ranged away from them to smell something he could see or hear in the darkness, interested in the nighttime wildlife.

Terry's pace was fairly brisk at first. He was used to walking for hours with K9 on patrol, keeping up a good speed so that he could cover a fair amount of ground. But at night, when there were nearly invisible obstacles and he had Erin on his arm, he needed to slow down. Before long, he relaxed the pace and Erin found it easier to keep up with him and not trip over her own feet. She could feel some of the tension falling away from Terry.

She looked up at the stars, visible through the tops of the trees. It was a clear night, and the stars sparkled like little gems catching the sun's light. "It's beautiful out."

"Yes, it is," Terry agreed. He pulled her close against his body and gave her a little squeeze. "This is… helping."

"Good."

They continued to walk. Erin expected Terry to talk, to tell her about what he was thinking and how he was handling the change of affairs, but he stayed silent. So maybe he didn't need someone to talk to. Just someone to share the silence with.

Erin wondered whether Vic really had been looking at the stars the night that Theresa had been killed. She was pretty sure that she had not. Vic had never shown a propensity to take off and look at the stars any other time. Certainly not to take Erin's car and drive around looking at them.

At least, not that Erin knew about.

What Vic might have done when Erin was normally asleep, she couldn't know. But most mornings, she had to be at Auntie Clem's Bakery with Erin, and Erin would have wondered if she were yawning and tired after spending extended nights out stargazing.

"Who's there?" a voice called out of the darkness.

Erin didn't have a flashlight with her, so she couldn't shine it in the direction of the noise, but she knew the voice and knew what she'd see if she did. A tall, slim woman with dark red hair, cloaked in black and a shotgun on her arm. A hood pulled over her head if the weather required a raincoat or sweatshirt. A rather odd combination of witch and warden.

"It's Erin, Adele."

She could hear Adele getting closer, but she was not on a pathway and it was a minute before a moonbeam caught her so that Erin could see her more clearly.

"And Officer Piper," Adele observed. "Out enjoying the vernal equinox?"

Erin thought about the dates. "Yes… I guess we are. It's a nice night for it."

Adele's head nodded gravely. "Quiet so far. Peaceful. A night to find balance."

Erin took in a deep breath and let it out, concentrating on one of her tai chi breathing patterns. Having been practicing for a while now, it was easier to focus on her breathing and find that focused, centered place where her body relaxed and her heart rate slowed. Balance.

"Nice after a stressful day."

"Has it been very stressful?" Adele asked. Her voice was low and musical. Erin sometimes wished that her life were more like Adele's, minimalist, quiet, and focused on being a part of nature.

"Yeah. I guess you heard about Theresa Franklin…"

"I did hear something about a woman being found in your yard. A rather strange occurrence."

"You could say that again."

"You don't know what happened?"

Erin looked at Terry to see what he would contribute. He said nothing.

"We're still trying to figure it out," Erin admitted. "I mean... the police are. It's nothing to do with us, of course."

"Are you concerned about prowlers? Trespassers in the woods? Is that why you're here?"

"No. I think... whoever did this, their target was Theresa. Not just a random woman walking around Bald Eagle Falls. If it was someone from out of town... they're probably long gone."

"And if it was someone from in town?"

"Then they're probably being super careful not to draw anyone's attention. They won't be out. They'll be acting like nothing happened."

Adele nodded. "Well, I'm sure our intrepid police force will sort it out."

"You didn't happen to see anything that night? Monday?" Terry asked.

Erin supposed she shouldn't be surprised that Terry couldn't keep from asking questions about the murder. He'd been kicked off the case, but he still wanted to know what had happened, and his investigator's mind wasn't going to shut off just because he'd been told he was done.

Adele didn't move, considering the question. Eventually, she answered. "There was some activity Monday night... but I'll have to think about it."

"If you saw anyone out and about, you should report it to the police," Terry told her. "It could be important."

Adele was not quick to agree. In her quiet patrol of the woods, she was often aware of things that others were not. Erin should have known to ask her earlier. If anyone had eyes and ears open around her land at night, it was Adele. But she wasn't always ready to jump to the aid of a police investigation. Erin tried to give Terry a look not to push it too hard with Adele. Erin could follow up with her later, more subtly. Adele didn't like authority figures and would clam up just as a matter of principle.

"Just think about it," Erin told Adele. "See what you can remember."

Adele nodded. "Enjoy your evening." She gave a slight bow. "Have a blessed equinox."

She melted back into the shadowy trees and was gone. Terry and Erin stood there for a moment, not moving on.

"She may know something," Terry said.

"I know. But she's not going to run to the police with it. She's going to need some time."

"And in the meantime, Theresa's killer walks free."

Which Erin wasn't sure was such a bad thing. It all depended on who had killed Theresa and why. If it had been someone defending himself or his family, then good for him. She hoped that he could live a peaceful life without consequences.

If, however, it was someone from one of the clans, that was a little more concerning. Though someone from the Jackson or Dyson clan wasn't as likely to be a danger to Erin or anyone she knew. No more than they had been before. It wasn't like Erin could identify the killer and he would be gunning for her. As long as she stayed away from clan politics, there shouldn't be any danger to her or anyone else in Bald Eagle Falls that she cared about. If the clan members killed each other off, that was bad, but not nearly as concerning as if there were some serial killer psycho who had attacked Theresa for no reason and continued to hunt in the woods or neighborhood around Erin's house.

And she didn't think that was what had happened.

Still, she had a chill and gave a little shiver. Terry noticed and rubbed her arm. "We should probably be getting back to the house."

"We can walk for a little longer if you like. I'll stay warm if we're moving."

"No. Let's go back. There's still time to put something short on TV and have that bowl of popcorn."

CHAPTER 26

It was good to have a quiet evening with Terry, who often wasn't home at night. It wasn't a romantic night, both of them still feeling rather out of sorts. Still, it was good to cuddle up together on the couch with a bowl full of popcorn and watch a movie without having to worry about whether Erin would be able to get up in time in the morning.

And she did sleep in. A couple of hours, anyway. And then she lay still in bed for a while, just listening to Terry breathe and watching his chest rise and fall. It was nice to be with someone, not to go to sleep alone every night. Their sleep schedules rarely matched exactly, but they were generally together for at least a couple of hours most nights. Lying in bed as the sun came up, listening to the birds chirping outside and her partner's long, even breaths was not something she normally experienced. It was pleasant, as long as she didn't think too hard about the reason that they were both still in bed.

Eventually, her busy brain wouldn't let her lie still anymore, and she got up quietly so that she wouldn't wake Terry up with restless tossing and turning. She had a quiet breakfast by herself— at least, it was quiet once she gave Orange Blossom his breakfast—

and sat down for a while to read and plan and ponder over all that had happened in the previous twenty-four hours.

She jotted a list on a blank page of her planner. People who had reason to kill Theresa. She didn't title it; she just started to list names. It was a pretty long list. Erin hoped that no one would ever see the need to write a similar list for her or, if they did, it would be much, much shorter.

Much of Theresa's life remained in darkness. She knew a little about Theresa growing up in the same area and in similar circumstances to Vic. The two of them were familiar with each other and dating for a time. She knew that Theresa's family had taken in her cousin, Bo Biggles, when his mother had abandoned him, and that he had been abusive toward Theresa. Was that when it had all started? When she'd started to have violent thoughts toward others and developed into the killer she would later become? Or was it before that, the influence of the clan or something in her genetic makeup?

She had been recruited by the clan, probably before she was ever out of high school. Perhaps at fourteen or fifteen years old. From what Jack Ward could dig up, they had trained her, and she had been an eager student.

Erin didn't know when her parents had disappeared. Sometime in the last year, from what Erin could tell. And again, Jack believed Theresa had killed them and disposed of the bodies in such a way that no one had been able to find them. Without any evidence of foul play, he could not get onto Theresa's family's property with a search warrant to find out.

She'd seized an opportunity to kill Bo Biggles and had almost gotten away with it, had nearly killed Terry and Jack, and had even had her hands around Erin's throat. After fleeing the scene, she had returned later, gotten in contact with Vic's older brothers, and convinced them to kill their father.

Quite a storied career for someone so young.

And then she had begun her campaign of harassing Vic and

everyone close to her. And one of those actions... had led to someone killing her?

Was it someone she had been calling and texting? That was the logical solution. But how many people had that been? And which of them had cracked, deciding to put an end to Theresa's cyberbullying?

Erin ran her thumb over the smooth surface of her phone for a few minutes, thinking it all through. At the center of it was Jack Ward. He was the one who knew the most about Theresa and her activities over the past few years. Even if all he had were suspicions, he still knew more about how she operated than Erin. She unlocked her phone and found his number.

Jack's phone rang a couple of times, and then he answered.

"Erin Price. A pleasure to hear from you!"

Erin smiled, remembering how crusty Jack had been when she had first met him. It was amazing how much a person could change in a few months. Or that her perceptions of him had changed. She now knew that, like Sheriff Wilmot, even if he put on a show of being a tough, unemotional cop, there was a gentle, tender-hearted man underneath.

"Hi, Jack. I guess you've probably heard about the excitement around here."

"About Crazy Theresa? Yeah. That was quite a shocker. How are you holding out? I understand it was pretty close to home."

"My backyard. But I'm okay. I didn't find her; someone else did."

"Good. You should probably lay off finding the bodies for a while. It isn't good for one's morale."

"I'll keep that in mind," Erin agreed dryly.

"So, did you just call to shoot the breeze? Or do you need something?"

"Can't I call you just to say hello?"

"Hello, Erin."

Erin smiled. "Okay. Yes. I wondered if we could talk about

Theresa. I'm... feeling sort of unsettled. I was hoping that if I had someone to talk with about it, maybe I would feel better."

"And Officer Piper can't help you out with that?"

"Well... he doesn't really know that much about Theresa. Not like you do." She paused for a few seconds. "And you probably heard he's off the case. So he can't make inquiries."

"But you can?"

"Well... *you* can."

Jack laughed. "As it happens, I am over your direction this afternoon. Would you like to get together? Maybe share some hot chicken at the BBQ place?"

"You're going to be in Bald Eagle Falls?"

"I am. Your police department has been left a little short-handed and doesn't have the deep knowledge of the clans that my boys do. We're going to get together, loan them a couple of men, have a big pow-wow over the case, see what we do and don't know."

"Well then, yes, that would be really nice. When are you getting in?"

"I'm meeting with Wilmot's crew about two. Should be out by six or seven and ready to tear into some chicken."

"Okay. Let me know when you're ready, and we'll get together."

"Will this include Officer Piper?"

"Umm... I'm not sure yet. Probably, I guess, since I don't know if they're giving him any shifts or not?"

"We'll play it by ear, I guess. Call you later."

∽

Erin was too restless to sit with a book or her planner anymore. She needed to move around. To get her hands working and distract her brain. Too much thinking, and it wasn't getting her any further ahead. Terry was just getting up, still bleary-eyed, as she was heading out the door.

"Where are you off to?" Terry asked, licking dry lips. "Shopping? A little retail therapy?"

"No, I'm going to go by the bakery. See how things went this morning and put in a shift if anyone ended up doing doubles today."

"I thought you weren't going to work today."

"I didn't want to have to get up in the morning, with the way the evening was going. But I need to do something. And to know that everything is running smoothly."

"Okay. Well, I'll see you later, then."

"Do you have a shift today?"

"Don't know yet. I'd better call in to find out what they want me to do today, if anything. Things were kind of left up in the air yesterday."

"All right. Well," Erin gave him a quick kiss, "let me know."

CHAPTER 27

*E*rin let herself in the back door of Auntie Clem's and gave the kitchen a quick once-over to make sure that everything was in order as she walked through to the front. Bella walked into the kitchen from the front and they nearly collided.

"Whoa! Hi, Erin, I wasn't expecting to see you today!"

"Couldn't stay away," Erin admitted.

"It was supposed to be a day off for you."

"Well, not originally, but things were pretty crazy last night, so I decided I'd better not try to make an early shift. But I'm here now, and I can spell someone…"

"Not me, I just barely got here. But Charley might take you up on that."

Charley was looking back over her shoulder as Erin walked through the door, having heard their voices. "Well, there's my dear sister. Have a nice sleep-in this morning?"

"Yes, it was good. Did you come in for the early shift?" Erin was dumbfounded. Charley was one who usually didn't get up until noon. Getting up early for her meant before eleven o'clock.

"Yep. I was here bright and early before the birds were twittering in the trees. Before the early worm even thought of crawling out of his hole."

"I didn't know you *could* get up that early."

"I didn't. I didn't go to bed."

"You haven't slept since yesterday?"

"Nope." Charley yawned and looked at the face of her phone. "More than twenty-four hours, now."

"Good grief. You're relieved. Go home and have a nap."

Charley laughed. "I was just getting my second wind."

"I don't want anyone chopping off a hand with a bread knife. You must be exhausted!"

"It really isn't that bad. I wouldn't recommend doing it regularly. But once in a while?" Charley shrugged. "You never pulled an all-nighter?"

"No. Whenever I tried to stay up with friends, I was always the first to fall asleep. It was kind of a running joke."

"I can believe it."

"Go on. Clock out. You've done your duty."

"I will. But Cheyenne is supposed to be in for the afternoon rush, so you really don't need to stay."

"We'll see. But you certainly don't need to."

Charley nodded and headed for the kitchen, reaching behind her back to untie her apron. Erin shook her head, watching her go.

"What a character," Bella laughed. "She's been getting pretty punchy. I could tell she must be tired. But she's really funny."

"I'll bet she is. Me, I'd be useless after that long without sleep. But luckily—I did sleep last night and had a lazy morning. So I need to do some work and get my engine running."

Erin ran the cash register while Bella served customers. Then when Cheyenne got there, Erin retreated to the kitchen to see what batters she needed to start on. Consulting her checklist and what was in the fridge, she found that Bella was already on top of everything. Timers were set on the ovens, and nothing would need to come out for another twenty minutes. Erin went into her tiny office to sort through the mail and other papers in her in basket.

She saw that her copy of the Bald Eagles Falls weekly newspaper was in her basket, and sat down with it to look through the sales and community events. It was always a good idea to stock up on whatever ingredients were on sale and to tie in to whatever holidays and community events she could.

It figured that the big above-the-fold headline was *Discovery of Local Clan Member's Body*. Erin's stomach flipped. Of course, it was the big news. It was the first edition of the newspaper to come out since Theresa had been killed, so they would be bound to run all of the gossip and whatever legitimate information they could find. Grim as it was, violent deaths sold newspapers. Maybe the story would even be picked up by one of the national syndicates. And the story would also have brought in a flood of customers that morning to discuss all the details. Good for Erin's bottom line, and she was relieved that she hadn't been there on the morning shift to have to deal with it all. She'd saved Vic the pain of having to hear everyone assume that Willie had killed Theresa, too. Changing their shifts around had been a good decision, even if Erin hadn't factored the newspaper's arrival into her thinking.

She wanted to just skip over the article and look for the information she had initially intended to. But she couldn't make herself turn the page without reading to see how much the newspaper had reported. She had mixed feelings when she saw Joshua Cox's name on the byline. Good for him for being able to land the lead story in the paper. That was a huge accomplishment and would look good on his resume. But she hated knowing that he was investigating the death himself. Mary Lou would not be happy about him potentially putting himself in the crosshairs of a killer again.

Erin skimmed the article, not expecting to find anything new. Joshua had talked to her and probably to everyone else he could find that might have some connection to Theresa or her death. But the police department was releasing little information. They had preliminary results back from the medical examiner, but hadn't made the information public.

Her eyes stopped on one paragraph near the beginning.

An unnamed source has revealed that Theresa Franklin was killed by strangulation.

Strangulation.

From the beginning, Erin had assumed the use of a weapon. A gun, most likely and, failing that, a knife. Maybe even some kind of bludgeon, if her attacker had been able to take Theresa off guard. But strangulation?

It was a totally different scenario from what Erin had imagined. Who had the skill and strength to do that? Especially knowing that Theresa had probably been well-armed at the time. Someone had either surprised or overpowered her and had known enough about unarmed combat to be able to subdue and kill her, and then to carry her from the murder site to Erin's yard to throw off investigators.

Had the police been right all along about it being Willie? Erin didn't know much about the time he had spent with the Dyson clan as one of their soldiers, but she was sure he would have been well trained in combat skills. She didn't know if he had been trained to kill for the clan, but she was sure that everyone would be expected to have at least some level of skills in case of a confrontation with the Jacksons or if they were assigned to take someone out.

The claim that someone in a police uniform had been near the scene gave her a chill. A law enforcement officer would know about strangleholds, if only as part of his training as to what *not* to do when subduing a suspect. Terry had an alibi. He'd been at the community center when Theresa had been killed. None of the other Bald Eagles Falls police had been on duty at that time, but any of them could have been out in uniform, hoping that people would assume they were on legitimate business.

Or it could have been one of Jack's officers from Moose River.

As she had told Terry, it could be someone who wasn't a police officer at all but had just put on a costume or uniform to look like one.

But Terry didn't even think it had been a legitimate tip, just a call to get the Bald Eagle Falls police off of the case.

Which was it?

Erin read carefully through the rest of the article, looking for anything else Joshua might have gotten from his unnamed source. No doubt it was Melissa. Joshua had grown up in Bald Eagle Falls, and Melissa and Mary Lou were friends. He would have grown up knowing that Melissa was the fount of knowledge for anything going on in the police department.

After putting the paper to the side, Erin scouted out the kitchen and snagged a few treats from each of the trays that hadn't been taken out to the front yet and arranged them in a box. She poked her head out the doorway to the front of the store.

"I'm going to take some treats over to the police department," she told Bella. "I'll just be a few minutes. Back by the after-school rush."

Bella gave her a knowing smile. "All right, boss. See what you can find out."

Erin couldn't suppress a guilty smile of her own. She shrugged and headed out of the bakery and down the street to the Town Hall, where the police department offices were located.

CHAPTER 28

Clara Jones was on reception at the police department, as usual. She wore a satiny, deep jade blouse that made her red hair look very striking and less brassy than usual. She eyed Erin's box. While she enjoyed the treats that Erin brought just as much as anyone in the department, she had learned to view Erin's offerings with suspicion, having allowed Erin too much latitude in the past.

"You can leave those here," she said sternly. "Everyone is very busy today. I'm sure they'll appreciate the baked goods, but you can't hang around here."

It was a public waiting area, so Erin was not in too much of a hurry to leave. She smiled at Clara. "You guys always work so hard. You deserve every bit of baking I bring." She opened the box and offered the goodies to Clara, who could not look at the variety of cookies and sweets without being tempted. Her hand hovered over the box as she tried to choose. All part of the plan.

"They still need to do more detailed analysis," Sheriff Wilmot's voice floated out to Erin as he walked down the hall around the corner with someone else, "chemical makeup and DNA and all that, but on a preliminary microscopic analysis, the fibers and hair are a match for Victoria Webster's apartment."

He stepped out of the hallway and his eyes immediately fell on Erin. He knew that she'd heard his comment. Jack Ward was one step behind Wilmot. He smiled when he saw Erin.

"Ah, Miss Price. With her hand in the cookie jar, apparently."

Erin looked down at her hand, holding the treat box in front of Clara. "Not exactly."

Jack chuckled. "Let's have a look at the evidence," he instructed, making a motion for Erin to show him the contents of the box.

Erin hesitated for a moment, waiting for Clara to make her selection. Clara quickly grabbed a brownie. Erin offered her a stack of napkins with the other hand, and Clara took one to put her brownie down on. Erin offered the box of goodies to Jack Ward.

"Now, don't get me wrong, Miss Price, we always appreciate your baking," Wilmot said, as he leaned over to peek into the box as well, "but you need to realize that the information we deal with here is very sensitive and… we really can't share details with you…"

"I haven't asked anything," Erin pointed out.

Jack selected a cookie and Erin moved the box closer to Wilmot.

"Nevertheless… Terry isn't even here. You really don't have an excuse to come around…"

"Other than bringing you cookies."

He grunted and helped himself to an oatmeal raisin cookie. An almost-healthy snack for the slightly tubby sheriff. He took a bite without waiting to get a napkin or take it back to his desk.

"As I said, we do appreciate it…"

"But you don't want me hanging around here."

He nodded, chewing.

"We're on for dinner?" Erin asked Jack.

"Of course. I'm sure we'll be finished here by six. And if not… we'll still need to take a break to let everyone eat and consider what's been discussed." Jack looked at Wilmot and raised an eyebrow.

"I'm sure we'll be done for the day," Wilmot agreed.

"Great," Erin said, "I'll see you then."

Erin left the box of goodies on Clara's desk and turned to leave. She didn't move quickly, and kept her ears open. Sheriff Wilmot picked up some papers from his mail slot behind Clara, and he and Jack turned around to return the way they had come.

"I haven't been here in town long," Jack said, "but I've already seen a couple of players around here that I think you would rather not have around Bald Eagle Falls. There is definitely something going on with the clans…"

∽

Once out of the Town Hall, Erin picked up her pace to get back to Auntie Clem's. It was a sunny clear day, the sky pale blue, the trees along the street and in yards nearby every imaginable shade of green. The brightly colored awnings of the storefronts of the other shops along Main Street were like a Welcome Home sign to her. She didn't often walk down the street during the day and probably needed to get out in the sunshine more often than she did. It helped to lift her spirits despite what she had just heard.

Shoppers bustled here and there, smiling their greetings and occasionally stopping to talk for a few minutes. While the close community of Bald Eagle Falls sometimes felt stifling, Erin could use the support and they all felt a little bit like family.

She saw Beaver partway down the street, leaning down to talk to the driver of an unfamiliar car. Her arm was casually on the roof and her body apparently loose and relaxed, although, with Beaver, that could be misleading. She always seemed calm and cool, even in the most dangerous of situations.

Erin wasn't close enough to hear what Beaver was talking to the driver about. Not like the day when she'd first spotted Beaver, talking in the street with a driver she had just rear-ended, smiling her wide, good-humored smile as he raged. Erin continued to walk down the street, pretending that she didn't notice Beaver while at the same time trying to get a good look at the driver of the car.

A middle-aged man, older than Beaver, with dark hair and eyes and an angry, stony expression. Beaver chewed on her gum as they spoke, smiling pleasantly and occasionally nodding. Was he a contact or informant of Beaver's? Someone she had just happened to run into? Or was he someone that she was suspicious about and had stopped on some kind of pretext? Was he a clan contact? Jack had just finished saying that there were members of the clan around town who really shouldn't be there.

Erin did her best to take a mental snapshot of the man so that she could describe him to Jack over dinner.

~

There were still a lot of curious customers as part of the after-school rush. Having read about Theresa's murder in the newspaper, they wanted to hear more or just to be in the same room with someone adjacent to the story. It was always amazing to Erin how much people wanted to hear about the latest crime or tragedy in Bald Eagle Falls.

She kept her eyes open for Joshua in case he came in with school friends to let him know that she had read his article, but he didn't put in an appearance. Hopefully, he was busy with friends, rather than off somewhere digging more deeply into the mystery.

Once the crowd started to taper off, she got started on kitchen clean-up and getting ready for the next day. It was always best to set things up for success the next morning, rather than rushing to get everything done in the hours before opening. She got a call from Jack Ward as she was finishing up, letting her know that he would be heading over to the BBQ restaurant soon. She called Terry to see whether he was interested in some hot chicken as well.

Terry sounded irritated at the invitation. "You know Jack Ward can't tell you any more about the investigation than I can."

"I know. But he might have some insight on Theresa. I'm not

trying to investigate Theresa's murder. The police can do that. I'm just… curious about hearing more of her background. He knows her better than anyone in the police department here. Unless Stayner went to school with her or knew her family, and I think he's too old for them to have crossed paths."

"Why do you need to hear more about her when she's dead? You don't need to worry about her ever coming after any of us again."

She was surprised Terry wasn't more curious about Theresa. Theresa had tried to kill him. Erin thought that he would want to know everything about her that he could.

But maybe he just wanted to put all of that behind him and to pretend that it had never happened. Maybe by ignoring it, he thought he could get over any remaining PTSD or brain injury symptoms. It was magical thinking, but that was not an uncommon way of coping with trauma.

So she'd been told by therapists in the past, anyway.

"Do you want me to come home for supper, then? Or do you mind me talking to Jack?"

"I don't see what good talking to him is going to do."

"I know. But do you mind? Do you want me to tell him I can't make it?"

"You do what you want, Erin. I can make a sandwich or open a can of soup."

"Okay. I'll try not to be too long."

She probably shouldn't have set up the dinner with Jack without checking in with Terry first. She hadn't anticipated that it would be a problem. Terry liked Jack well enough, and she would have expected him to jump at the chance to hear more about the case from Jack, since he'd been kicked off.

Erin picked up her purse. She hesitated for a moment; she knew that Terry didn't want her to go to dinner with Jack, and his "do what you want" did not mean that he would be happy with her choice. But he hadn't said *not* to go, and Erin wanted to see what Jack could tell her about Theresa's life and death.

CHAPTER 29

It wasn't until Erin met with Jack and sat down with him that she realized people would be talking about her. She should have thought it through; she knew that a man and a woman meeting for dinner would be seen as a date, whether either of them had anything romantic in mind or not. But she hadn't thought about it in time. She saw the way the waitress looked at her and swore to herself. All of the locals knew that she was seeing Terry Piper. Showing up there with another man was going to attract all kinds of gossip.

"Erin? Everything okay?" Jack asked.

Erin rubbed her forehead. "Yeah. It's nothing. I'm fine."

"Headache?" he asked sympathetically.

"Oh yeah... a big one."

He nodded. "Have you got an aspirin? We could probably track one down."

"It's fine. I don't need anything."

"Okay."

They browsed over the menus, probably not something that either one of them needed to do. They already knew what was on the menu and what they were going to order. There might be other things on the menu, but hardly anyone would consider getting anything other than the hot chicken, in one variety or another.

"Soo... how did things go with the police department?"

Jack took a sip of his water and shrugged. "About as expected. It's always good to have another set of eyes, a different perspective on a case. Sometimes someone else will see what you have missed. But there isn't a lot of evidence on this case. Everything we do have points toward Willie Andrews."

"But he was set up."

Jack blinked at her. "Oh? what makes you say that with such certainty?"

"Because it doesn't make any sense. If he had killed Theresa, why would he take her down to the yard and call it in as if he'd just found her there? If he'd killed her in Vic's apartment, then he would have just called and said that he'd killed her when she broke in. Why take her out of there? And if he was going to take her out, then why put her down in the yard and call in? That doesn't make any kind of sense."

He shrugged. "He found that it was harder to handle a dead body than he expected. Tired himself out and decided that was as far as he was going to take her. He had a cover story he figured would fly."

"Willie isn't an idiot. He's a really smart guy. If he'd killed her, he wouldn't have taken her out of there and he wouldn't have stopped when he got down to the yard."

"Something unforeseen happened and he didn't have a choice. He had to go with the cards he was dealt."

"I don't buy it."

Jack considered this for a long time. The waitress brought their chicken and Erin had a few bites.

"It doesn't much matter what I think anyway," Jack said with a shrug, picking up a piece of chicken. "I'm not the one who is going to make an arrest in this case. That will be up to Sheriff Wilmot and his crew. I've lent him a couple of my boys to help finish the investigation and keep things quiet here. That's really the extent of my involvement. It doesn't sound like a complicated case. Despite any questions or shortcomings, it won't be hard to convince a jury of what happened. One look at Willie, and they'll be convinced without too much hand-holding. He has the right background. A good motive. They can put him at the scene. There's no one to support his story of just stumbling across the body in the middle of the night, not even his girlfriend."

Erin put her hot chicken down and had a sip of water, waiting for the burn to subside. "That's the other thing. Where was Vic? I can't figure out for the life of me why she wasn't home. She's always home at that time of night. And don't tell me that Willie told her to make herself scarce. If they conspired to kill Theresa or to dispose of her body, they would never have separated."

"Maybe they had a fight. A disagreement over what to do."

Erin hated to tell him that Vic and Willie argued regularly. Most couples tried to keep a semblance that they agreed with each other most of the time, but Erin was close enough to Vic and Willie to know that they had disagreements. Some real humdingers with shouting and slammed doors. No physical abuse, as far as she could tell, and they still professed their love for each other, but no one could claim that the two of them always got along and agreed on all of the important points. Their relationship was fiery. Passionate.

"What about other suspects?" Erin asked. "You said that there were clan members in town. Someone else said that there were several strangers in town. How do we know that this wasn't done by one of the clan members? There's just as much reason to believe that."

"Except that there aren't any signs that it was clan. It doesn't look particularly like a clan hit. They wouldn't be so unprofessional as to leave a body in the middle of the yard like that."

"You think that Willie did, and he's a former clan member."

"*Former* being the operative word. It's a long time since he was working with the organization. He's untrained. Let himself go to seed."

"He has not!"

"He's anything but a disciplined soldier. He bounces from one job to another, doesn't take orders from anyone, doesn't claim any amnesty under the clan. It's been years since he was working with them actively. He may do a job for Dwight or Nelson now and then, but those are paid, aboveboard jobs. Computers, security, technology. We're aware of that."

"You are?"

"We keep a pretty close eye on everything that happens in Moose River in connection with the clans. We have to, if we're going to keep things running peacefully."

"What about these clan members or strangers around town, then? Why are they here?"

Jack nodded, pursing his lips. "I don't know yet. That's a good question, and I don't have an answer for you. I need to do a little poking around and see if I can find anything out. And see whether my boys turn anything up during their time here. They know the major players in the clan."

"I've seen Beaver talking to a couple of guys. Are you working with her?"

Jack raised his brows. "Who?"

"You know Beaver, you dealt with her when Joe and Daniel—" Erin saw the twinkle in Jack's eye and shook her head. "Do you know what Beaver is working on? Maybe she knows something. Or maybe she has an informant who knows something."

"Beaver and her agency have not passed any information on to me. In fact, her agency would prefer to have police involvement pulled from the case altogether. Just leave it to them."

"Why?"

"Interagency politics can be funny. We're all supposed to get along with each other, help provide the resources that the other needs, share information. But in reality… there are personalities, politics, power grabs. Nothing dramatic like on TV cop dramas. It's a lot more subtle than that. But there is enough that it's noticeable. A little resistance here, a little holdback there. My department isn't really involved in this case, other than to provide a little extra staff support for Sheriff Wilmot. But Sheriff Wilmot has definitely been told to back off and to hand his investigation off to another organization."

"Who? The FBI?"

"I can't give you any details."

"Who handles organized crime situations around here? Is it the FBI?"

"Let's not get ahead of ourselves. There is no indication that this is an organized crime case. Willie Andrews looks good for it. One single person. No organization attached to him. No need to get other agencies involved."

"Is that why they're pushing for it to be Willie? So that they don't have to hand the case over to someone else?"

"No. No one is trying to railroad Mr. Andrews."

"That's not how it looks from my perspective."

"Maybe you need to take a closer look."

Erin was surprised. She had expected Jack to be on her side. He wasn't part of the Bald Eagle Falls police department, so he had a more unbiased viewpoint.

She fiddled with her chicken, no longer hungry.

Jack looked around the restaurant, saying nothing for a time. Then, "Who have you seen Beaver with?"

"A couple of different men that I don't know."

He nodded, encouraging her to go on. Erin concentrated on the two different times she had seen Beaver talking to strange men in the time since Theresa had been killed. The younger blond man at the restaurant and the dark-haired older man in the car on Main Street. She described them the best she could to Jack. He rubbed his chin, thinking about it.

"The young one... I don't know. Of course, she has a number of CI's around here, as you well know. That could describe several people."

If someone else had given Erin that description, she could have imagined it to be Jeremy or one of his brothers. But she knew it wasn't any of them. She knew all of them by sight. Maybe it was a young man from the clans and maybe not. Maybe it was just someone she had run into. Maybe an informant.

"The older one…" Jack mused. "I saw one of the Jackson clan men here earlier that could fit that description. Payne is his name."

"Pain?"

"P-A-Y-N-E. Though P-A-I-N would certainly be apt for an enforcer from the clan. Especially combined with his first name."

"Which is?"

"Phillip."

"Phillip Payne? Tell me that isn't what his parents named him."

"Afraid so. And I guess it became a self-fulfilling prophecy. What would you expect a kid named Phillip Payne to become?"

"A dentist, maybe."

Jack grinned. "Maybe that was what they had in mind. It could have been him that Beaver was talking to."

"Why would she be talking to him?"

"That would be her business, not mine. I don't know what all she is involved with. As far as anyone but an elite few people around here know, she's an 'underemployed' treasure hunter. She may have just been feeling him out, or she might know something about why he is here."

CHAPTER 30

The house was dark when Erin drove up to it. Not completely dark. The porch light was on and one lamp in the living room. But if Terry were home, there would be a lot more lights than that on, unless he had fallen asleep. He hadn't sounded tired when she had talked to him earlier. Hadn't said that he was suffering from a migraine or any other issue.

But he had not been happy with her.

Erin let herself in and, after punching her pass code into the burglar alarm, ignored the animals and took a quick look around the house to see if Terry was there. There was no sign of him. But she did eventually find a note on the kitchen table, apparently scribbled in haste, that said simply, "Going out. Back later."

No hint of where he was going or when he would be back. And he hadn't bothered to call or text her to give her any warning. She took her phone out and checked it, just in case she had missed a text or had a voicemail message from him. But there was nothing. He hadn't even tried to reach her.

Erin fed Orange Blossom and Marshmallow, not doing much more than petting them briefly and scratching their ears, then went across the yard to Vic's. She climbed the stairs and knocked tentatively on the door.

Usually, Vic came over to see her, not vice versa. But Vic always said that Erin was welcome. But Erin didn't like to make assumptions. As Vic's landlord, it would be easy to make Vic feel like she had to let Erin in.

There was no answer. But it was clear from the lights and noise within that Vic was home. Erin raised her fist and knocked more loudly. This time, the voices stopped. In a moment, Vic pulled open the door and faced her, expression angry. Erin drew back in surprise. Vic's mouth opened and for a moment she couldn't seem to find words.

"I didn't know it was you," she finally said, apologetic. "Come in, Erin. I'm sorry."

"You didn't do anything."

"You probably thought I was going to light into you. And I was, but I didn't know it was you."

Erin stepped into the room. "You were expecting someone else?"

Willie was already there, sitting in an easy chair, so Vic hadn't been expecting him.

"The police." Vic let out a loud, exasperated sigh. "They are… encouraging us to come in and have an interview with them." She motioned to the couch. "Sit down. Make yourself at home."

Nilla came racing across the room and stopped just inches from Erin, then started to sniff her earnestly. Erin pushed him away with her foot. "Nilla. Chill. It's just me. Why do they want to talk to you?"

Vic looked over at Willie. He didn't say anything. "Well… we're the prime suspects in Theresa's death, of course. They don't have enough to charge either of us, so they're hoping that if they can talk to us, they can squeeze something out of us… more evidence, a confession, I don't know. And we," she pointed at Willie and herself, "are not inclined to oblige them."

Erin nodded her understanding. "They said that they matched the carpet fibers and hairs to… here."

"Who said?"

"Sheriff Wilmot. I overheard him when I was taking some cookies over to the police department."

Vic grinned. But her smile seemed thin and forced. "You and your cookies."

"I guess that's why they want to talk to you."

Vic shrugged. "So it would appear. But they're barking up the wrong tree. Neither of us had anything to do with it. And carpet fibers…" Vic shook her head. "That doesn't prove anything. There have got to be a dozen houses in Bald Eagle Falls with carpet from that very same roll. You buy what the store has in stock. They can't prove that came from my apartment."

"And I guess they're going to do DNA testing on the hair…?" Erin shrugged. "That's what he said, anyway. Before he realized that I was there."

"That can be challenged," Willie said confidently. "It's a key principle of forensics. When you walk into a place, you leave something behind and you take something with you. Anyone who has been in this apartment, or has been near anyone who has been in this apartment, could have one of our hairs on them. You have animals, you know how their fur gets transferred from one thing to another. You get cat hair on your car upholstery when the cat has never been in your car. It transfers from them, to you, to something else."

Erin nodded and made a mental note that she needed to have her car vacuumed.

"Yeah, I guess… but they're going to try to use it to put Theresa in this apartment." Erin allowed herself a look around. "Even if she was never here."

"She wasn't," Vic asserted.

Erin knew that there had been no sign of Theresa or any kind of struggle when she had entered the apartment looking for Vic. "But for hair and fibers from the apartment to get onto Theresa's body, then someone who had been in the apartment must have touched the body."

Willie shrugged. "Or someone was in contact with someone

who had been in the apartment… once you get two or three contacts out, you're suddenly talking about half the population of Bald Eagle Falls. And remember, so far there hasn't been any real testing done yet to see if they are matches for this apartment. Just someone looking at them with a magnifying glass and saying that they look the same. There hasn't been enough time for real forensic testing or, like you say, DNA analysis. This is all speculation."

"It just doesn't make any sense to me," Erin said. "The whole thing… it all seems 'off.'"

"What does?" Willie challenged. "I came over to see Vic. Came across Theresa's body. Called it in. That's it. Someone was trying to set one of us up. Vic or me or even you or Terry. Trying to throw the police off the trail of the clan or whoever it actually was that killed her. Make it look like it was a personal vendetta."

"How did you know that Vic wasn't home?"

He shook his head. "I never said that."

"You did. Not tonight. The night it happened. You said that she had gone out, but she hadn't told you where she had gone."

"I don't recall saying that."

"But you did…" Erin frowned, puzzling it through. "But if you just came to see her, and stumbled across Theresa's body on the way, then you wouldn't know that she wasn't home. You would assume that she was."

"Well, it was obvious when she didn't answer her door to the police that she wasn't home. She didn't come out to see what was going on, like you did. If she'd been home, she would have wanted to know what I was doing in the yard and what the police were there for. But she didn't. She wasn't there."

"No…" Erin shook her head. "When Terry told me that she wasn't answering the door or her phone, I had to go see, make sure she wasn't in here, hurt. If someone killed Theresa, they could have hurt her too." Erin avoided saying killed, not wanting that image in her head. It was bad enough picturing Vic alone behind the locked door of her apartment, bleeding from some undisclosed wound.

"I didn't want to let the police into her apartment."

"Neither did I. But your concern for Vic would have overruled any worries about the police. They let me come in by myself to make sure that nothing was wrong. They wouldn't have stopped you."

"How the police treat you and how they treat me is vastly different," Willie pointed out. And it was probably true. If he had wanted to go into the apartment to check on Vic, maybe they would have barred him, for fear that he would destroy evidence or that he had already hurt her. They would have insisted that they go in themselves for a welfare check, or have gotten Erin to go in as she had, letting herself in with her key. But the police had not been worried that Vic was in her apartment hurt because Willie had already told them that she was out.

"You came in here?" Vic asked. "After Theresa was killed?"

Erin nodded. "Just in and out, to make sure that you weren't hurt. And I didn't let the police in." She looked at Willie. "We both protected your privacy."

"Well... thank you." Vic looked perplexed. She was probably having mixed feelings about knowing that Erin had been there when she wasn't, that Erin had been worried she was hurt or worse, and that Erin and Willie had kept her rights from being violated. Vic glanced at Willie and then away.

Something itched at the back of Erin's brain. She tried to just observe the feeling with interest, not trying to figure out what was wrong or what she was trying to remember. She was far more likely to remember the stray thought if she pretended she wasn't trying to reach it. The brain was funny that way.

Her own words kept coming back into her consciousness. "We both protected you." The facts started to click into place. They started to build a picture, to make sense in a way that they hadn't before.

"You're protecting her," she said to Willie. "That's what this had been all along. You trying to protect Vic."

Willie nodded and shrugged. "Of course I want to protect Vic.

That's only natural. I want to keep her from any harm or having her privacy invaded by the cops. No one wants the police poking around their things while they're out. You didn't exactly enjoy having a search warrant served on your home, did you?"

"No." Erin wasn't going to be distracted from the picture that was starting to form. "You knew that Vic wasn't here because you had already been inside."

Willie and Vic just looked at her, neither saying anything.

"And there's no way that you could have walked by Theresa's body on the way to the loft without seeing it. You wouldn't walk by a body without doing anything, pop upstairs to see whether Vic was home, and then come back down to report what you'd found."

"You never know what you would do in the face of something like that," Willie said in a calm, even tone. "Until you have actually been in that situation, you have no idea how your brain would react and what you would do."

That was just hot air. Looking for an excuse. Erin knew better. Willie was calm and cool under pressure. He didn't freeze up. He didn't do stupid impulsive things. Had acted slowly and logically. She knew how she had reacted upon finding a body unexpectedly. And she knew how he would react.

"If Theresa's body wasn't in the yard when you went up the stairs to look for Vic, then it must have been somewhere else. Like where the police have already put it—*in her apartment.*" Erin looked around, her eyes feeling unnaturally wide. "Right here."

"I found Theresa's body and then I came up to the loft to make sure that Vic was okay," Willie said. "Obviously."

Erin thought over the fleeting images in her head of that night. The movement in the dark backyard. Seeing Willie out there and wondering what he was doing.

"No. That's not what happened," she said with certainty.

CHAPTER 31

She and Willie looked at each other for a long time. Erin eventually looked away, but she still waited for Willie's explanation.

"Willie," Vic prompted. "What happened?"

Erin was surprised to hear that Vic sounded just as much in the dark as she was. She had assumed that the two of them would have talked, would have discussed in detail where each of them had been and what exactly had happened while they were separated. But Willie hadn't told Vic the whole truth either, if Erin was to believe what she said.

"Okay..." Willie looked at each of them. "Of course, you won't say anything to the police." He met Erin's eyes. He wasn't going to tell her his story unless she agreed.

Erin nodded.

"No pillow talk," Willie warned. "This isn't something you can say to Officer Piper casually in bed or over dinner."

"Okay."

Willie looked around as if the explanation might be painted on the walls. Something he could just read off to her and not have to put it into words himself.

"I did come up to the loft. And Vic was gone." He looked at her. "And there was no body in the yard."

"You found Theresa in here," Erin suggested.

Willie nodded. "Yes."

"And you had a fight?" Vic asked, her voice hitching higher. "What happened?"

Willie blinked. "What?"

"This is exactly what I was afraid of. All of your talk about tracking her down and killing her. You came here, and there she was, and you just went after her… that temper of yours…"

Willie scowled. He shook his head at Vic.

"I didn't kill her."

"What?" Vic asked sarcastically, "She just fell down the stairs and broke her neck?"

That might have been a good explanation. If she hadn't been strangled.

"She was already dead."

They all looked at each other, waiting for the others to talk.

"She was already dead?" Vic repeated. "Then who killed her?"

Willie stared back at her.

"You thought it was me?" Vic demanded.

Willie nodded. "Of course."

A body abandoned in Vic's apartment. An ex-girlfriend. Someone who had stalked and threatened her. Of course that was what Willie would immediately assume. What else was he to think?

Vic shook her head. "It wasn't. I didn't see her, let alone kill her."

Willie frowned, perplexed.

Erin was still building the picture in her mind, fitting more and more of the clues together. If Vic had killed Theresa and Willie had walked into the apartment to find Theresa dead, then of course his first instinct would be to move the body somewhere else and to get Vic out of there, make sure she established an alibi somewhere else. So Vic had left, and Willie had moved the body out of the apartment.

But Vic had truly sounded like she had thought Willie had killed Theresa. And Willie sounded like he had thought Vic had killed her. They hadn't met over the body and made a plan together. Each had been protecting the other, assuming they knew what happened, but neither really knew.

It left too many blanks. Erin tried to nail it down as much as she could.

"So you moved the body… down to the yard?"

Willie made a noise of disgust. "Well, that wasn't exactly the plan. Yes, I took her out of here and down the stairs. Which is a lot more work than you would think. I put her down to catch my breath. But there was someone in the woods." He motioned toward the back of the loft. "I saw movement, heard footsteps. But no one came out. I didn't know if it was a trespasser, or Adele, or an accomplice of Theresa's… there were plenty of people that it could be, but no way to know who it was or what their intentions were."

"You didn't call out? Ask who was there?"

"If whoever it was hadn't seen me yet, I didn't want to draw any attention to myself and the body I had just carried down the stairs," Willie pointed out. "And if it was someone from one of the clans, I wasn't aiming on getting shot."

Or Adele. Adele had said that she had seen something that night, but she didn't know what it was or wasn't willing to talk to the police about it yet.

"No matter who it was, it wasn't good news for me. Someone who had seen me and would report what they had seen to the police? Someone from one of the clans or who would want to avenge Theresa's death? Who would want to blackmail me? There really wasn't a good outcome from anyone in the woods seeing me with a dead body."

"No. I guess not," Erin admitted.

Vic was still staring at Willie. "You just assumed that I had killed Theresa and you immediately went into action to dispose of the body without even talking to me?"

Willie nodded and repeated the same answer as before. "Of course."

"A friend knows where the bodies are buried. A true friend helps you dig the hole," Vic said, giving a little laugh.

Willie nodded, but didn't seem to think there was anything humorous about it. But give the guy a break; he'd been a murder suspect for a few days now and had only just discovered that the person he thought he was protecting hadn't even been involved.

"So the only thing you could do was to call the police and report that you found her there," Erin said. "Admit that you were there and that you found a body. No one can tell them anything worse. And if it's an accomplice, he disappears when the cops show up."

Willie nodded briefly. "Obscure the facts as much as possible. Keep them from suspecting Vic." He glanced over at her. "Put myself in the hot seat."

"Well… now that you know Vic didn't do it, you can tell the police the truth."

"No, that's not going to cut it. They've already figured that I moved her from here down to the yard. Confessing what they already know won't do any good, and it won't prove that I didn't kill Theresa. Or that Vic didn't. In fact, it would make Vic the prime suspect, and that's something that I'm not about to do."

Erin wanted to do the right thing. She wanted to tell them, "If you're innocent, nothing bad is going to happen to you," but she knew only too well that they wouldn't believe her. She wasn't even sure that she believed it herself. She'd seen Charley arrested for a murder she didn't commit. She'd been in that police hot-seat herself, knowing that if she didn't come up with some way to prove what really happened, that she was going to end up in prison. As much as she would like to tell Willie and Vic that everything would work out if they did the right things, the words would be hollow. She wouldn't even believe herself.

"We need to tell someone..."

"No, we don't. You said that you would keep your mouth shut. You can't tell this to anyone."

"But..."

"You can't, Erin. You know that. And don't suggest Terry. I know you love him, but you know very well that he'd be happy to get me for murder. He tried to put Rip Ryder's death on me and now he's trying to get me arrested for Theresa's."

"He's not on the case anymore."

"And I wish that made me feel better, but it doesn't. He still thinks what he thinks, and the rest of the police department is all going to be lined up in a row behind him."

Would Sheriff Wilmot still pursue Willie as the lead suspect? Probably. Stayner? For sure. He wasn't going to look any farther than the end of his own nose if he didn't have to.

"What about Jack Ward? He wouldn't be so biased against you."

Though he had already said that Willie was the most likely suspect. She might be able to convince him otherwise if she had enough information.

"Jack Ward?" Vic asked. "What good would involving the Moose River police department be? It didn't happen there, it happened here, and this is where the charges are going to be laid."

"He's here in town and brought a couple of his officers to help with the case. And he knows Theresa. If he told the sheriff—"

"It's not safe to bring Jack Ward in on this either," Willie insisted.

Erin leaned forward. "He said that there have been clan members here in town. People who shouldn't be here. That's a good sign, isn't it? It points to other people that could have done it. Plenty of people had motives to kill Theresa Franklin. If we can show that someone else could have done it just as easily..."

"That would be good, yes. But you don't need to tell Ward everything we know for him to come up with that. You don't need to tell him anything about Vic and me."

Erin nodded slowly. Willie and Vic didn't have any proof that the story they had told was true. Just because it fit together nicely, that didn't mean that Erin had it right or had the whole story yet. There were still a lot of holes. Many unanswered questions.

"So…" Erin looked at Vic. "Where did you go?"

Vic raised her brows. "What?"

"I don't understand why you weren't home when Willie got there. You didn't really go to look at the stars."

"How do you know?"

"Because… you've never gone out to look at the stars before. If you were an amateur astronomer, I would know it."

"I can have interests that you know nothing about."

"You don't even have a telescope."

Vic looked for an answer to that. Willie chuckled. "She's got you there, Vicky."

"You shut up," Vic snapped.

"Do you think the police believe your stargazing story?" Erin asked.

"Sure, why wouldn't they? They don't know me as well as you do."

"But they searched your apartment… so they must know that you don't have any telescopes, star charts, books about stars, or anything like that."

Vic made a growling noise and rubbed her eyes. "Erin… I'm tired. If we're working tomorrow, we'd better get to bed."

CHAPTER 32

"I'd like to hear the answer to that question too," Willie told Vic.

Erin looked from one to the other, shaking her head. "Didn't you guys talk about anything?"

"You don't ask a question you don't want to know the answer to," Willie told her. "Are you telling me that you and Terry discuss everything?"

"No, of course not. He won't tell me police stuff, so that puts a damper on things."

"And there are things that you don't tell him." His eyes were steady on hers. "Things from your past. Things that you don't think will interest him. Things that you think might upset him and are better off left alone. Feelings you don't want to share. Opinions you know he would disagree with."

Erin shifted uncomfortably. "Yes."

"And if you think that someone you love might have done something…" He looked over at Vic again, and she started to blush, "…illegal or dangerous, then you don't necessarily ask about it. Sometimes it's best not to know."

"Well, if both of you are saying that you had nothing to do with it, then we need to find out who did. Clear your names."

"I couldn't figure out why you wouldn't just claim self-defense," Vic said, looking down at her hands as if she were talking to herself.

"Same with you," Willie said with a wry smile. "But as long as you weren't talking about it... I assumed you had your reasons."

They all fell silent. Erin looked at Vic, waiting to see if she would kick Erin out or if she were willing to continue the conversation.

"Okay," Vic said finally. She fiddled with a button on her shirt. "But it isn't like it's an exciting or informative answer."

Erin would just feel better if she knew the full story. Then she had something to work with. If she knew where everyone was at particular times, she might be able to come up with something. Alibis that would show that her friends couldn't have killed Theresa or provide alternative theories that someone else could have.

"Well... you both know now that Theresa was calling me and texting me. Stalking me electronically, I guess. And maybe everyone else in my life too." Vic gave a wide shrug. Willie and Erin both nodded their agreement.

They had all thought that they alone were being targeted, but it had been all of them. Theresa had been one busy woman.

"So, Monday night, she called me. Woke me up. It was making me crazy, her calling me any time, night or day. Or getting these texts or pictures I didn't want anyone else to see."

Vic looked guilty, but Erin didn't think she had done anything wrong. Of course she hadn't wanted anyone else to see whatever the taunting messages had to say. Who would want to share that kind of thing?

"Of course not," Willie agreed. "But you could have shown me or told me about it. Sometimes it feels better to get it off your chest."

"And you would have been perfectly happy with that?" Vic challenged. "You were already crazy mad at Theresa. You've been looking for her since before Christmas. Telling you about this would have just riled you up more. And you were already suspicious about the calls and texts, even though you didn't know what they were about."

It was Willie's turn to look uncomfortable. Erin couldn't detect a blush under his darkly stained skin, but she was pretty sure there was one. He didn't like Vic mentioning their arguments in front of someone else.

"So..." Vic went on with her story with a sigh. "I was really ticked off, especially after being woken up in the middle of the night. I need to be able to sleep. I told her I'm a baker, I have to get my sleep or I can't function in the morning."

And that had probably gone over really well. Theresa didn't respect them for being bakers or small business operators, for the work that they put into the business day after day, getting up in the morning before she would have dreamed of getting out of bed. Theresa thought that Vic should have chosen the same sort of lifestyle as she had. Working for a criminal organization. Staying up late and sleeping in the morning. Loafing around most days and taking jobs from the clan or some other contractor when she felt like it.

"She said that she had decided... that if she could just talk to me face to face, she could... make whatever proposition she wanted to. And when she was done, if I said I didn't want anything to do with her, that would be the end of it. She would stop calling or texting me. I would be dead to her. She would pretend I didn't even exist anymore."

Erin didn't like the sound of that. Dead to her? Maybe Theresa had planned to kill Vic if she didn't cooperate. That was far more likely than her backing off.

"So you left to go meet with her," Willie said. "Where did you go? Why did it take you so long to get back?"

"Well... it wasn't here. She said neutral ground, but it wasn't really. She picked a place... it's about halfway between here and Moose River. Out in the middle of nowhere. I guess I figured that she was still in Moose River, and we were meeting halfway between the towns. At a place where we had been before."

Erin waited for more, but Vic didn't describe the place. A friend's farm? A campsite or hiking trail?

"Where?" Willie asked. "And what happened when you got there?"

Vic shrugged. "She wasn't there. Because she was back here. I thought she was in Moose River, but she was already in Bald Eagle Falls. I went there and nothing happened. She wasn't there. I tried calling and texting her, but couldn't get any response."

Because Theresa was already dead. That would mean that the police department had those messages, because they had access to Theresa's phone. They knew that Vic had been nowhere near Theresa at the time of her death.

"Where was this?" Willie asked again, watching Vic's face.

"Just this… place out in the middle of nowhere. Like a… natural area. Where people might get out to walk the trail or take pictures of the rock formations. Stuff like that."

"Or park and make out?" Willie suggested.

Vic's face turned an even darker shade of red this time. Erin was very impressed with Vic's range of color. "Yes, maybe," she agreed.

"*Not* neutral ground. Somewhere you'd been with her before. She wasn't just trying to talk to you; she was trying to relive old memories. Take you back to when you and she were dating."

"Except she wasn't there," Vic said, spreading her hands apart in a helpless gesture. "So, no face-to-face talk, no resolution. I still had to worry about her calling and harassing me."

Except someone had obligingly murdered Theresa. And apparently, that person was not Willie.

"So…" Erin pondered, "did she intend to be there? If she hadn't been killed? Or did she send you away for another reason?"

"I figured it was just to mess with me. I looked around and waited for a while, and then I figured she had just done it to prove that she was smarter than me or could get me to do whatever she wanted."

Erin looked at Willie. "What do you think?"

He was frowning, forehead wrinkled in concentration. "I'm trying to work out the timeline. Vic, you were home an hour after I called the police. Maybe a bit more. How long did it take you to figure out that she wasn't going to show up and to come back here?"

"I don't know. I waited around for half an hour or something like that. And then it's an hour traveling time in either direction. So, I got there an hour and a half before I got back here."

"Half an hour before you called the police," Erin told Willie.

He shook his head.

"And Terry said there was about a forty-minute window for time of death," Erin told him. "Forty minutes from the last activity on her phone to the time you called it in."

"No... there's something wrong here. Vic would have had to leave Bald Eagle Falls two and a half hours before she got back. An hour driving either way and half an hour waiting for her."

Vic nodded. "About that."

"But... an hour and a half before you got back, you were still asleep in your bed."

Vic shook her head. "No."

"You were."

"Says who? That would be right before you got there. You know I was gone by the time you arrived."

"I figured you must have left here in the twenty minutes between when Theresa texted me and I arrived at the apartment. But you're saying you left an hour before that."

"I guess. She texted you? That's why you came to the loft?"

Willie hesitated. He pulled out his phone and unlocked it, tapped around a few times, and turned it around to show it to Vic. Erin looked at the screen too. Willie wasn't exactly trying to hide it from her.

You leave your precious possessions just lying around? the text from Theresa's message read. And below it was a picture of Vic, asleep in her bed.

Erin's jaw dropped. She stared at it in disbelief. And Willie was right, of course; the message was time stamped about the time that Vic should have been arriving at the meeting place between the two towns, looking for Theresa.

"But…" Vic stared at the picture. "I wasn't there. I wasn't sleeping. I was out there looking for her! How did… how did she get a picture of me sleeping?"

"It must have been taken at a different time," Erin said. "A different day." She looked at Willie. "You never took a picture of her while she was sleeping…?"

"If I did, wouldn't I recognize it when Theresa sent it back to me?"

"Then she'd been here. In the apartment," Vic said in a choked voice. "She's been here at night inside my apartment watching me!"

Erin felt sick. Theresa could have done anything. Vic was lucky that all she had done was take a picture. "How did she get past the burglar alarm? I thought that was all set up so that it couldn't be bypassed."

"I… I guess I don't always remember to set it," Vic admitted. "I know you've had trouble over at your house, but… with us coming and going at different times and having to take the dog out in the middle of the night sometimes, it's just such a pain to always have to arm it…"

"I know," Erin agreed. It was a pain. She hated having to keep hers armed, to tap in the code every time she needed to enter or exit the house. But it gave her some sense of safety, knowing that no one could enter unless they had a passcode. She could sleep at night without worrying about intruders.

"I figured I didn't have to worry about that." Vic rubbed her temples. "But I guess when Theresa started calling me, I should have known better."

"Do you know when the picture was taken?"

Vic squinted at Willie's phone and shook her head. "No... I can't tell anything from the picture. Willie wasn't there, but he isn't around every night..."

Willie didn't work shift like Terry, but sometimes he was out of town. Or sometimes they had arguments. "Do you think it was this week? Sunday night?"

Vic shrugged helplessly. "I don't know. It could have been."

They all looked at each other. "Why would she do that?" Erin asked. "Send you away and call Willie here? What was she planning to do?"

Willie shook his head slowly. He turned off his phone and put it back away. "I don't know. But whatever it was... she never got a chance to do it."

CHAPTER 33

*E*rin's phone vibrated and, for a split second, she thought that it would be Theresa. She had gotten so wound up about those calls. She had a sick, anxious feeling whenever she heard her phone ring or felt it vibrate, worried that it would be another message from Theresa. And worried that Vic or Terry would see it.

But Theresa was gone now. She wasn't going to lure her away or make threats or rant at her. Despite all of Erin's worry about Willie or Vic being arrested for Theresa's death, it was a relief to know that Theresa was gone and would never be troubling her again.

She let out a slow breath and looked at the phone to see Terry's name. She tapped the message.

Where are you?

Clearly, Terry had returned home. Erin tapped a quick message back. *At Vic's. I'll be right there.*

"Terry's back. I've got to go." Erin hesitated, looking at Vic. "Do you want me to get someone to cover your shift tomorrow? Need a break?"

"No." Vic shook her head. "I'd rather be kept busy and

distracted. If I don't go in, I'll just end up lying in my bed, unable to get back to sleep or to think of anything but Theresa."

"Okay. If you change your mind, just text me. I can get started on the morning baking by myself and call someone in for the opening."

"I'm not going to leave you in the lurch."

"You're not. Other people can cover it. I want you to rest if you need it."

"I plan to be there. But I'll text you if not," Vic agreed.

"Okay. See you tomorrow." She nodded goodbye to Willie as well and headed for the door. "Don't forget to set the alarm," she reminded them, looking at the keypad as she opened the door.

Erin crossed the yard quickly, seeing Theresa's covered body in her mind. She was glad that she hadn't actually seen the body itself. She didn't need more nightmares. This time it wasn't dark. The security lights had been fixed.

Terry was waiting for her at the back door. Erin glanced back over her shoulder as she entered.

"Thanks for fixing the lights."

Terry nodded. He shut the door and followed her into the kitchen. "There wasn't actually anything wrong with them. They weren't burned out. They were just… unscrewed."

Erin looked at him. "Theresa?"

"I can't see Vic or Willie wanting the yard to be dark. I don't think it was some kid's prank. There isn't anything to vibrate them and make them unscrew by themselves."

"Theresa, then. Did you know…" Erin stopped, wondering how much she could or should say to Terry. "You saw the messages on Theresa's phone? Who she called or sent texts to?"

He sighed. "You know I can't talk to you about that."

"No, I know you can't tell me anything confidential. But if I already know something, you can."

And conversely, if he already knew something, she wouldn't be breaking any confidences with Vic and Willie.

Terry went to the fridge, looked into it for a moment, then

closed it again. Erin looked at the clock. It was getting late. Probably not a good time for her to start making dinner for Terry. If he were really hungry, he could make himself a sandwich or something small. But from his body language and the fact that he had just closed the fridge again, she didn't think he was actually hungry. He was just looking for something to occupy himself.

"Why don't we get ready for bed? We can cuddle. I just want to be with you."

Terry gave her a tired smile and a nod. "Yeah. That sounds nice."

She followed him into the bedroom and they both changed for bed.

"You said that Theresa's last phone activity was about forty minutes before Willie called the police. That's the window for time of death."

Terry nodded as he changed. He threw his shirt over Orange Blossom, who was sleeping in the middle of the bed. Blossom didn't twitch a muscle.

"Was that the message from Theresa to Willie?"

Terry raised his brows. "He told you about that?"

"We were talking…"

"I really should get you to provide consulting services for interrogations. You have a way of worming things out of people." His smile was genuine, less forced this time.

"So was it? Was that the last thing sent from Theresa's phone?"

"It could be."

Which, to Erin, was pretty much confirmation that it was.

"She sent a picture of Vic sleeping."

"Mmm-hmm."

"And you think that's motive for Willie to charge over there and kill her."

"It would be a pretty good motivator for me."

"What if Vic wasn't even in town when Theresa sent that picture?"

Terry considered this as he folded his clothes neatly, including the shirt he had thrown over Orange Blossom. Blossom stretched and purred and looked at them through squinted eyes.

"That would be an interesting point to consider. Like how did she take the picture if Vic wasn't home? But it doesn't change the fact that Willie *thought* that Theresa was in Vic's apartment while Vic slept, whether it was true or not. The motivation is still there."

"Why would Theresa send Vic on a wild goose chase and then call Willie to the apartment?"

"It sounds like she wanted a confrontation. And she got one."

"But if she knew Willie was going to run over here to rescue Vic, then how could he take her off guard? How could he strangle her? Wouldn't she have met him with her gun out?"

Terry pushed Orange Blossom to the side, lay down, and waited for Erin to join him. "That would make sense, of course. But she wasn't called Crazy Theresa for nothing. She did things that no one else would have. Things that defy logic. She probably wasn't thinking. She thought she could deal with Willie without her gun. You know that… she has chosen hand-to-hand combat over guns and weapons before."

Erin again felt Theresa's hands around her neck, and shuddered. Theresa had also taken Terry down without a weapon. And had nearly dispatched Jack Ward with a knife. And on all of those occasions, she'd had a gun handy if she'd wanted to use it.

"But in those cases, she had the advantage of surprise. She had the drop on us. With Willie… he knew that he was going to meet her. There was no element of surprise. She baited him."

"And maybe he was supposed to walk right into a trap. Race into her bedroom and not see Theresa pasted up against the wall out of his view lines. Or maybe she was expecting to hold Vic at gunpoint and Vic got away or distracted her. We don't know if they were both there or not."

"Vic wasn't."

"That might be what they're telling you. It isn't necessarily the truth."

Erin wanted to argue, but knew there was no point. She lay

down with her back to Terry and snuggled into him, nestling into his warm body. She believed Vic. But the police wouldn't believe her without proof. Maybe the GPS in the bug would show them where Vic had been at the time of Theresa's death.

"What if it *wasn't* Willie?"

"Erin…"

"I know you believe it was him. Lots of things pointing to him. He was there, he had motivation, all of that. I know. But what if it was someone else?"

"Okay. Who?"

"That's just what I'm wondering. Who else *could* have done it?"

"Well, your name pops up further down on the list."

"Just because I was here?"

"It was in your yard. Obviously, the homeowner has to be considered."

"But do you think that I could have beaten Theresa? That I could have surprised her, overpowered her, and strangled her to death?"

She could feel Terry shake his head. "No," he said immediately. "I would rule you out pretty quickly. You *can* strangle someone bigger and stronger than you, but you need some other advantage. Surprise. A ligature. Rage. Training in hand-to-hand."

Erin was glad to hear that he had never seriously considered her a suspect. She didn't like being the subject of a police investigation. It was very uncomfortable. Especially as she had grown closer to Terry.

"Who could have, then?"

"Willie."

"He's not the only one."

"Someone else from the clans. Dysons or Jacksons. Despite her experience and propensity for violence, Theresa was still a young woman. Not a lot of experience. Less upper body strength than a man. Somebody that she knew and wasn't expecting to attack her could still get a drop on her."

"Uh-huh."

"But there weren't any recent calls or messages with known clan members on her phone."

Erin frowned. "None?"

"Looks like the only people she was in contact with here were Vic and the people closest to her."

"Does that mean that Theresa wasn't with the clan anymore, or just that she was doing her own thing for a while until things cooled down?"

"Probably that she was too hot for them to use for anything for a while, so she was taking a break."

"Hmm." Erin filed that away for later. "Who else?"

"Who else? Vic herself."

"Not Vic," Erin disagreed.

"She's taller than Theresa. You don't know what training she may have had just from her father and brothers. I imagine they wrestled. Tried out different holds and moves on each other like boys do. Her father may have shared his training with them. I don't know how much upper body strength she has. Does a transwoman retain the upper body strength of a male body? Does she lose it if she's on hormones? Does Vic work out? Lift weights?"

"Not that I know of."

"So that's an unknown, but other factors fit. She could have taken Theresa by surprise. Pretended she wanted a hug or kiss to get in close, got an arm around her neck…"

Erin shook her head, trying to rid herself of the violent images that popped into her head at his suggestion. "No. It wasn't Vic."

"You don't know that. I don't know who else to suggest."

"Police?"

His muscles tensed. "Who?"

"I don't know. The police get training in how to subdue suspects."

"Yes, of course. But we're specifically taught *not* to employ any choke holds."

"Some of them might have other training. Martial arts."

"Anyone could have martial arts training, not just a cop."

"That tip that was called in about there being a police officer around at the time she was killed. What if it was true? What if one of the other Bald Eagle Falls officers was there? Or Jack Ward or someone else from Moose River?"

"Yes, of course that's a possibility. But the dispatcher knew where everyone was coming from. She knew where they were at the time the call came in."

"Where they *said* they were."

"Yes, okay," he agreed. The police department did not have live GPS tracking of all of their units.

"So there are possibilities that it could have been someone other than Willie or Vic."

"That someone else would have had to get there sometime between when Theresa sent that last message and when Willie called it in. That is a very narrow window. Willie was there for some time before he called it in."

"How do you know that?"

"From signs on Theresa's body. Her pallor. Her temperature. She'd been dead more than ten minutes. And because I know that even if all he did was walk in and find a dead body, he would take a few minutes to check out the scene."

"That's biased."

"Yes. Because I know Willie. He's careful."

"Okay." That was true.

"Say Willie was there for twenty minutes. Then the window in which somebody else gets access to Vic's apartment, surprises Theresa, kills her, and possibly moves the body, is reduced from forty minutes to twenty."

Twenty minutes. Erin had to admit that the chances of someone slipping into Vic's apartment during that specific twenty-minute interval by chance and killing her seemed highly unlikely.

She snuggled closer to Terry, though it wasn't really possible to get closer since she was already against him. His arms tightened around her in a firm hug.

"You should try to get some sleep."
Erin yawned. "I don't know if I can."
"Shh."
"Where were you tonight?" she asked him.
"Shh. Go to sleep."

CHAPTER 34

*E*rin knew that she and Vic were both tired as they worked Friday morning, after the discussions of the night before. Still, neither of them said anything about it, pretending to be as bright-eyed as on any other morning. Since it was Easter weekend, Erin was busily producing more sugar cookies in cute Easter shapes, hot cross rolls, and marshmallow eggs. Also, white dinner rolls for Sunday dinners.

Erin smothered another yawn and focused on her checklist, keeping track of what they needed to have ready by the time they opened.

There was a knock at the back door. Erin frowned, exchanged looks with Vic, and went to answer it.

"Are you sure you should?" Vic asked. "We're not expecting anyone."

"It's probably just one of the guys."

Erin opened the door and was surprised to see Beaver standing there. She nodded a greeting and chewed her gum.

"Mornin' Miss Erin. Miss Victoria."

"Good morning. You're up awfully early. What can I do for you this morning?"

Erin thought of the day-old bread program that she had instituted to provide free bread for anyone unable to pay. Beaver drove around that battered old station wagon and was almost always dressed in the same clothes. Even though Erin knew that this was probably just part of her cover as an underemployed treasure hunter, Erin wondered if Beaver might be having problems making ends meet. She had helped Jeremy with the deposit on his apartment. Jeremy was working, so he shouldn't need help making the rent. But you could never tell looking at someone what their actual financial situation was.

"Up late rather than early," Beaver informed her. "Haven't been to bed. Listen... I know you're not open yet, so this is sort of an imposition, but... well, I'm starving." She wiped her forehead, shiny with sweat, with the back of her arm. "I wasn't expecting to be so active all night, so I've long since burned off all my calories, and nothing opens for a couple more hours. I've only got a five-minute break, so even going to Jeremy's or to the 24-hour gas station on the highway is out of the question."

"Sure, happy to help," Erin told her with a laugh. "What can I get you?"

"Whatever you've got. Muffins, rolls, heels of a loaf of bread. I'm not picky. Just gotta get something into this gaping hole."

"Okay, hang on." Erin busied herself putting together a box of baked goods for Beaver and added a couple of the take-out packs of butter and jam and a plastic knife.

She was disconcerted when she turned around to face Beaver and found her studying the interior of the kitchen with unexpected intensity. Beaver relaxed into her usual fluid slouch and smiled. "You're an angel. What do I owe you?"

"Just throw something in the tip jar the next time you're around," Erin said, waving her hand. "The till isn't open yet, and half of this is day-old that we would give away anyway. Happy to help law enforcement." She studied Beaver. "You're working this morning—last night? On a big job?"

Beaver's chin lifted slightly in the barest nod. She looked around the kitchen again as if someone else might be lurking in the shadows, listening in. "Stay alert. Report anything that doesn't feel right to the police."

"What—?" Before Erin could form a coherent question, Beaver was withdrawing into the darkness.

Erin shut the door, bolted it, and turned to Vic. "That was weird, right?"

Vic nodded. "It kind of was," she agreed. "I mean, we all know Beaver… she's wired differently than the rest of us. But that did seem a little… ominous."

"Yeah."

"You think we should still open today?" Vic inquired.

Erin rebelled against the idea of closing when they had already planned to be open, already started baking. It was a holiday weekend; people would be spending more money than usual for big family meals. "We have to."

"If it's dangerous…"

"It's not dangerous. That's just Beaver being Beaver. She loves to tease." Erin brushed away any anxiety Beaver's words had produced, pushing it to the side. She couldn't let Beaver gaslight her. Especially not on Easter weekend.

"You sure?" Vic persisted.

"Yes. It will be fine. If there was a danger, there would be cops all over the street telling people to go home and stay there."

Vic nodded. "Yeah, you're probably right."

∼

Despite their initial misgivings, the morning went fairly smoothly. Lots of customers; they moved a lot of product. Holidays were good for the bottom line, and Erin always worked hard to plan exactly what people would need in connection with their holiday plans.

Mary Lou stood at the counter placing her order, which Erin noted was bigger than usual.

"Company for Easter dinner?" she inquired.

"Campbell is going to come by. And Roger may be able to get out on a day pass. No guarantees, but we're praying it all works out."

Erin smiled. It had been a long time since Roger had been put into the care facility he was in, and she knew that his family missed him. "Fingers crossed," she told Mary Lou, showing her crossed fingers.

Mary Lou nodded. Erin added a couple of extra cookies into Mary Lou's order. As she handed the carefully packed baked goods across to Mary Lou, her gaze caught on a young man in a hoodie standing outside the front window of the bakery. His back was to her and, for an instant, she thought it was Joshua, waiting patiently outside for his mother to finish her shopping. But he turned slightly and she saw from his profile that it was not one of the Cox boys. His hair was blond like Vic's brothers' rather than dark like the Cox boys', but it wasn't Jeremy or one of the other Jackson boys either. Erin stared at him for a minute before she could place him.

The young man who had been with Beaver at the restaurant the day that she and Vic had eaten there with Jeremy. As Erin was gazing at him, he turned and looked into the interior of the bakery and, for a moment, their eyes met. Then he turned around again and looked up and down the road before slouching across the street and making his way down it, head down so that his face was nearly invisible.

"Happy Easter, Erin," Mary Lou said, in a loud, clear voice, as if Erin had not heard her once before.

"Oh, I'm sorry. Happy Easter," Erin agreed, tearing her gaze from the young man to meet Mary Lou's eyes and make sure she saw that Erin's best wishes were genuine. She nodded and touched Mary Lou's shoulder briefly. "I hope it's a great one."

Mary Lou smiled and turned to go.

"Do you think...?" Vic started.

Erin blinked at her, understanding that she was supposed to complete the sentence in her own head without Vic having to say it out loud, but she was out of sync with Vic. Usually, they could complete each other's sentences or start talking on a random topic without any introduction, and the other person still knew what she was talking about. But Erin had gotten too distracted.

"Sorry, do I think what?"

"That…" Vic gave a little nod toward the window. "Do you think that constitutes something we should report…?"

"Oh." Erin thought about it, but she couldn't identify anything in the young man's behavior that had been reportable. She couldn't very well call the police dispatcher and say that she was concerned that a young stranger had been standing in front of her window, and now was gone. "No, I don't think so."

There was a bang outside, followed by a burst of firecracker pops. Mary Lou, standing at the door with her hand on the handle, paused and looked out. The other customers waiting in line turned around to see what was going on.

"Everybody get down!" Vic ordered in an authoritative bark. "Get down below the window! Now!"

The customers looked around at each other, confused, checking to see what everybody else was doing. Vic strode out from behind the counter and started pushing women down, pulling her gun out of her bra holster and crouching down to get as low as possible as she moved among the customers.

"Mary Lou!" she grabbed Mary Lou's sleeve and pulled down. "Get down. Get away from the door."

Erin realized she was standing there, frozen, watching everyone else as if it were a show on TV. She forced herself to crouch down, then to crawl along the floor behind the display case and out from behind the counter to the open area everyone else was in. Staying as low as possible, Vic pulled the blinds on the window on her side to lower them. Erin reached for the string on the window closest to her to do the same.

There were more pops outside. They seemed far away, and Erin thought that they were all just overreacting. But Easter wasn't July the Fourth. Who fired off firecrackers in the middle of the day for Easter?

There was a smash of broken glass and the sound of something whizzing through the air. Erin yelped and jerked back from the string as though touching it had triggered the explosion. Glass fell at her feet and across her knees. Erin reached up and gave the string a good yank to the side. The blind came whooshing down.

"Get everyone in the back!" Erin ordered. There were no windows in the kitchen. It was protected from the street. And she knew the back door was securely bolted.

"Go on," Vic told the ladies, spreading her arms and shooing them like a flock of birds. "Around the counter and into the kitchen. Go, go!"

They obeyed in a confused babble of voices, asking what was going on. Mrs. Peach, Erin's elderly neighbor, was doing her best to walk on her knees with the support of her walker. Erin took a second to straighten out the walker, which was veering to one side, and to pat Mrs. Peach reassuringly on the shoulder. "Just a little way," she encouraged. "You'll be safe in there."

"I should go home. I need to put the laundry in the dryer."

"Soon. Just a few minutes. This is your chance to tour the kitchen!"

Mrs. Peach smiled in confusion and kept pushing her walker forward. Erin reached up to lock the front door. She flipped the sign over to Closed and pulled the blinds over the door. Then she followed the rest of the women, her knees aching, around the counter and into the kitchen.

They never closed the door between the kitchen and the front, but Erin did so anyway, regretting that it was just a lightweight, hollow-core door with no lock. With the door shut, they could no longer hear the gunfire from outside. Erin leaned against the door for a minute to catch her breath. Her heart was racing.

"Stay away from the door," Vic advised. "Move to the side so that the wall and cupboards are between you and the front."

Erin inched to the side. She looked around at the customers, huddling wide-eyed in her kitchen. "Is everyone okay? Is anyone hurt?" She didn't think anyone could be, but at least one shot had come through the window and there hadn't been enough time to see if it had hit anyone.

They all looked at each other, but no one seemed to be injured.

"Now, should we call the police?" Vic asked with a weak laugh.

Erin shook her head. "The dispatcher's lines are going to be jammed. Everyone is going to be calling in."

She pulled out her phone, though, and texted Terry.

ACB ok. all in back

Then she dialed the number for The Book Nook across the street. She didn't know the numbers of all of the businesses along Main Street, but she knew that one.

"Erin?" Naomi's voice sounded tearful. "What's going on?"

"I don't know yet. Is everyone okay over there?"

"Yes."

"Are you somewhere safe, away from the windows?"

"In the stock room."

"Okay. Stay there. Do you know the numbers for any of the other businesses on Main?"

Naomi sniffled. "The General Store. And Monica's." Her voice was a bit stronger.

"Call them. Make sure they're okay and away from the windows and have them text me their status. Then to call anyone else they know on Main to do the same."

"Okay. I can do that."

Erin hung up. She texted Terry again.

Book Nook ok.

Vic was looking at her for instructions.

"Nothing else we can do," Erin said. She looked at the oven beside Vic. "That timer is going to go off in thirty seconds, just so you're not startled. Just put them on top to cool. Those hot cross rolls"—she pointed—"they should be cool enough to eat. Why not pass them around? Everyone will feel better with something in their stomachs. I'll be in my office."

CHAPTER 35

*E*rin crawled across the kitchen to her office, knowing that everyone would be wondering what the heck she was doing. Time to do a little filing until the crisis was over? Check her email?

She pulled her mouse and keyboard to the floor and angled the monitor so that she could see it, then brought up her text messaging app. It would be much easier to message Terry using her computer than her phone. She watched status reports coming up on her phone screen and transcribed them in a string of messages to Terry.

General Store ok

Monica's one reported injury but safe for now

Grocery ok

Chinese restaurant ok

She could hear sirens nearby and hoped that Terry and the other officers would be safe. They would be wearing vests and helmets. They would surround whoever was shooting and arrest him. Then it would all be over.

There were more sirens than she expected. It sounded like more emergency vehicles than they had in Bald Eagle Falls. Maybe Jack Ward was still in town, and the men he had lent to Sheriff

Wilmot had their own vehicles. Maybe Beaver had called in other forces during the night.

The status messages slowed. People started sending questions, impatient to know what was going on.

Is it over? Can we come out?

who was shooting?

what is going on?

Erin sent everyone replies to stay where they were unless the police gave them other instructions. She couldn't hear any more shots or sirens.

Eventually, she heard a knock on the back door.

"Erin?" Vic called.

Erin kept low and joined the rest of the ladies in the kitchen. They were all sitting on the floor around the room. They looked reasonably comfortable, all things considered. Their faces were white and anxious, but no one was crying or having hysterics. No one was trying to escape the confines of the kitchen. Erin duck-walked to the door. She leaned up against it, ear to the door.

"Who's there?"

"All clear, Erin."

Erin looked down at her phone screen, waiting for confirmation from Terry. *Anyone* could come to her door and say, "all clear."

In a few seconds, a new text scrolled down from the top of her screen.

Situation resolved. Answer doors to first responders.

Erin stood up, turned the bolt on the door and opened it slowly, still cautious. It was Beaver.

"Knocking on your door twice in one day," Beaver said casually. "Police are saying it's all clear. But everyone is to stay here; they'll be coming around to take statements."

She was acting like a messenger rather than the agent in charge. An act for anyone who didn't know that she was actually an undercover agent. Erin was careful not to blow it.

"Okay, thanks. Do you know what happened?"

"Some kind of argument." Beaver shrugged and chewed her gum. "Maybe the police will know more." She leaned in the door to look around at the ladies sitting around the floor. "Everyone is okay? No injuries?"

Erin nodded. Beaver reached over and brushed broken glass from Erin's pants. She touched Erin's shoulder and adjusted her stance. "What's that?" She pulled Erin's arm toward her and rotated it into an uncomfortable position. Erin resisted, then saw blood on her elbow. She tried to turn it farther to see where it had come from. Beaver leaned in close and pincered something in the fleshy part in the back of Erin's upper arm. She held up a tiny splinter of glass, red with blood.

"Just a sliver. Slap a bandage on it and you'll be fine."

"Oh. Thanks."

"Best not to stand close to windows when people are firing."

Erin glared at her. "I was shutting the blinds."

Beaver nodded. "Good thinking."

"Vic's idea."

Beaver nodded a greeting to Vic. "Good plan, Miss Victoria."

"Can we go home now?" Mrs. Peach asked plaintively.

"Just a few more minutes," Erin told her. "Then you can go home. Maybe one of the officers or one of the other ladies can drive you."

"Nothing wrong with my legs," Mrs. Peach told her. "I'm not a cripple yet."

"You're a beast, Mrs. Peach," Vic told her.

Mrs. Peach looked uncertain. "Is that a good thing?"

"It's a good thing. You're one tough broad."

Mrs. Peach colored at that. "Thank you."

∼

It was a while before the police made it to Auntie Clem's, working their way down the street to all of the businesses on Main Street to take witness statements. Erin assumed that they went to the businesses with injuries first. Luckily, there were not a lot of injured and no deaths. The gunplay had been confined to the street and the people involved had not entered into any of the stores. Maybe due in part to the business owners having the sense to lock their doors immediately.

Terry entered the bakery, along with several law enforcement officers that Erin did not know. They were, she assumed, some of the officers from Moose River or Beaver's agency. Terry broke out of his cop role long enough to give Erin a hug, holding her tightly in his relief that she was safe and unharmed, other than a small cut on the back of her arm.

"You were a big help," he told her. "Having reports coming in through one text channel was a lot more manageable than everyone trying to get through to the police dispatcher at the same time. Knowing that everyone was safe behind locked doors was a big relief and let us focus on what was happening on the street without worrying about civilians popping out their doors and getting in the way."

Erin held her face against Terry's chest, feeling his warmth and smelling his sweat, the anxiety finally starting to drain from her body. "I'm so glad you're okay."

"Of course I am. And I'm glad that you're okay." He stroked her cheek with his thumb and kissed her on top of the head.

"It all happened so fast. There wasn't really time to stop and think about the danger. Until we were all battened down and I could hear the sirens and was thinking about you being out there with the shooter."

"No law enforcement officers were injured."

"That's good."

He gave her another squeeze, then let her go. K9 gave a little whine and, even though he was on duty, Erin scratched his ears. "It's okay, bud. You did good too, didn't you?"

He nuzzled her hand and gave it a brief lick.

"We need to get some pictures in the front," Terry said,

motioning to the customer area at the front of Auntie Clem's, "and then you can tidy up and go home."

"Go home?"

"I doubt you're going to be able to get any business the rest of the day. Main Street is blocked off for the time being."

Erin looked around at the customers in her kitchen. "Well, I still have these people to serve. Assuming everyone still needs rolls for their Easter dinners." She raised her voice for the last statement and, around the room, women nodded. Gunfire or no gunfire, they would still be having family dinner on Sunday. After serving the customers who were there, she would consider going home. But maybe the police would open up the street again in an hour, or people would make their way around to the back of the bakery. Erin had a mobile point of sale device for her phone that they used when they sold baking at community events. She could take payment that way. It would take a little longer but was still workable.

"Let's get someone in to take those pictures, then," she told Terry, "so we can get on with it."

~

It was taking longer than Erin had expected for the police to get statements from everyone and to clear the front of her shop for her to get everything fixed up. She set up a folding banquet table in the parking lot with a big carafe of fresh coffee and free baked goods for the law enforcement officers. News of the food spread quickly, and it wasn't long before she had a steady stream of cops she knew and cops she didn't know stopping by for refreshments. Erin listened in on the chatter, picking up as much information as possible about what had happened.

"Hey," she smiled as Jack Ward came to the table for his coffee and muffin. "I thought you would be back home by now."

"Well, that was what I had originally expected, but when we started to get reports from certain quarters that something was going down tonight—last night—it called for a change in plans."

Erin nodded. "I'm glad you stuck around. Our little police department probably needed all of the help they could get."

"Things were a little... dicey."

"This was the clans?" Erin asked, putting together what she had overheard from the other officers.

"Power play by the Jacksons. There have been rumblings for a while, a lot of movement, new trafficking routes. I didn't think that it would come to a head this quickly. It can take years to be able to get enough on these guys to make significant arrests. But the feds came through with a boatload of new information about parties involved and shipment details, so they were able to break it open last night and today." He shook his head. "Having gunplay break out on the street was not something anyone anticipated. But some parties were pretty desperate to escape our net."

Erin appreciated Jack, who was much more open with her than Terry or any other law enforcement personnel in Bald Eagle Falls. It wasn't like he was giving her information that wouldn't eventually make it to the papers. Every investigative journalist in the area was going to be calling, looking for details after a shoot-up on Main Street of Bald Eagle Falls. It might even warrant a special edition of the local newspaper.

"Did you get that guy that you were telling me about?" Erin wrinkled her brow, trying to recall the name. "Payne?"

"Ah, we did." Jack took a swig from his coffee cup and put it down on the table. He pulled out his phone and tapped the screen a few times, then turned it to show Erin the picture on the screen. An older, dark-haired, tough-looking man sat in the back of a police car, staring defiantly out. His hair was cut short, almost shaved down to the skin. "Is that the man you saw talking with Beaver?"

Erin shook her head. "No. The guy she was with... he had longer hair and facial hair. A thin mustache and beard." She used her finger to draw the shape on her chin.

"He couldn't have just shaved them off?"

Erin tried to remember what she could of the man's face and looked again at Payne. "No. I'm sure it's not the same man."

"Okay. Well, do tell me if you see him again. Or tell someone in your police department."

"The other man I saw her meeting with in the restaurant, the younger guy, I saw him on the street in front of Auntie Clem's just before the gunfire started. I don't know if he was involved, but it was right at that time."

"Long, blond hair?"

Erin nodded. "He was wearing a hoodie, had it pulled down over most of his face."

"Being a young guy, I'm going to assume he was an informant. Maybe someone in the Jackson clan who was feeding her information. She had a lot of intel."

"Yeah. He reminded me a bit of Vic's brothers, so maybe they were cousins."

"There is a lot of intermarrying in the clan, even now, so certain family features do become more prominent. They could well be related." Jack shrugged. He put his phone away and picked up his coffee again. "There have been a number of extra people around town. Hopefully, anyone who wasn't arrested will make themselves scarce and things will quiet down again for a while."

"That's what they said after the drug waypoint was seized. That the clan wouldn't be back any time soon. But it's been less than a year."

"Well, apparently, they decided to make another play. What can I say? They don't take lessons from me."

CHAPTER 36

*E*ven though Erin was home earlier than usual, she was exhausted after the busy day. She wasn't sure why serving the police coffee and making a few sales out her back door should make her so tired. But maybe that wasn't what had caused her exhaustion. She hadn't been sleeping well, and the adrenaline rush caused by the shoot-out on Main Street had burned through whatever physical reserves she'd had at that point.

"We should make something to eat," she told Terry, collapsing into a chair at the kitchen table. She knew that was a bad idea, because she probably wouldn't be able to get up again. Terry opened the fridge, then the freezer door, apparently not finding anything that appealed to him or that he had the energy to make.

"Why don't we order in?"

It was a luxury that they didn't usually indulge in. Everything was so close in Bald Eagle Falls that it made a lot more sense to just pick up whatever they needed. Or, in the case of restaurant food, to just go to the restaurant and eat there, leaving the restaurant with all of the cleanup too.

"We shouldn't," Erin said. But she didn't have the energy to get up and make something or go to a restaurant to eat. "It's so expensive. And silly when they're only traveling a couple of blocks to deliver."

"Tonight, we need it." Terry sat down on the chair across from Erin's and put his phone on the table. "I don't even have the mental energy to put something in the microwave, do you?"

"No."

She should be able to just warm something up. It wasn't that complicated or difficult. But she just couldn't.

Terry started tapping on his phone. Putting together an order for one of the restaurants, Erin was sure. She should be taking care of him. Making sure that he didn't do more than he had to and took a break. She didn't want him to end up in the grip of another of the migraines that he'd been experiencing since his encounter with Theresa. They were few and far between now, but that didn't mean that they couldn't come back full force if he was overstressed and exhausted.

But try as she might to talk herself into just getting up and making a couple of sandwiches, Erin couldn't manage it.

"Just relax," Terry advised. "There's nothing that says you have to prepare a meal every night. I'm taking care of it. Don't get stressed out."

"I should do something."

"You were shot at. You helped the town deal with an emergency. You've fed half the population of the town. And how much sleep did you get last night?"

"Not much. But a couple of hours."

"Go to bed. Close your eyes for a few minutes while we wait for the food. I'm sure plenty of other people will be ordering in tonight, so there may be a wait. I'll wake you up when it comes."

"I can't sleep during the day."

"Then just close your eyes."

Orange Blossom yowled for attention, but Erin couldn't muster up the energy to get his treats out. That would involve walking across the kitchen, taking them down, opening the can, taking a couple out of the container…

"I'm not going to bed," Erin told Terry. "I'm just going to put my head down for a minute and close my eyes."

She rested her head on folded arms on top of the table, like she used to do at school when the teacher read aloud to them. That had been a long, long time ago. Erin closed her eyes. She didn't even have the energy to yawn.

Terry stayed at the table with her, tapping on his phone. Orange Blossom tried clawing at Erin's thigh to get her moving, and Terry growled and waved his hand at Blossom, making him gallop away. Time drifted by. Eventually, the doorbell rang and Terry got up from the table with a deep sigh to answer it.

"Oh. Adele."

Erin raised her head and rubbed her eyes. Adele wouldn't be there to talk to Terry. She turned her head to look toward the door. Her legs felt like lead, too heavy to move.

"She's... are you awake, Erin?"

"Yes, yes," Erin made one more unsuccessful attempt to get up. "Why don't you come in here, Adele?"

Adele and Terry murmured too low for Erin to hear, and then Adele entered the kitchen. She sat down in the chair that Terry had vacated, and Erin heard Terry settle into the couch with the squeak of springs.

Adele looked Erin over. Erin wiped the side of her face, making sure she hadn't drooled too much. She probably had a big red splotch where her face had been resting on her arms.

"I probably shouldn't have come," Adele said. "You need some sleep."

"We're just waiting for dinner, so you're not interrupting anything."

"I heard about the excitement in town today."

Erin nodded. "It was exciting, all right." She turned to show Adele her upper arm and pushed back her sleeve to reveal the bandage. "See, I was even injured."

Adele smiled. "I see that. Will you recover?"

Erin laughed. "They tell me I will. Maybe even without a scar."

They both chuckled over it.

"Everything going okay over in your direction?" Erin asked. "Are the woods quiet?"

"I have been trying to keep it free of pests."

"Of the two-legged variety?"

"Yes. Exactly. It has been an unusually busy time this equinox."

"Have you had intruders in the woods? There have been some people around town who shouldn't have been there. Or at least... didn't belong there."

"Strangers don't usually venture into the woods, not knowing where they will come out. But there have been people ducking in and out, with all of the commotion in town. But before this, that woman... she was around a few times. Spending too much time creeping about, watching the houses."

"That woman? You mean Theresa Franklin?"

"The one who was killed. Yes."

"You saw her in the woods? Watching the house?"

"Yes. Sent her on her way a couple of times."

"Well, she shouldn't be bothering you again."

"I should hope not," Adele agreed dryly.

"And the night she was killed. You said that you might have seen something, but had to think about it. Did you see someone other than Theresa that night?"

"Yes."

"Willie?"

Adele considered this, her eyes grave. "Yes," she agreed eventually.

"He isn't the one who killed Theresa. He just carried her body out of the apartment. Trying to keep Vic from being blamed for her death."

Adele kept her own counsel, not indicating whether or not what she had seen had coincided with Erin's conclusion. But then, how would she know the difference? She wouldn't know whether Willie had killed Theresa before carrying her down the stairs or whether he had found her in that condition.

"Is that it? Did you see anyone else?"

Adele didn't answer. She got up from the table. "Why don't I make you some tea? You look exhausted. I know you're waiting on dinner, but maybe something to hold you over…"

Erin remembered Terry making her tea after discovering Theresa's body, not letting her talk until she'd had something to drink.

"Then will you tell me?"

Adele put the kettle on and looked through a basket of teabags. "It's probably still too early for sleepy tea. But maybe a soothing chamomile?"

"No." Erin rubbed her eyes. "How about mint?"

Adele nodded and pulled one out of the basket. She selected Erin's favorite mug from the cupboard and waited for the kettle to boil. Adele never made any decision impulsively, so Erin waited for her to finish thinking things through while they waited.

Adele returned to the table with a cup for each of them. She didn't force Erin to add sugar like Terry had. That seemed like a very long time ago now.

"Vic wasn't around, was she?" Erin asked, with a downward inflection that said she already knew the answer.

"No. She left very early—or very late—quite unlike her."

"At least two hours before Willie got there?"

"Yes."

"And was there someone else there in between? Did you see?"

"I don't just stay and watch your houses. There are other parts of the woods that I need to monitor. Places that don't have burglar alarms or phones to call for help."

"Yeah. Does that mean that you did see someone or not?"

"You're sure that there was someone there between Vic and Willie?"

"Besides Theresa? Yes. Because Willie didn't kill her. And she didn't kill herself."

Adele sipped her tea. "You know I don't like to be mixed up in law enforcement issues."

Erin imagined that Adele had found herself on the wrong side of the law too often. If being a practicing witch wasn't enough for people to suspect and report her to the police, her ex-husband had been a con man and a scoundrel. He had undoubtedly brought far more police attention on Adele than she liked.

"I know that. But Willie needs you to speak up and tell what you know."

"After what happened today… I don't think you'll need my word."

Erin frowned, studying her. She sipped her tea and tried to sort out what Adele was saying. What did the shoot-out and arrests of the clan members in Bald Eagle Falls have to do with Theresa's death and whether they could arrest Willie for Theresa's murder?

"I don't follow."

"Not right now. You need to relax and get a good sleep tonight. No one is going to arrest Willie Andrews tonight."

She was right about that. And Adele was generally right about the other things she had speculated about in Bald Eagle Falls. She was quiet, watched carefully, and thought deeply. Which meant you could take her word for it on most things. As long as her husband wasn't involved. And Rudolph Windsor was doing time for kidnapping and his involvement in other clan dealings in Bald Eagle Falls. From the last time that the Jacksons and Dysons had battled over business in town.

"If they do arrest Willie, will you come forward?"

"If it became necessary. But it will not."

"How can you be so sure?"

Adele shrugged. "Let us wait and see."

Erin sighed and sipped her tea. It was good and helped to wake her up a little more, chasing the cobwebs away.

CHAPTER 37

*E*rin couldn't remember much about the dinner she and Terry shared that night. She was still sitting at the table when Terry brought it in, and Adele left sometime before or just after that. Erin thought they'd had Chinese, but she had no memory of eating it or getting ready for bed.

When she awoke in the morning, feeling clear-headed and rested, she could see immediately that she had overslept. Sunlight was pouring in around the blinds on the windows. Erin sat up, her heart racing.

"Shh, it's okay," Terry mumbled, reaching for her.

"I slept in! What time is it?" Erin snatched for her phone on the side table.

"It's okay. I talked to Charley. She's taking care of things."

Erin sat back. "You talked to Charley?" She held the phone in her hand, ready to call someone, but now had no need to.

"Yes. It's okay. Everything is covered. You don't need to race over there."

A hundred different worries darted through Erin's brain, but she took a couple of deep breaths, trying to push them away. Charley and the others were taking care of Auntie Clem's, so she didn't need to worry. They had the plans and checklists for the week. They knew what she wanted done. And Auntie Clem's was open. That was the biggest thing.

"Okay. Okay."

Terry nodded. "It's just fine. How are you feeling this morning?"

"Good. How long did I sleep?"

He rubbed his eyes and looked at the time on his phone. "About ten hours."

"Wow. What a sleepy head."

"After everything that happened yesterday, I'm surprised you didn't need even more than that. Are you sure you don't want to go back to sleep? Cuddle and laze around for a while?"

"No. I need to talk to Beaver."

Terry blinked at her. "Beaver?"

"Yeah." Erin studied him. "I suppose you know everything already. They briefed you yesterday. Or the night before, when you weren't here."

"They? Briefed me on what?"

"The feds. They gave you a heads-up on what was going to happen yesterday. How it was all connected. Why Beaver lied."

"No... we were told to be careful, to watch for any clan activity. But... I don't know what else you're talking about. Why Beaver lied about what?"

"She has the phone. *She's* the reason that the Bald Eagle Falls Police Department was told to back off of Theresa's case. So you wouldn't interfere with *Beaver's* case."

"I suspect that she was involved in monitoring the clan activities and trying to prevent things from blowing up like they did," he said cautiously.

"Oh, she was," Erin agreed. She remembered Beaver coming to Auntie Clem's during the pre-opening hours, face shiny with sweat, starving after working through the night. Warning Erin to keep her eyes open for any trouble.

She got out of bed and heard Orange Blossom jump to the floor as he heard her getting up. By the time she reached the bathroom, he was winding around her legs, yowling his complaints, encouraging her to hurry up and feed him before he starved to death.

"I'll be there in a minute," Erin laughed. "Just relax. You're not going to die."

It was lucky that he hadn't woken her up at her usual rising time. Often, if she slept in on a rare day off, he was on the bed pawing at her face or knocking things off the side table trying to get her attention.

After using the facilities and splashing water on her face, Erin headed to the kitchen, carefully avoiding the animals underfoot, and filled each pet food bowl. She wanted to see Beaver as quickly as she could, but she would need to eat and dress, at the very least. She should probably shower and make herself look presentable. And she should call Charley and Bella at Auntie Clem's and see how things were going and what time they would need her to be there.

~

It was another hour before Erin managed to make it to Jeremy's apartment. It was probably too early to be waking Beaver up, considering the fact that she hadn't slept the night before, but Jeremy would still have work and might have awakened her with his preparations. Regardless, Erin was tired of being kept in the dark about what had really happened to Theresa on Erin's property Monday night.

She knocked on the door. She didn't hammer on it like the police would, but she wasn't shy about making herself heard, either, fully expecting that Beaver would still be in bed.

It was only thirty seconds before the door was opened. Beaver was in her usual camouflage cargo pants and a green halter top, her arms and shoulders bare, showing impressive muscle definition.

Beaver leaned against the doorway and chewed her gum,

looking at Erin and then looking past her to see if anyone else was with her or watching.

"Come in." She moved out of the way.

Erin entered and shut the door behind her. She sat down on the couch and Beaver leaned against the kitchenette island, drinking what Erin assumed was a protein shake.

"Surprised you're not at Auntie Clem's," she told Erin. "I thought that the day before Easter Sunday you would be run off your feet."

"I should be. But after everything that happened yesterday, I crashed. Slept in late. But Charley arranged things, so I'm okay for another hour or two; then I'll go help with the afternoon shift. Business will probably peter out about noon, but we'll keep it open late just to make sure we've got all of the last-minute planners covered."

Beaver nodded.

"You probably crashed too," Erin guessed. "With not sleeping the night before, you must have been exhausted."

"Depending heavily on pharmaceuticals," Beaver told her, as if that were perfectly natural. And maybe it was for her.

There was certainly a history of the military using amphetamines on missions where soldiers needed to stay awake and alert for long periods.

"Do you have Theresa's phone?" Erin asked without any further preliminaries.

"The police have Theresa's phone."

"I didn't get it when Terry told me that there weren't any contacts with the clan on Theresa's phone. I should have. That meant that either all of her contacts with the clan had been erased, or she'd had two phones. One for personal stuff and one for work."

"Or maybe she wasn't involved in any clan business."

"Of course she was. Why would she just come here and stop communicating with them? It doesn't make any sense."

"Because she was obsessed with Miss Victoria. And in

harassing everyone in her constellation. Her boyfriend, her brother, her best friend…" Beaver raised her brows at Erin.

Her words confirmed that she had seen Theresa's personal phone, or that someone in the Bald Eagle Falls police department had told her who Theresa had been in contact with. But Erin was sure she hadn't returned the favor and shown them Theresa's business phone.

"That was just the icing on the cake," Erin asserted. "She was here for clan business. Just like Phillip Payne and the rest of them."

"Payne wasn't here because of the rivalry between the two clans," Beaver informed her. "He was here to bring Theresa back into line."

Erin shrugged impatiently. "Theresa had another phone."

Beaver blinked slowly. That was as good as a nod to Erin. Beaver would continue to be cagey and admit nothing out loud, but Erin could read the signals.

"You took that phone, and that's what you've been working with since she died, gathering together all of that intelligence and feeding it back to your agency, so they would be ready when the clan moved in."

"That would be a wise approach."

"You were at Vic's apartment between the time that she left and the time Willie arrived."

"You don't have any evidence of that."

"You were seen."

Adele had said she didn't want to be involved in anything to do with law enforcement. She wasn't referring to the case against Willie. She was talking about Beaver being there. Beaver was law enforcement and Adele did not want to get in the way of her operations.

Beaver raised a brow. "By you? I don't think so. By Miss Victoria?" She considered, then shook her head. "No. No one saw me there."

"It doesn't matter who. They aren't going to talk. Not as long as you do the right thing."

"Which is...?"

"To tell the police department that Willie didn't have anything to do with Theresa's death and to leave it alone."

"The police department has already been told to leave it alone."

"So that you could continue with your operation against the clan. They're still going to try to arrest Willie as soon as your agency backs out of Bald Eagle Falls again."

Beaver chewed her gum slowly, considering it. She gave her head a slight shake. "You don't need to worry about Willie. Or Vic."

"Theresa told Vic to go to their old rendezvous to meet her so that she could have Vic's apartment to herself. Why did you go up there? Was it part of your assignment? To take Theresa out?"

"Despite what you may have seen on TV, agents are not assigned hits on US citizens. If they wanted to remove Theresa from the picture, they would arrange for her arrest."

"If they had enough evidence."

Beaver nodded her agreement.

"But if there wasn't enough evidence, then you couldn't do anything about her."

Beaver's eyes rolled up toward the ceiling. "Not lawfully," she agreed.

"Then... what? Why would you go up to Vic's apartment when you knew Theresa was there?"

Beaver took a few swallows of her protein shake. "Why would *you* speculate?" she asked eventually.

Erin had been thinking about it ever since the instant she had woken up. And she could only come up with one solution. "Because you thought Vic was in danger. Theresa was going to kill her."

"But law enforcement cannot step in before the crime is committed. All I would have had on Theresa is burglary."

"You could arrest her for that."

"But she would be out again in a day. Jails are overcrowded.

No judge is going to withhold bail for a simple break and enter. If Theresa could pay, she'd be right back out."

Erin was starting to see the shape of things. Faced with the dilemma of knowing that Theresa was a threat to Vic, but that there was nothing she could do as a law enforcement agent to stop her, Beaver had stepped over the line. Whether she thought she could get away with it as an unfortunate death in custody, an accident because Theresa had resisted arrest and struggled against Beaver, or whether she had intended from the start to be long gone before anyone discovered her presence there, Erin didn't know. But she had taken a considerable risk for a friend. For her boyfriend's sister.

"But then why involve Willie?" Erin asked. "You *were* the one who sent him the picture of Vic sleeping, weren't you?"

Beaver raised her brows innocently. "That text was sent from Theresa's phone. It must have been sent by Theresa."

"Why? I don't understand why you would do that."

Erin frowned, trying to fit the pieces of the puzzle together. She knew she was close. She just couldn't get the last few pieces to fall into place.

What effect had sending Willie that picture had?

Beaver knew that if Willie believed that Theresa was in Vic's apartment, watching her while she slept, making some kind of unspoken threat, that Willie would get there as quickly as he could.

Theresa had been dead when Beaver had sent Willie that message. Erin didn't know how long Theresa had been dead. The police had set the time of death window as between the time that Willie had been sent that message and the time that Willie had called in.

That was the key. No medical examiner could establish time of death to the minute. He would set a wide window of several hours.

Terry had said that he was sure Willie had been at the scene longer than he said because of Theresa's pallor and body temperature. That she appeared to have been dead longer than Willie's testimony suggested.

And she had. She'd been dead before Willie had even received that message. Maybe as much as an hour before. Maybe just minutes after Vic had left to meet with her to plead face-to-face that Theresa leave her alone.

"And you have an alibi from the time that message was sent to Willie until he called it in."

Beaver smiled. "Of course I do. I was at Sheriff Wilmot's office."

CHAPTER 38

It would only have taken Beaver a minute or two to get from Vic's apartment to the police department in the middle of the night after sending the message. There was no traffic and it was only blocks away. Her alibi would be well-established by the time Willie's call came in.

"But Willie was never supposed to call it in, was he?" Erin challenged. "He was supposed to assume that Vic had killed Theresa in a confrontation and to dispose of the body."

"I was rather surprised to hear the call come in," Beaver agreed. "With Willie's knowledge of caves, mines, and tunnels, I would think he would have his choice of places to dispose of a body where it would never be discovered."

"Someone saw him. There was someone in the woods, and he couldn't take the chance of them reporting him transporting a dead body. He had to beat them to it and report the dead body himself."

Beaver nodded. "Of course. He's no idiot, Willie Andrews."

"If they arrest Willie, you'll come forward and tell them what really happened?"

Beaver sipped her shake. "I would… help them come up with an alternate theory of the crime."

Erin shook her head. "People are going to think that he did it and just got away with it."

A shrug from Beaver. "So what? They think he defended his girlfriend from a psychotic killer. They're not exactly going to be upset and calling for his blood."

Erin had to admit that she hadn't come across one person who had been the least bit upset about Theresa being killed. Her parents were gone. No other close family members. With her history of violence, she had no close friends. Maybe no friends at all.

"So you got away with it."

"With what?" Beaver smiled.

"Does your boss have any idea? Or do you just wink and nod at each other and not discuss it?"

"I've talked to my boss. But what is discussed between us is, of course, sensitive, confidential information."

"Is he the man I saw you talking to?"

Beaver raised her hands palms-up. "I have talked to a lot of people. I don't know what conversation you might have seen. Things have been… rather busy the last few days."

CHAPTER 39

Amid all of the chaos of the week, even with the carefully written notes and lists in Erin's planner, she hadn't done everything she needed to for Easter Sunday. There was no ladies' tea, as the church ladies would be going directly from Easter services to their homes to prepare their big family dinners rather than visiting with each other at the bakery. But all of the stores in town, and probably even in the city, were closed and there would be no Easter ham or leg of lamb. Not that she was sure she had the time or energy to prepare such a big meal anyway. And while she had initially planned to invite Vic and Willie over, and Adele, and Jeremy and Beaver, and anyone else she thought might be alone or lonely on Easter, that had not worked out. She had been too distracted by Theresa's death and trying to find the answers to what had really happened.

Erin sighed and looked over the stores in her pantry. She could make mashed potatoes from a box and some vegetable side dishes from canned or frozen vegetables. There wasn't much in the way of meat choices other than deli slices in the fridge and flaked ham or tuna in a can. She supposed she could make some toasted ham and cheese sandwiches, and some gravy from bouillon to pour over the mashed potatoes or to dunk the sandwiches in. That was going to have to do.

Of course, she had plenty for dessert. She had taken the rest of the Easter treats home with her after closing on Saturday, so there were plenty of hot cross rolls, hand-dipped marshmallow eggs, and cut-out cookies to follow the meal. Terry wouldn't complain about that. He wouldn't complain about anything she made for dinner, of course, even if all she did was to open a can of soup. He was too sensitive about her feelings toward religious holidays. He wouldn't want to make a big thing of it being Easter.

The doorbell at the back door rang. Erin tripped over Orange Blossom as she hurried out of the pantry to answer it. Vic and Willie had a key and codes to the alarm, so she wasn't sure why either one of them would need to be let in. It flashed through her mind that maybe it was the police, needing to look at something else they had failed to investigate before or hoping to arrest Willie for Theresa's murder. But Beaver had assured her that the investigation would fade out and no arrests would be made.

She unlocked and opened the door for Vic, who was holding a casserole dish covered with tinfoil, her hands protected with oven mitts and steam swirling out from under the foil covering.

"Careful, it's hot!" she warned as she sidled in through the door. She glanced back over her shoulder. "Willie is coming. He's just being slow."

She marched into the kitchen and set the casserole dish down on top of the stove.

Erin sniffed the air. "That smells really good!"

"Ham and noodle casserole. Ma's recipe. Tastes like a little bit of heaven!"

Erin felt a warm rush of appreciation. "You didn't have to do that! Will you stay and have some with us?"

"Sure, of course. We already went to Easter service while it was cooking, so we have plenty of time."

Erin saw Willie coming down the steps from the loft apartment and opened the door for him, keeping her foot across the door to prevent Orange Blossom from leaving. Blossom snorted and went back into the kitchen, rubbing against Vic and standing up on his hind legs to better smell the casserole and beg for some.

Willie displayed a couple of bottles of wine and entered.

"This is great!" Erin told him. She rapidly revised her plans for dinner. Maybe a couple of vegetable side dishes to go with the ham casserole centerpiece...

There was a knock at the front door. "Oh! Just a minute..." Erin told her company, hurrying to get it.

It was Brandy, one of the cooks from the family restaurant. She handed Erin a take-out bag, the savory smells of potatoes and cream with herbs wafting up from it. "Your scalloped potatoes," she told Erin. "Happy Easter!"

She gave a little wave, then turned around to go back to her car. Beaver and Jeremy were coming up the sidewalk. They waved to Brandy, then approached Erin. It was Jeremy who was carrying a covered dish, not Beaver. He grinned his wide, easy grin and tossed his head to flip his long hair over his shoulder. "Green bean casserole. Actually, it's cheddar-pecan green bean casserole."

Erin's mouth watered just at the words, even before the smells of the cheese and pecans hit her. "This is..." she shook her head and tried to prevent the tears welling up in her eyes from overwhelming her. "This is so nice! When did you guys plan all of this?"

Beaver chewed her gum, smiling comfortably at Erin. "Mostly yesterday. Though talk started a few days ago. Everybody knew how much time you were putting in at Auntie Clem's and... on other things. Vic happened to have occasional access to your planner and knew you weren't getting your own Easter preparations done."

Erin turned back toward the kitchen and shook her head at Vic. "A spy in my own bakery!"

Vic nodded, laughing. "Guilty as charged."

Terry emerged from the bedroom dressed in freshly laundered chinos and a light blue shirt, smelling of soap from his late-morning shower. K9, watching all of the action from beside the couch, got up to sniff and greet Terry.

"What's all the ruckus?" he asked, the dimple appearing in his cheek.

Disturbed by K9 getting up, Marshmallow hopped around in a wide circle and stopped at Erin's feet to nibble at her toes.

Erin held up the bag from the family restaurant. "Is this your doing?"

"You didn't expect me to make them myself, did you?"

She laughed. "Well, let's get everything set out in the kitchen. We can serve ourselves buffet-style."

Adele came in quietly through the back door as Erin set things out, displaying her own offering. "Corn pudding casserole."

"You didn't have to do that! Are you going to join us?" Erin knew that Adele didn't like crowds. She didn't always stick around when they had a large gathering.

"For a bit." Adele glanced around at the other guests. She was still uncomfortable around Vic after what her husband had done. She forced a smile. "And can I assume that… everything is working out?"

"Yes. Yes, everything is good." Erin looked at Beaver. "Or so I'm told."

Adele nodded. "Good."

Another knock on the front door sent Erin hurrying back across the house to answer it. Joshua stood there with a casserole bowl, held between mittened hands. He was a little pink and smiled at Erin, then looked back over his shoulder at the car that had brought him to the house.

"Loaded cauliflower casserole. From Mom," he said unnecessarily.

"Tell her thank you so much," Erin told him. "You can bring it into the kitchen."

She obviously couldn't take it from him with bare hands.

"Did Cam make it home for Easter?" she asked.

"Yes. And Dad." Joshua's eyes shone. It had been a long time since the family had all been together.

"Oh, that's good news. I read your article in the paper Thursday. It was really good."

"Thanks! There will be another one next week. About the shoot-out. Can I come by later and talk to you about it?"

"Oh, it didn't have anything to do with me. You should talk to Terry."

"I want to talk to you."

"Hmm." Erin didn't give him a firm answer, thinking about Mary Lou and how she would feel about it. She didn't like Erin encouraging Joshua in his investigative journalism, worried that it might lead him into trouble. Still, they had both seen how having a story to write changed his whole demeanor. It was what he lived for. Mary Lou wasn't going to keep him away from it.

"Got room for one more person?" Jack Ward was coming up the sidewalk carrying a couple of bottles of soda.

Erin shook her head. "Why aren't you back in Moose River?"

"Still following up on some details with the feds. No point in going home just to turn around and come back again."

Erin had never asked him about his family situation, but guessed that he must be unattached. If he had a wife or girlfriend back in Moose River, then he would go home for Easter, even if he had to turn around and return to Bald Eagle Falls the next day.

"Of course you're welcome to join us. The more, the merrier." Erin touched Joshua's shoulder before he could return to the car. "Tell Mary Lou thanks. It was so kind of her to think of me."

"Casseroles." He shrugged. "It's what they do."

"Well, we are going to have a king's feast, thanks to your mom and the others. I hope you all have a very happy Easter."

"We will," Joshua agreed. He nodded and walked back to the car where Mary Lou or Cam was waiting to drive him home. Erin lifted a hand to wave, even though she couldn't see whether the occupant waved back at her.

Erin ushered Jack into the house, then looked up and down the street to see if that was everyone. She looked at the house next door to hers. Mrs. Peach. She shut the door to prevent any animal escapes and tiptoed down the sidewalk to the city sidewalk, over one house, and up Mrs. Peach's sidewalk. She knocked on the door. It took a few minutes for Mrs. Peach to make it there on her walker.

"Erin. Happy Easter. What can I do for you?"

"Well... I've ended up with a big feast over here, and there is going to be way too much for us to eat. I was wondering if you could come over, help us to put a dent in it. I hate to interrupt your Easter plans, but..." Erin trailed off. She didn't hear any voices inside Mrs. Peach's house or smell a ham dinner.

"Oh no, I couldn't," Mrs. Peach demurred.

"Please? You would be doing me a huge favor."

"Well..." Mrs. Peach patted her hair and looked down at her dress. "I'm not really dressed for visiting..."

"Oh, you'll put the rest of us to shame. No one else is dressed up." Erin gestured to her own black slacks and t-shirt. "It's casual. So can you?"

"I suppose," Mrs. Peach said. "If you need my help, it wouldn't be neighborly to turn you away."

"Thank you so much! Can I give you a hand?" Erin offered her arm to the older woman.

"Just down the steps. I really am fine. I only use the walker for longer distances."

Mrs. Peach took Erin's arm for stability and carefully stepped down the concrete stairs. At the bottom, she let go and walked along behind Erin.

"You go on. You don't need to wait for a tired old lady. I'll be there in a minute."

"It's such a beautiful day. I want to enjoy the weather," Erin told her. She took in a long breath of fresh air and looked around at the beautiful green trees, lawns, and flower gardens. "Isn't spring just the best time of year?"

"It is lovely," Mrs. Peach agreed.

Erin walked with her up her sidewalk and helped her up the steps. They walked into the house, buzzing with people with smiles on their faces and redolent with the smells of the donated casseroles all lined up on the counter. Terry had seen to getting out glasses, plates, and cutlery, and they were all ready to begin.

"Thank you so much, everyone," Erin told the group. "This is the best surprise. I don't know how… just thank you."

"Let's eat!" Willie declared.

And they did.

∾

Erin was halfway into a food coma when her phone rang. She sleepily pulled it out of her pocket to look at the screen.

Reg. Twice in a week. Erin yawned and answered it. "Reg. Hi. How are you?"

"Everything is fine," Reg said, in a tone that suggested that Erin had accused her of being in trouble. "All back to normal."

"Back to normal… after your games? Did you enjoy watching them?"

"Oh, they were really cool," Reg declared. "You wouldn't believe the things that some people can do."

Erin nodded. "I always think that when I watch the Olympics. You never really know what a body is capable of until you watch something like that. We really don't use the abilities that we have, rarely explore them to see what we are really capable of."

"You're telling me! I saw some pretty unbelievable stuff."

"So, are you having a good Easter?"

"Most of the folks around here celebrate Ostara rather than Easter, so we've already had our celebrations. Is that what you're doing today? Easter?"

"Yes. Today is Easter Sunday."

"Well, if some lady with sparkles shows up and claims to be the goddess Eostre, don't believe her."

"Um... okay. I won't." Erin shook her head in disbelief. "Are you taking care of yourself, Reg? Everything okay?"

"Yes. Yes, everything is going to be fine now."

Erin hoped that it was true.

Did you enjoy this book? Reviews and recommendations are vital to making a book successful.

Please leave a review at your favorite book store or review site and share it with your friends.

Don't miss the following bonus material:
Sign up for mailing list to get a free ebook
Read a sneak preview chapter
Other books by P.D. Workman
Learn more about the author

Sign up for my mailing list at pdworkman.com and get Gluten-Free Murder for free!

JOIN MY MAILING LIST AND

Download a sweet mystery for free

pdworkman.com

PREVIEW OF ON THE SLAB PIE

The pie crust is tender, but the case is tough!

It all starts with a body.

Erin thought she'd seen and heard it all. In Bald Eagle Falls, everyone seemed not only to know everyone else's business, but to discuss it at length. Yet she had always assumed that her neighbor Mrs. Peach, who had no man in her life, was widowed.

Mr. Peach's unexpected reappearance, a prison breaking, and a body in the woods combine to form the toughest case yet for the gluten-free baker to solve!

Like baking mysteries? Cats, dogs, and other pets? Award-winning and USA Today Bestselling Author P.D. Workman brings readers back to small town Bald Eagle Falls for another culinary cozy mystery to be solved by gluten-free baker Erin Price and her friends.

Have your gluten-free cake and eat it too. Sink your teeth into this sweet treat now!

CHAPTER 1

"I've never even heard of a slab pie before." Erin studied the materials that her best friend and assistant Vic had assembled for her. "It must be a Southern thing, is it?"

"Suppose so." Vic shrugged. "I've never lived anywhere else, so I couldn't tell you. I guess if you never heard of it in Maine…"

Erin shook her head again. "In the North, the only pies I ever saw were round pies made in pie tins."

"Well, if you have a whole crew to feed, it's a lot less trouble to roll your pastry out onto a cookie sheet, add the filling and a top crust if you're doing one, and pop it in the oven. Then you just cut it into squares to serve. A lot less fuss and bother than cutting and filling half a dozen round pies."

"And people do double-crusted too?"

"Most of the ones you see now are dessert, and they just do a single crust. But you can make meat and potato pies, and then you do a double crust, so you can pick it up and eat it for lunch."

"Like an individual-size meat pie."

Vic nodded. "But a lot less bother. It would be pretty fussy to make individual meat pies for your whole field crew or mining shift. Or for a mom with a dozen kids, putting them in everyone's lunchbox."

"I never even thought of such a thing. But it's very practical."

"And good for a picnic or fair." Vic grinned widely. "You can get really fancy, laying out your fruit in a pattern or picture. Looks good, tastes even better, and it's quick and easy to serve."

"Okay," Erin agreed with a nod. "I'm convinced. That's what we'll do for the Statehood Day picnic."

"Great. We can do a run-through now, and I'll look up some recipe ideas tonight so you have something to start with. Then we can come up with something traditional but unique."

Erin wasn't sure she would be able to repeat the success they'd had with the mile-high stack cake at the Fall Fair, but she and Vic would come up with something good. She had perfected several gluten-free pastry recipes in the time since she had first opened Auntie Clem's Bakery, so that part would not be difficult. She was sure that it would cook up just as well in the large cookie sheet as in a pie pan. Though it might need to be a little stronger to make sure that the pieces in the middle were substantial enough to remove from the pan without crumbling, even if they would be eating them with a plate and fork rather than out of hand. They would come up with something that would work with a tweak or two.

∽

After they had closed shop and gone home, Erin had a light dinner by herself—Terry was on an evening shift with the police department, and Vic was having dinner with her boyfriend, Willie—and debated going out for a walk.

It was a beautiful day, and she knew that she should take advantage of the cooling evening. She and Vic had vowed to spend more time watching the sunrises and sunsets and enjoying the natural beauty around them. What was the point in working all day indoors and never getting out to enjoy the beauty around them? Not only was Bald Eagle Falls a paradise in the midst of some of the most gorgeous scenery Erin had seen, but she literally had the woods in her backyard. Or separated from her backyard by a fence. And the woods were hers, inherited from her aunt Clementine along with the house and the storefront that had been the original Auntie Clem's Bakery, the only gluten-free and allergy-friendly bakery in driving distance.

She could take a short walk through the woods, enjoying the lowering light shining through the dappled leaves of the brilliantly green trees, return to the yard for her tai chi practice, and then head to bed for a few minutes of reading and, hopefully, quickly drop off to sleep.

It was always harder falling sleep without Terry there. Unless, of course, Terry was also having trouble sleeping, and then they just kept each other awake tossing and turning and kicking each other. But Orange Blossom, the cat rubbing against her legs and complaining that his kibble bowl was already empty, would snuggle with her in bed, and he was never too restless. He didn't seem to have any kitty worries or trauma that kept *him* awake at night.

"You don't need any more to eat," Erin chided him. "You're getting too fat. You want Doc Edmunds to put you on a diet?"

Blossom yowled more loudly. He had the loudest voice of any cat Erin had ever heard. The windows were open and she didn't want any of the neighbors complaining that he was disrupting their evening.

"Shh. You don't need anything else. You need to be quiet now."

But he wasn't quieting, and Erin eventually broke down and added a little more dry kibble to his bowl, hoping that would satisfy him. Marshmallow, the brown and white rabbit, had quietly eaten his dinner and lolloped off to the living room to sleep it off without any complaints. But then, he never complained. Orange Blossom more than compensated for Marshmallow's silence.

She decided to make her escape while he was occupied with his second course. Then at least if he started howling for more, she wouldn't be close enough to hear him and he would eventually get the message and have a nap.

After stepping out the back door onto the porch, Erin took a deep breath of the warm, sweet air. Even though she had grown up in the northeast, moving to Tennessee had been like coming home. She had only vague memories of the times she had visited Clementine before her parents' deaths, "helped" her aunt in what had then been her tearoom, and dug around in the garden or thrown rocks into the river. But the smell of the plants and flowers growing around her and the wind blowing over the lakes was unique. It took her right back to her childhood, confirming that Bald Eagle Falls, Tennessee would always be her home no matter where she lived.

She wandered into the woods beyond her fence, following the animal trails that had become familiar to her since she had returned home. She didn't know the woods nearly as well as Adele, the woman she employed as a groundskeeper in exchange for her use of the summer cottage and a small salary. And she wouldn't be comfortable walking around it late at night by herself like Adele did. But there was plenty of daylight left before she started worrying about that.

She could feel the tensions of the day and any stress over upcoming events or promotions or worries about employee scheduling or short supplies on flours that she needed falling away. Her muscles relaxed and she breathed more deeply. It was a good idea to take more time to enjoy the nature around her.

Erin could hear a crow cawing loudly nearby and wondered whether it was Skye, Adele's crow. He wasn't exactly Adele's pet, but he came to her for food and companionship, and sometimes when Erin was out in her yard, she would feed him a few peanuts or some other treat.

The crow's voice mixed with another loud bird. A magpie, Erin decided, listening to it. Both were scavengers and were probably fighting over some tasty morsel dropped by a passerby or the remains of a fox kill. The path she was taking would bring her closer to them. For a moment, she hesitated and considered taking a branch off in another direction to avoid disrupting them. But she was curious about what they were fighting over. If it were Skye, then he wouldn't leave just because Erin showed up. He knew her and would just ignore her unless she had a treat for him.

In a moment, she could see them both. The crow on the ground, his wings flapping, making himself big, and the magpie dive-bombing from above. Erin got closer. She probably didn't want to see exactly what they were fighting over. Scavenging birds weren't exactly known for eating fresh fruit or flowers.

She crept a little closer, her eyes on the ground, trying to discern any objects in the shadows of the trees. Late in the day, the shadows were long and it was hard to make out the shapes in the foliage. Tree stumps, litter, whatever it was the birds were squawking over so excitedly.

Erin let out a soft cry when she got close enough to make out the shape of an animal in the undergrowth. And not something dead; it was still alive. She hurried closer, shooing the birds away.

"Get out of here! Go on! Get out!"

She leaned down to peer under the bush and found herself looking into the round green eyes of a kitten.

CHAPTER 2

The kitten was not as young as Orange Blossom had been when she had found him, barely old enough to have left his mother. This cat was probably half-grown, but terribly thin, his coat patchy and bloody in places where the birds had attacked him.

"Oh, look at you." She knew that he would be too skittish for her to just reach down and pick him up. Even if he was hurt, he would still try to leap away, avoiding her. "There, little one. Are you okay? Where did you come from?"

There were feral cats around town, of course, though with both traffic and predators to deal with, they did not have long lifespans. And there were barn cats from nearby farms, and many people in Bald Eagle Falls didn't believe in keeping their cats indoors where they were safe, but insisted that a cat needed to roam outside. Erin looked around for something that would help her catch the cat so that Doc Edmunds could see to its injuries.

Terry had caught Marshmallow—when he had been feral—by throwing his coat over him. Erin had layered a loose blouse over a sleeveless t-shirt. Not being able to think of any other solution, she unbuttoned the blouse and took it off, moving very slowly and, she hoped, in a non-threatening way. The cat continued to watch her with big, round eyes, perhaps unsure whether she had actually seen him or not. Or maybe just hoping that she would walk away and leave him alone to lick his wounds.

Erin threw her blouse over the cat, and miraculously, it actually covered him. Erin had never been the best at sports. But she had never played any sport that involved throwing clothing, either. She shuffled a bit closer and bent over to pick up the cat inside the shirt, wrapping it tightly around him so that he would be still and she could transport him, as she had seen others do.

As soon as her hands closed around him, he slithered out from under the shirt, darting away and hiding behind a tree to watch whether she would pursue him or not. She could see his sides heaving and quivering.

"Poor thing. Just let me catch you, and I'll take you somewhere they'll make you feel much better."

He didn't look disposed to do as she said. Erin could hear Skye —if it was Skye— cawing high overhead. Disappointed that she had chased him away from the potentially tasty morsel?

Erin looked around for help. If Adele was nearby, or another neighbor, maybe the two of them together would be able to trap the cat.

A few feet away, she saw a boot. And was it a pile of clothes? Or the shape of someone sleeping on the ground?

Adele had previously mentioned that someone had been sleeping in the woods, as she had found areas where the grass and vegetation were still crushed down from someone being there for an extended length of time. After all that had transpired, Erin had assumed that the person in the woods had been Theresa, watching Vic and those she interacted with from a distance before making her move. Theresa and Vic had been a couple before Vic's gender transition and Theresa had decided she wanted to renew their relationship. But Vic was not interested in Theresa, and as was often the case with crazy Theresa, things went quickly from bad to worse.

But that was in the past. Vic was fine. All of Erin's friends associated with Vic were safe and well, and Theresa had failed in her aims, foiled by someone who had been watching her as she watched Vic.

Erin shifted her stance and shuffled sideways a bit, not towards the cat, but in the direction of the dark shape with the boots to get a better look.

She would not confront someone who was sleeping in the woods by herself. She would get Terry or Adele with her shotgun to back her up. She had no desire to face an angry vagrant on her own.

It was starting to get darker, the sun setting over the horizon. That made it harder to make everything out. But she knew something was wrong. Something was very, very wrong with what she saw.

Erin fumbled for her phone. It took several attempts to get it out of the small purse she had brought with her, slung diagonally across her body. For some reason, her fingers felt numb and fat and weren't working the way they were supposed to.

When she was baking, her hands flew, she was so familiar with the processes of stirring, rolling, shaping, and all of the other things she did automatically while she was preparing the goods for sale at Auntie Clem's Bakery that sometimes she just watched her fingers, surprised that they knew what they were supposed to do and moved so automatically and gracefully. But that wasn't the case as she clumsily separated her phone from the purse and tapped at the screen, trying to unlock it multiple times and then unsure what to press when she finally got past the lock screen.

Her sluggish brain fed her the instructions. Tap the phone icon. Find Terry's face in her favorites list. Tap on it a couple of times until the phone figured out she wanted to call him and tried to make the connection. She stared at the phone, waiting for something to happen. It was a few moments before she realized that he had answered but that she hadn't put the phone up to her ear to answer or pressed the speaker button. She lifted the phone to her face.

"Terry?"

"Erin? Is everything okay?" His tone was light, but with just a hint of concern. He knew only too well that as idyllic as everything might appear to be in Bald Eagle Falls, things didn't always go as expected and there were dangerous people or circumstances to contend with. Or maybe he was just worried that Erin might have chopped the tip of a finger off while getting a bedtime snack or had forgotten that he was on shift and was expecting him home.

"Umm… no. I guess not. There's something in the woods."

"In the woods?" his concern raised his tone another notch higher. "What is in the woods? Where are you?"

"I just went for a walk. And I stopped because I saw Skye and a magpie fighting over something, and then I saw that it was a little cat."

"A cat." He blew his breath out in relief. "You had me scared for a minute there. Don't tell me that you're adopting another stray."

"No… I didn't see… there is something else here. I saw the boots, and then I smelled something, and…"

"Boots?" he echoed, trying to make sense of her babbling. "What did you smell? Is there a fire? Some homeless person camping out back there?"

"No… it's… well, maybe he was camping here. But he wasn't. And there's no fire. It's okay."

"He? Who is there? Do you need me to send someone on his way?"

"I need you. And… I don't know who else. Everyone, I guess." They didn't have a very large police department. Something like this would require all hands on deck. "You see… it's a body."

~

On the Slab Pie, Book #18 of the *Auntie Clem's Bakery* series by P.D. Workman can be purchased at pdworkman.com

ABOUT THE AUTHOR

Award-winning and USA Today bestselling author P.D. (Pamela) Workman writes riveting mystery/suspense and young adult books dealing with mental illness, addiction, abuse, and other real-life issues. For as long as she can remember, the blank page has held an incredible allure and from a very young age she was trying to write her own books.

Workman wrote her first complete novel at the age of twelve and continued to write as a hobby for many years. She started publishing in 2013. She has won several literary awards from Library Services for Youth in Custody for her young adult fiction. She currently has over 80 published titles and can be found at pdworkman.com.

Born and raised in Alberta, Workman has been married for over 25 years and has one son.

∼

Please visit P.D. Workman at pdworkman.com to see what else she is working on, to join her mailing list, and to link to her social networks.

∼

If you enjoyed this book, please take the time to recommend it to other purchasers with a review or star rating and share it with your friends!

- facebook.com/pdworkmanauthor
- twitter.com/pdworkmanauthor
- instagram.com/pdworkmanauthor
- amazon.com/author/pdworkman
- bookbub.com/authors/p-d-workman
- goodreads.com/pdworkman
- linkedin.com/in/pdworkman
- pinterest.com/pdworkmanauthor
- youtube.com/pdworkman

Find P.D. Workman's books at

PDWORKMAN.COM

Scan the QR code below

Made in the USA
Monee, IL
17 June 2022